# Wild Beasts and Plague
## short stories

David Porter

**by David Porter:**

*Old Men's Dreams*, a novel
Walk in My Shoes Publications
ISBN 9780993489808

*A Rebel's Journey, my life and times*
Walk in My Shoes Publications
ISBN 9780993489822

**Co-authored:**

*GCSE Drama Study Guide*
Rhinegold Education
ISBN 9781785581731

*AS and A Level Drama and Theatre Study Guide*
Rhinegold Education
ISBN 9781785581748

*Cambridge Technicals Level 3 Performing Arts*
Hodder Education
ISBN 9781471874888

 **Walk in My Shoes**
PUBLICATIONS

First published in 2018 by

**Walk in My Shoes Publications**
11 Irex Road
Lowestoft
NR33 7BU

The right of David Porter to be identified as author of this work
has been asserted in accordance with Section 77 of the
Copyright, Designs and Patents Act 1988

ISBN 9780993489839

**Wild Beasts and Plague**

**Contents**

# Introduction

My autobiography, *A Rebel's Journey,* was self-published in early 2018. It described in over 150,000 words and with 300+ pictures, a varied life and was, for his grandchildren who might one day ask who the hell was I really?

It was an epic task taking more than three years to research, write and design, drawing on the more than 50 volumes of my page-a-day diary, press cuttings, photos, memories, mine and others.

While awaiting design and amendments, I finished and self-published on Amazon the third version of a novel, *Old Men's Dreams,* based on a play based on a film script based on a short story.

There still remained boxes of old ideas and part-worked material, earlier novels, over 40 plays and new ideas that just keep coming. As old age and the need to downsize gathered pace, I decided to rewrite and publish some of those old stories, poems, plays and ideas in this collection, *Wild Beasts and Plague,* along with some new material.

**Wild Beasts and Plague,** *a 2017 story from an idea first thought of in the 1970s, based on a prophecy from Ezekiel.*

**The Watcher** *written while teaching at Kirkley High School, was published in National Writers Magazine, 2002.*

**Third Time Lucky** *was a short story, then a film script for a cost-free short film contest in Norfolk in 2011 that went nowhere.*

*Judging Books*, 2016, written out of frustration at a stand-up world where those who cannot stand are always an after-thought.

*The Quiet Man* written in 2016 after a cruise holiday and from a series of older ideas about having to cope with the criminal stupidity of others.

*The Representative* written during my time in Parliament 1987-97, and revised in 2016 for this collection.

*Things to Do Before You Die, 2060*, 2012, a sci-fi story for a competition – no chance!

*Private Asylum*, 2017, from a short story idea first born in the 1980s.

*The Spiral Escape*, a mid-1970s story to illustrate a film idea. It's an escape from a city frozen in time, leading to the need for another escape. One day there'll be cities built under the sea!

*Travelling,* a 2016 short story from my 1970 play rejected by ATV as 'zany, allegorical and over-ambitious' but I have 'flair and imagination'.

*Saint Rosa, I Die* from my play that reached the finals of the Sunday Times/National Union of Students Drama Festival in 1969 performed by my college, New College of Speech and Drama.

*17 The Crescent* is from a partly autobiographical novel I wrote in the early 70s about my three years in a strange student house.

*A Reunion of Clowns* is from another of my 1970s novels about life beyond college and into teaching where the past is *not a foreign country and the present is not as clear as it appears.*

***Open Relationship*** *was written first as a story in the mid 1970s and rewritten in 2017. It's based on fact up to a point. The theatre company was real; the relationships have been exaggerated for dramatic effect.*

***The Dreams of Nigel Barnes****, a story originally from the 1980s, revised in 2017 for this collection.*

***Groups of Five*** *is a story about drama teaching I first wrote in 2010 before I retired from teaching and revised in 2017.*

***My Friend, The Don*** *came from an idea during the 1980s about finding money unexpectedly and was rewritten in 2017.*

***Who Will Speak At My Funeral?*** *was written in 2017 to bring this collection of stories – new and revamped – to a natural close.*

# Wild Beasts and Plague

I'm safe in this trench. Well, safe as can be.

It's warm and so far dry. Close by me are an old canvas bag and a small improvised holdall I dragged along when the wild beasts and plague hit us.

The Lord certainly sent his vengeance on us. I remember those churchy people spouting on and on about it for months before it happened. Ezekiel, whoever he or she was, said *'How much worse will it be when I send my four dreadful judgements – sword and famine and wild beasts and plague.'*

We had the sword as the wars started. All over, everywhere. I never really understood what we were fighting about. Or actually, who we were fighting in  clumsy ambushes, childish reprisals, occasional hand to hand slugging it out.

We had neither the weaponry nor the knowledge to hit back at them.

The famine came as rations were tightened to starvation point. Only the already strong made it. Those who couldn't fight, trick or steal their way to food, simply died, growing increasingly weaker, big eyes staring condemnation and anger from pinched faces before hope faded.

The churchies claimed that Ezekiel promised there'd be survivors, sons and daughters brought out of the sword, famine, wild beasts and plague. I'm not sure what sons and daughters are, but a few of us did survive the famine and the sword as the soldiers hunted us down. It was the wild beasts and plague that did for me.

Some people said the wild beasts were all in the mind, every terror imaginable. Well, that makes them real enough. The mind is the last frontier of humanity. I never saw one myself, but Miro told me they were like every animal that ever was alive, unnaturally mixed kinds, with big mouths, teeth that cut leaving paralytic poison to seep into us.

It was even said that some were beasts who lived in the waters but had been brought up to kill us off. I hate animals. One day Distus was certain they were all robotics; the next that they were hideous aberrations caused by pollution and cross breeding.

None of us could tell the difference anyway. They were the beasts that we were told would be unleashed. And they would not stop till … what? I don't know.

The plague was worse. The medicos claimed that this was a plague that could have been sexually passed around. Or it was carried on the air we breathe. Or it came from contaminated food. The water was polluted and all the clean ups over the years had made things worse.

Victims begin to feel faint, slightly dizzy, staggering before falling, unable to move yet horrifyingly alive as great red itchy sores burst through their skin and relentless vomiting begins.

Machines don't catch plague and don't need water. Or our food. So why do they want our world? It was a question we all asked a lot. Until there were too few of us left to wonder any more. We were just hanging on.

When they came for us, I'd hurt my knee so couldn't run. I crawled. That was what saved me as the beasts fanned out round our little cluster of derelict houses, smashing their noisy way into each systematically.

It was the crawling that saved me, yes, it must have been. Well, saved me for a time. Someone had told me there was an old graveyard not far away. They used to bury the dead in it, I overheard some people explaining. I'd never seen it, nor was I sure what it looked like. But as I navigated my way over the rough, withered, dry, dirty earth, I realised I'd found it.

With darkness gathering and no street lights like we used to have – robots don't need lights – I was starting to panic for a place to hide. I had to rest. Just to catch my breath and let the pain in my leg subside a little, would be enough.

I scraped forward, over another mound and toppled headlong into a trench, desperately grabbing soil around me as I fell, with no idea how far down I would go. Dirt trickled down with me, before stopping, leaving me closed in, but not too tightly. That did my knee no good, but I hoped below the surface, I wouldn't be seen.

It amazes me that even in my bad state, the urge to survive is strong enough to make me lie still to focus on thinking. What next for me? I reach for the handful of cereals I'd kept in the bag, wishing I'd taken more as Miro vomited and no longer cared about our food stash.

I must've dozed off, because as I stretch my leg and shift to my side to relieve myself into the soil I appreciate daylight above. Something is approaching.

There are several of them, judging by the sounds on the ground. These are not robots encased in mock-human outers. These creatures communicate with each other by sounds, shrills and groans in a tongue I don't recognise. Robots communicate silently.

They're not robots, then. Nor are they human survivors. The back of my cold neck and bumps on my arms register dawning realisation - these are the wild beasts.

I have to breathe out slowly, without noise, my brain is swimming. Perhaps they don't know I'm here. They cannot see me. Can they smell me? This is their place. A wild abandoned human area would be ideal for them. Nobody would come and check out wild beasts.

Perhaps, maybe. What if …? My rush of thoughts is leading nowhere and I need to let my bowels open, must dribble my twice daily trickle. I feel tight and this space is suddenly too small and close. I must gulp the air above me. In the light.

The first shovel of earth hits. I splutter and frantically brush it off my head. The second follows swiftly and I have to repeat the action. Before the third arrives, I turn on my side and hold my hand up ready to protect my head.

The beasts are filling the trench in. I will be covered.

Unsure whether this is fear, I feel faint, slightly dizzy. If I was walking, I'd be staggering about. I scratch at my left cheek, attack an itch that is beyond irritating. My back needs a scratch too.

With each load of dirt, I am brushing it off and patting it down as I realise that I am being slowly raised towards the light.

Another few shovels of earth and I will see them and they see me. Will I scream? Will I be able to get away? I scrabble upwards, gulping air, hauling myself towards the surface and freedom, my chest both itching and sore.

And I see the wild beasts. I vomit profusely.

# The Watcher

Period One ended and for a split second, as he recovered some paper from the floor, his notes from the desk and squared the back row of chairs, he looked forward to his coming free period. And a cup of coffee in the staffroom.

Still an hour till break, but another coffee would be a treat he deserved after that bunch of Year 9s, the rising fourteen-year olds, the inmates of institutions of tomorrow.

Then he remembered his free period was gone. Snatched away cruelly on the daily cover sheet for all to see.

He was down for some heavy duty boredom in the school hall. Public exams were under way with a vengeance and the coffee would have to wait.

He had to sit and watch for an hour. Oh Lord!

At least Beth would be there, unless she was in the overflow exam area, the gym. If she was in the hall he could spend the hour looking at her, looking out for her, and that would make it all bearable.

He picked her out at once, even as the hall door closed, his eye practised over the years at finding faces, even in identical school uniform. Beth was half way down a row at the far end of the hall.

***************************

For the first quarter of an hour, he did his usual mental exercises. Planned the rest of the day, his evening, tomorrow's lesson tweaks and a departmental meeting. He then moved into more detailed planning of his summer holiday and wished his oldest kids were coming along too.

He stood and paced across the front of the hall, looking severe, just to make sure they were all heads down. All except that little shit with the silly name he couldn't recall.

Sitting back down, it was time to count the left-handers. There seemed to be 39 of them, so if there were fifteen rows of kids with 12 in a row, the percentage of left-handers was … He abandoned it.

The next ten minutes went on putting the world to rights in a conversation with somebody that was convincing, righteous and inspirational. To him.

He slipped next year's draft timetable from his jacket pocket. Management were having a laugh – expecting as much teaching as that! Ridiculous. Still, once September came, he'd get stuck in, as usual.

He glanced at the huge wall clock as it continued its slow, ponderous advance. Two colleagues were on either side of the hall, towards the back, pacing, watching.

God. Half way through. How long actually is eternity?

Maths exam tomorrow and two free periods, so probably more watching.

He surveyed the bowed heads before him. Young minds, many already beyond repair by the time they arrived at the school. A couple were bright glimmers for the nation's future. Well, at least the town's.

He'd been doing this too long. Too long teaching. But Beth was there, brightening lives, a ray of celestial light in the gloomy hall. A breath of fragrant youth, a taste of great beauty of heaven beyond.

GCSE English Literature. He used to read the question papers the moment he entered the invigilation, but no more. Now he sat and daydreamed, watching as weary, seasoned invigilators do. Watching as the little darlings toiled away or frittered the time, their great culmination of statutory schooling.

There was talk of employing non-teachers to take on this ghastly task. It couldn't come soon enough for him.

His eyes kept returning to her. She was an attractive 16-year old now. Her blond hair neatly parted and held off her face with a silver clasp. She didn't look up, perhaps not sensing his eyes on her. If only more worked as hard a she did.

How many generations had he watched? He recalled several faces, a few names. He reflected how year by year some quite awkward and unappealing girls flowered during the closing months of the summer term into stunners.

And their legs! The warmer days brought out legs, shapely and obviously smooth, no wonder half the male teachers and most of the lads were is a state of permanent heat.

Years ago when he'd started teaching secondary, the top years were little older than he was. Ideal. Ideal for lusting after, for aching. And he'd recognised the sign on the face of that young PE teacher walking across the yard only yesterday while he was on break duty.

After he was married, there was always temptation. Even the ones who used their agile bodies as weapons were not truly aware of the power they held over men. Or were they?

Time for another turn around the front half of the hall. He was the senior colleague, so another walk down a few aisles, perilously close to the work, jangling keys in his pocket, just as teachers for generations have felt obliged to pile on the challenges of the teenagers before them.

Beth was special. He longed to glimpse her work, to see if she was on schedule. Not that he could've helped; he just wanted to know. His old shoes had a slight squeak – another requisite for the time-worn role of watching he played out.

Yes, she was doing fine, but didn't look up. She knew he was there, of course, but ploughed on, her teenage writing racing across the sheets.

Past her; back round a row towards the front. With professional educationalist eyes in the back of his head he sensed her look – not at him, but sideways.

He forced himself to walk till he reached the front and swung round to face the desks. Suspicion confirmed. She'd snatched a lightning glance at Damian Gregson.

What a creep. The lad was a worthless, waster sort of boy, handy with a chat-up line and a laugh to impress young girls. And he had noticed that Beth, even Beth, was fascinated by something about the boy.

What would Gregson make of himself? At best he'd work as a mechanic in some deadbeat job; at worst, he'd do shifts at the turkey factory out of town earning good money till he made a girl or girls pregnant after which he'd age into a morose adulthood, as such men do.

Beth deserved better. He held the thought for a moment in his mind and studied it from all sides, the light of his own views shining through it. What did he picture for Beth?

Well, a man much like himself, naturally. Younger ...

And then he found a word for what he felt. He was jealous! Jealous that Beth was drawn to Gregson's shallow charm and was therefore vulnerable to him.

Jealous of a 16-year old boy! He could fight it, no question. He could handle it, deal with it and package it up, no problem. But in that moment, that stab of jealousy shocked him. That girl made him feel that way, old as he was and old as the kids saw him.

It was the kind of instant pain that could lead to unpremeditated murder. He struggled for breath for a moment while he regained composure and could look impassively round the hall. That boy definitely had something – an air of self assurance that he himself had never really had.

The watcher spent the next fifteen minutes mentally strangling, running over, poisoning, sending threatening/warning letters, whispering to the police about Damian Gregson. It didn't help, but time passed.

Beth's school skirt was far too short. Very attractive and appealing but an animal like Damian Gregson would be unable to resist the suggestion of what the lovely legs hinted at. Just like his father.

Yes, the watcher had watched Wayne Gregson do his exams a generation ago and had experienced the same jealous loathing at his ability to be so at ease with the most attractive girls on the block in his year class.

\*\*\*\*\*\*\*\*\*\*\*\*\*\*\*\*\*\*\*\*\*\*\*\*\*

Finally, like release from a long, confined prison term, he found himself standing, confirming the position from his wristwatch and addressing the whole hall. 'Stop writing, now!'

In obedience to his superiority, one hundred and fifty nine hands surrendered their pens and looked to him for further orders. He repeated the stop command and added, 'Put your papers in order. Wait for them to be collected. I remind you, nobody may talk.'

Beth was almost the first to have her papers ready as his colleagues worked the rows collecting. She looked slightly high coloured – she'd been concentrating and giving it her best for the full two hours. He'd expect nothing less.

The two junior staff had almost gathered in the full harvest of wisdom. He stood his ground at the front, glaring at the students, daring anyone to speak. He waited a full twenty seconds after the last paper was in before pointing and barking, 'This row, file out quietly.'

In a matter of moments the hall was emptied, each keen to share the horrors of their common ordeal. Beth was near the rear of the exiting line of legs, backs and hair as it merged into a seething mass of jabbering exuberance in to the foyer.

He nodded thanks to his colleagues and clutching the entire pile of work he pushed through the crowd making for the exams office.

He spoke to none, but veered towards Beth, then stood deliberately close to her, taking advantage of his height to lean forward with a slight tilt of his upper body so he could speak through the hubbub.

'How did it go, Beth? You managed, didn't you?'

She flashed him that smile to die for, her eyes full of affection and he felt so happy that at that moment Damian Gregson was well away from her as she answered.

'Oh yes, thanks, that was OK, Dad.'

# Third Time Lucky

William thought of himself as a bit of a film buff. To everyone else he was a nerd. But here he was, part of the team of like-minded students making a film of their own for a youth short movie making competition.

It was early in the grey morning outside the Hippodrome, Great Yarmouth in Norfolk. William, while making the final unnecessary tweaks to his basic pair of cameras on tripods, looked around at the students already arrived and a couple just approaching.

Early for 20-somethings, perhaps, but William liked getting up and on with the day. It might bring some good news. A day might help him realise his dream.

*To find a girlfriend.*

This film was the vehicle to that desirable outcome. He'd not had much success so far. Back at secondary school in Hertfordshire he'd eaten his heart out as the girls he liked looked right through him, laughed in his face when he bucked up courage to ask, ignored him so it was impossible to approach or went out with every other boy in Year 10. Then Year 11. Then sixth form.

At university in Norwich, he really thought he'd find one. Same story, though, only ten times worse. But William was at heart an optimistic soul, knowing that he had plenty of time, she was somewhere to be found and every rebuff only strengthened him.

The group gathering in front of him was a complete mix of yawning, stretching, reluctant youngsters. William panned the camera around them, lingering a fraction longer on the girls' faces. He provided himself with mental back-stories for these people.

Simon, who somehow had claimed the role of director for himself, finished his McDonalds' coffee and dropkicked the cup towards the litter bin. An economic studies undergraduate, Simon was tall, rugby playing, good looking, casual, easy-going sort of youth with a touch of arrogance born of family wealth and a smile of disdain always playing on his lips.

William had seen Simon manage time with two separate girls at a party where he'd been invited out of someone feeling sorry for him. Simon didn't need the degree in economics as he had family connections and quite why he was in Norfolk rather than the LSE or Oxbridge William decided was down to him not knuckling to his A-levels when it mattered.

'Are we ready, sometime today?' Simon demanded.

Chris shouted out loud, 'Well, I am. As usual.'

Chris was one of life's natural sidekicks, William decided. When a natural leader like Simon emerged, Chris – short, stocky, not very bright, beer expert and loudmouth about his sexual prowess – may have been all talk. But Chris was obviously more successful than William.

Sally didn't look away from her hand mirror as she painted her eyelids, but snapped at Chris, 'For God's sake, Chris, take the broomstick out of your bum and get real, will you. Some of us have to make up for a shoot, OK?'

William liked Sally. At least he liked her outward looks, her long dark hair, slender hips, breasts that were a big asset judging by how much of them were on display, even on a cold day like this. She was from somewhere up north – William didn't care, he'd been thinking that she may have a kind heart under that exterior. She'd be quite a catch, impress everyone, make them think better of William ...

Emma's irritability with Chris crossed her face and Josh joined in. Emma was a local girl who'd decided, like many East Anglians, that Norwich was quite far enough way for university and was so local that she had suggested to Simon that filming in Yarmouth was a great idea.

She was flirty, quite bright, willing and a possible, noted William as she moved away from Josh. He, a little older than the girls was one of those rather camp drama students who fill the profession on stage and off it. He could sing and dance a little and William had noticed he could throw some Oscar-winning hissy fits when he was in the mood.

William missed what started them off, but there was a snappish, ill-tempered little interchange that could have passed for improvisation. Simon wanted to get on with it, knowing the gear they'd borrowed had to be back in Norwich too soon.

He heard Lucy say, 'Can we just calm down and start the scene?' in that sensible, down to earth way of hers. William had often thought of her – she was not in this for all she could get out of it - she was articulate, a good actor, a genuinely caring person. Mmmm. But then William noticed Sally staring at him and he could only think of her.

'What exactly are you doing? Are you filming me, Thingy?' Chris clowned that 'that was the point'; a few onlookers thought they were watching something real.

'No, I'm just getting everything set up. And I'm William, by the way.' But it was lost as Sally's foot was trodden on by Josh who had taken to jigging about like a wild bird, for some reason.

Simon raised his voice and clapped his hands, 'Right, guys, we'll take that as a warm up. Let me remind you we are making a film. In other words this film is about students making a film about making a film. You know it's on a shoestring

17

...' which caused murmurs and nods, sighs and a few looks at the sky. They'd heard it before.

'...but we are what we are and I'd like to win this competition. The publicity will be useful.' He looked over at William, 'You, camera-man, sorry, your name has slipped my mind, you know you are doing sound as well? We'll both do the editing but anyone wants to help, that's OK with me.'

This was the cue to get into an agreed position, displayed around the frontage of the circus building. Simon continued in lecture mode. 'The outside of this Hippodrome is our first scene as it's the finest example of the early 1900s purpose-built circus building that still has a facility for flooding the arena with water for the finales... we need a circusy feel and as we're not allowed inside ...'

Simon droned on about the history and ghosts and events at the circus. He'd read up well, and some looked marginally impressed.

William decided to get some of it on film – a documentary of their success in mind – and panned the group. He reached out an arm to stop Sally moving into shot. She paused, looked at his arm and pushed it aside.

'Sorry, Sally, I was just – '

'Yeah, OK, Will, no probs.'

'It's William. Sally ...'

She turned to face him, looking in his face and seeing him for the first time. He had gone red and his mouth dried up but he managed to come out with – 'you know how in a group, you get a feeling that you have something in common with only one or two?'

She neither replied nor moved off. 'I feel we have something in common, Sally.'

'Yeah, like what?' Her eyebrow was raised.

'A love of film, a desire to make this work and to really advance our careers.'

She nodded. 'Sounds like you've been rehearsing that line. What do you actually want?'

William, having come thus far, was at the limit of his nerves, conscious that others would notice he was talking to her soon blurted out, 'Well, I er, um, I wondered if you'd go and have a drink with me, you know, after today's shooting, just us, you know?'

There, he'd asked. She stood looking at him, realised that he was serious and not being a complete bitch, replied, 'Well, thanks, no, erm, after the shoot, I'm
going to town. My mum's birthday is next week, need stuff, you know. And later I'm going for a pizza with Simon.'

'Oh, yeah, that's cool, Sally. I didn't know you and Simon –'

'We're not. We're just going out for some fun, you know, and some of the others will be there as well, sorry, Will.'

'It's William.' But she walked away, grinning.

Simon noticed and walked towards her and said to William over her shoulder, 'What did you say your name was?'

'William!'

'Well, Willy, I hope you're not distracting Sally from hearing my history lecture on the Hippodrome.'

'Of course not,' William muttered, 'great lecture.'

Josh, who hadn't had anybody paying him any attention for a whole five minutes, chirruped, 'Oh Simon, love, can I have some help about my motivation here? Am I a bit camp?'

Chris responded, 'Act, Josh, it's not your real life!'

Emma warned him not to start off again. Chris said, 'I'm not, Emma, my love, just saying.'

Simon shepherded them into position with a quick word to each. William watched Sally through his lens, upset but determined she wouldn't know that.

Simon called, 'OK Willy Boy, stand by, Scene 1 ...'

'It's William,' pointlessly muttered as Simon clapped his board which set off everyone into an improvised piece of circus-like physical theatre, a cross between inmates in an asylum and students playing inmates in an asylum.

Most onlookers wandered away, feeling that they'd already seen the best.

*************************

William imagined the script instructions. *Exterior. Outside a pub. Night.*

There was the team, all except him, of course, gathered around a parked car, doors open. They were drinking, glasses from the pub, stuffing pizza into their mouths having that good larking around time that William half wanted to be part of, and half didn't.

Let them have their fun – it was all so shallow. Only Lucy stood apart, drinking
slowly before sneaking a quick glance at her phone, clearly less involved than the others.

From his distance, William noted that Simon and Sally appeared rather close; Emma and Chris seemed quite affectionate, too. Josh was part with them, part eyeing up the talent on the other side of the car park where two adjacent park benches were a focal point for several groups of young people.

Charlotte was on her phone chattering to her absent boyfriend when she caught a reflection on the camera lens William was holding. 'Emma, look over there…'

Emma stopped canoodling with Chris to look. 'Hang on, isn't that what's his face?'

Chris wasn't interested. 'Could be anyone, Emma, just give us a kiss…'

She pushed him aside, 'No, Chris, it is him! Weirdo! You know.'

He finally but reluctantly took the trouble to check it out. 'OMG! You're right, it IS him, that one,'

Charlotte cried out. Josh was now onto it. 'He's filming us, what a perv!'

Sally said, 'He asked me out today' which was their cue to release howls of laughter; William receded into the shadows, cursing that he'd been spotted.

Simon roared, 'You should go if he asks you again and we can all film it secretly and have a bloody good laugh – *YouTube*, the lot.'

Josh did a swirl, 'And I thought he fancied me!'

'William,' Lucy said quietly, 'his name is William.'

At the mention of it, they nod and spread arms, as if – so what? Topic closed.

****************************

William managed to get inside the house where his landlord's family were noisily and possibly happily all watching telly in the lounge. If they heard him entering the hall, shutting the door and going upstairs to his little room, they gave no indication.

Why would they? He was just the latest tenant.

In his room he transferred the disc from his camera to his laptop and watched back the footage he'd shot outside the pub. He paused on Sally, stared at the image for a moment and then connected to his printer.

Her face came out on a slightly less than perfect A4 print which William carried to the wall where he taped it firmly. Taking a marker pen he obliterated her face in
repeated, savage, diagonal slashes.

The photo joined others, a series of images – all women, all obliterated with wild marker pens, so they were no longer visible. Or pretty. William lay back on the bed and admired his handiwork before drifting off.

*************************

Next morning, 'first thing', chilly but bright, Simon was decidedly impatient. They were outside the Pleasure Beach, the extended funfair and amusements area which made Yarmouth famous.

Still waiting for Sally and William, Simon thought constant pacing, sighing and looking at the time on his phone would bring them. 'Where the hell are they?'

'You don't suppose they got off together, do you, in the end?' suggested Chris with a grin.

Simon snapped back, 'Don't be stupid. She was fine when I left her last night.'

Emma yawned and held her coat closer around her.' Maybe it's too early. Do we have to film this early every day?

Lucy looked incredulous. 'It's half ten, gone!'

Josh finished what he thought of as a warm-up and offered, 'Got to shoot before it gets too crowded.'

Chris suggested, 'Perhaps Wierdiam went on to perv on someone else last night, got arrested and will be here when he gets bail?'

Some were amused as Sally ran up, somewhat out of breath, her long dark hair blowing about, 'Sorry, I am late, everyone. Sorry, Simon.'

He snubbed her as Josh asked, 'Rough night was it Sally?'

'Now all we need is Big Willy with his perv camera and we're off.'

Sally wasn't best pleased at Simon's reaction. 'So, I'm not the only one late, am I? So fuck you, Simon.'

'Yeah, you did, Sally and I got the tee shirt and the herpes. Can we move on?

Sally's jaw dropped and she drew breath for a good row; Emma ready to join in at his crossing a line with that remark when William was sighted struggling across the road with his gear in his arms and round his neck.

Only Lucy helped him, while the rest watched and Simon tapped his foot. 'Sorry, Simon, I feel a bit sick …'

And as if to confirm it, William retched into the gutter. An old woman passing by leading a pint-sized-pooch physically recoiled in disgust. Somebody would have to clear that up. Lucy offered him a tissue from her bag and looked for something bigger to tackle the mess. 'Sorry, Simon…'

He wrestled with the tripods and cameras with unresponsive fingers. Simon's patience was finally gone, 'Last chance, I can get someone else if you stayed up too long past your bedtime last night.' Josh laughed dutifully but William was no nearer being ready.

Simon's fists clenched ready to thump William, but Charlotte slotted her phone away in her pocket and calmed Simon by assisting William.

Josh decided to be awkward. 'I'm ready. Remember I have a monologue here and I don't want any of you buggers upstaging me, yeah?'

Chris said, 'I won't if you leave mine alone in the next scene, deal?'

Emma spluttered, 'you boys are lucky you've got monologues, my part is so small I'm wondering if I'm really needed.' Charlotte would have none of that – 'I think you'll find my part is the nothing one, just an add-on.'

Lucy smiled at them, 'It's all experience, though, isn't it? For your CV and life.'

'Says the only girl who's actually got lines worth speaking!' snapped Sally, just checking her hair in a pocket mirror again.

William's voice cut across them. 'Right, ready! Stand by for action!'

'I say action, thank you, Wilco, not you...' pointed Simon.

With a simple shrug, William panned the camera, focussing on Charlotte.

Chris asked, as if just aware of where they were, 'Why are we outside this fun palace, Simon?'

'Pre-season, winter closure Pleasure Beach is a symbol for the shut down emotions of the broken hero, as he struggles to find an identity for himself, you know ...'

They nodded warmly, but clearly didn't have a clue. Josh whined, 'Can we start, I'm freezing my best mates off here.'

Simon barked the 'action' order and a rather stilted, chilly piece of mime began with Josh providing a voice-over of torment and anguish about a long winter and dark nights of the soul.

*******************************

Serving as a late breakfast and an early lunch, Simon halted proceedings so they could mill about and get warm. Lucy arrived back with three large brown bags of McDonalds which they fell on as if they hadn't eaten for days. William was last.

Half the chips had gone from his bag and his burger was squashed. Only Lucy noticed. 'William, I can't eat all these chips...' she began, but Charlotte overheard, 'Ta, Luce, I'm starving,' and she took the lot.

Lucy smiled at William who wasn't surprised, as she was called away by Emma to talk about somebody she'd just seen on a pushbike, leaving William with Charlotte, stuffing her face.

William swallowed, checked the others were all looking elsewhere and asked Charlotte, 'can I just say something, Charlotte?' She shrugged as she wiped her mouth on the now finished brown bag.

He began, 'you know how in a group, you get a feeling that you have something in common with only one or two?'

She reached for her mobile. 'I feel we have something in common, Charlotte.'

She nodded at the screen which he took to be progress. 'A love of film, a desire to make this work and to really advance our careers.'

Her hand passed across the screen, checking emails and social media, and just gave him, 'mmmm', so he ploughed on. 'I er, um, I wondered if you'd go and have a drink with me, you know, after today's shooting, just us, you know?'

'I get it,' Charlotte smiled at William, 'you're asking me out? Too late. Simon has already asked me for tonight.' She handed him the wrappings from the food and rejoined the others.

She straightway texted the news to her boyfriend and told Emma who told Chris who told Sally who told Josh who told Simon as he talked to Lucy. Everyone laughed, except Lucy.

\*\*\*\*\*\*\*\*\*\*\*\*\*\*\*\*\*\*\*\*\*\*\*\*\*\*\*\*\*\*

Outside Emma's family home, they gathered in the evening. She stood outside, happy to play the hostess. Nobody clocked that William wasn't among them.

'Come on in guys, everybody's out so we can make ourselves at home... though I'm glad you brought some drink, I don't think my dad would be happy...'

They piled into the front room and Chris asked Simon, 'how do you think it's going?'

Simon grabbed a bottle of beer from the supermarket bag that Lucy was carrying and as he moved towards Charlotte conceded, 'We're getting there. Slowly.' He completely ignored Sally.

Josh asked, 'Hey Charlotte, are you bringing your boyfriend?' as a means of stirring Simon up.

She shook her head. 'Not tonight. Oh, you mean, what's his name?' Others laughed as Simon stood very close to her, which made Sally suggest, 'perhaps he's in the garden with a camera!'

Emma responded, 'We could go and have a look. Shall I leave the curtains open?'

Josh nodded, 'Why not? Give him something to look at.'

Lucy asked simply, 'Did anyone think to invite William, then?' But nobody bothered to answer, the music went on and they were off.

As darkness deepened, William crept near the window, afraid he'd be seen by neighbours and the chilling group inside. He focussed the camera through the window, caught Simon and Charlotte laughing and froze the shot.

\*\*\*\*\*\*\*\*\*\*\*\*\*\*\*\*\*\*\*\*\*\*\*\*\*\*\*\*\*\*\*\*\*\*\*

Later, in his room William put the still of Charlotte laughing on his screen. He stared a moment, then thumped the desk, angry. He printed it off and reached for his marker pen. Changing his mind, he opened a drawer to find a craft knife and shredded the image of Charlotte so violently he accidentally sliced his underarm, just above the wrist.

He stared as a few drops of blood dripped onto the script. Then he cut himself some more.

\*\*\*\*\*\*\*\*\*\*\*\*\*\*\*\*\*\*\*\*\*\*\*\*\*\*\*\*\*\*\*\*\*\*\*\*\*\*\*

Next morning they gathered outside the Sealife Centre with no delays and got straight into a scene of free dancing-cum-movement that represented aquatic environments. All went well till Simon started pacing.

'Cut! Cut! What the hell? You're not a bunch of GCSE students doing a bad warm up, you are supposed to be more creative. Let me have the shooting script? Oi, you got it, Big Willy?

'I've got it here, Simon. And it's William'.

'Yeah, yeah, let's have it. Here. Now.'

As William walked over with it, Charlotte smirked at him in a provocative way while looking up from her phone, never missing an opportunity to check it. Simon noticed blood on the script.

28

'What the fuck is this? Blood?'

'Sorry, Simon, I, er... cut my arm...' He showed them the still raw cut.

Sally peered at it, 'looks more like your wrist, mate!'

Charlotte looked at William as if he was a specimen on a slab. 'Gutted were you, I turned you down?'

Lucy's reply was, as ever, practical, caring. 'You ought to put something on that, William.'

Emma responded, 'I've got a small first aid kit in my bag, my mum is a nurse, always insists I carry it, let me see....'

Chris raised his eyebrows, 'Florence Nightingale!' which provoked a fresh outburst from Simon, 'Bloody hell! We'll have to stop for a scene from *Nights in A&E* right here on the streets of Yarmouth.'

Emma smiled at Simon, 'That's funny, Simon, blood-y hell'. She wrapped William's wrist as the others lost interest and left them to it.

With no hesitation, William swallowed and spoke directly to Emma's head bowed over his arm. 'Emma, I just wondered, well, you know, I just feel that of all the people in this group, that you and I have got something in common.'

'Hey, stop there, if this is a try-on, forget it, you know I'm with Chris.'

'Yeah, but, just a drink and a talk. I feel that none of us has really, well, talked. At least I haven't. Talked and listened, that must be nice. Tonight, a quick drink...'

Simon returned to them as Emma tied off the dressing. 'All done? What's this cosy little head to head? Don't like the look of that! You want advice, Emma, you just ask me, ok?'

'Or I can ask Chris?'

Simon twisted his face in disgust. 'When you want a real director, ask me.'

He gave her a knowing grin and she smiled back. Chris didn't like it but was powerless.

**********************************

They descended on the Regent Bowls that evening, playing in pairs - Simon with Emma, Chris with Josh, Lucy with Sally, and Charlotte keeping score, all while having a running conversation on her mobile, 'Look, I'm sorry, OK. Yeah, I know. Well, we're nearly done, and then you can see the film and see more of me... OK well come down here now, instead of moaning, I'm here, everybody's paired up, except me keeping score which is about much fun as... yeah, well sorry, last night, no.... er, we just filmed on a bit and ended up round Emma's house, you know... No, he is nothing to me, you're so jealous. No, Simon is just directing, OK.'

In the game, Simon and Emma were soon points ahead, lording it over the others, high fiving like it was going out of fashion.

'You'll be sorry for this later, Emma,' hissed Chris, which received the response, 'I don't think so, Chris.'

Suddenly Josh cried out, pointing – 'Oh no, he's over there, look!'

Everyone swivelled to see William scurrying out the building. Josh called out to him, but he'd gone. They found that amusing. Lucy looked at the door William had gone though with a rather sad expression. Chris turned back to the game to see Simon with his tongue down Emma's throat.

******************************

That evening, William was back in his room looking at the wreckage, the absolute mutilation of his images, faded dreams and fantasies. After a moment of thought, he opened his wardrobe door to pull the cord from his old, worn, childish dressing gown.

He sat at the desk and removed his shoelaces. He tied two plastic bags together with the cord and laces to make a noose, one end on the door handle outside, the other threaded over the door and into his room.

With a sense of grim inevitability, William put the chair in place, checked for stability before stepping onto it, attached the tight noose round his neck and kicked the chair away.

He swung, his weight crashing him back into the door as he fought for breath against the cord. The plastic bag slipped undone and he dropped to the floor.

It was almost funny and if he hadn't been shaking from the adrenalin rush, he'd have laughed aloud. Picking himself and the chair up, he looked in the mirror over the sink. His neck was very red. Why had nobody filmed that?

******************************

The next day they were outside a seafront pub. It was no warmer than before, but they all felt a sense of the end being

31

in sight now and soon they could go on to other things. William alone was late.

Simon addressed them all, his tone rather subdued from his usual. 'Well, I don't know what we can do today, guys. That twat tried to hang himself last night, and he's in the James Paget Hospital, so, suppose we ought to see him.'

They already knew this, but it was still shocking. Lucy told them, 'No, he's not in hospital now, they sent him home.'

Sally, amazed, demanded 'How do you know that?'

'I rang him on his mobile.'

Charlotte confessed, 'Didn't know you had his number.'

Josh offered, 'I didn't know he had a mobile!'

Lucy said, 'I wrote all our numbers down at that very first script read-through we did....

Sally gathered her bag to leave, 'Yeah, we didn't know how weird he's turned out to be. Lucky escape for me, I reckon.'

Charlotte nodded, 'I was just thinking the same.'

Emma sighed. 'And me too. I had a lucky escape.'

Chris would have none of that. 'I don't think you did, Emma, not last night. I wish you had gone for a drink with the weirdo, instead of how it turned out...

Emma shook her head at him, 'Chris, you don't own me.'

Simon cut in, 'chill a bit, Chris. Get over it. You can have her back now anyway. I'm done. Josh laughed out loud, 'You straights are so complicated!'

Lucy asked, 'Are we going to see him, then?'

Simon shook his head. 'I dunno, Lucy, I'd rather go for a drink, but you go, and find out if he's coming back, as long as he promises not to top himself again!

Chris jeered, 'Yeah, send Willy Wonka our love!'

Lucy stated simply, 'His name is William.'

*******************************

In his room William dozed on the bed, his neck bandaged and his head thumping. They'd given him something but it hadn't yet kicked in.

Lucy, reluctantly shown in by the landlady, stood taking in the damaged photos, the debris before sitting herself on the desk chair. 'Hello, William, I'm sorry to disturb you. Somebody from downstairs let me in. How are you feeling?'

'Lucy, so good of you to come ... how did you know I was back home?
'
'I went to the hospital and they said you'd been discharged.'

'I'm OK now. A bit sore round the neck and the police are coming round to talk to me a bit later. I feel a complete bloody idiot.'

'I thought they'd have kept you in longer.'

'Needed the bed, I believe.' There was a pause. 'Are the others coming?'

She shook her head and smiled. 'I doubt it. Simon was talking about the pub.'

'I suppose that's the end for me, they won't want me to film it now...'

Lucy asked, 'Will you be sorry?'

'Not really. Are you enjoying it?'

'Not really. But I signed up for it so I'll see it to the end. You never know, it might be good eventually.'

William said with a sign, 'Yeah. There are some good actors in it. It's just that they don't think much of what I do, or of me. It's been hard.'

Lucy reached across to put her hand on his. 'I know it has. William... I just wondered, well, you know, I just feel that of all the people in this group that you and I have got something in common.'

He stared back at her, not sure if she was taking the piss.

\*\*\*\*\*\*\*\*\*\*\*\*\*\*\*\*\*\*\*\*\*\*\*\*\*\*\*\*\*\*\*\*\*\*\*\*\*

On a much warmer evening as the summer had edged closer, William and Lucy walked side by side, not actually touching.

Lucy looked around, 'They're shooting along here, in one of these side roads; I can't remember which. If we walk along, we'll see them, though we are early. The last scene is the night one, you know?'

'Better to be early, isn't it? I just don't know what they'll say. What will Simon want?'

She thought a moment. 'Well, he has to finish it, time and money and all that. I think he'll want you to finish the shoot in your own style.'

'Thank you, Lucy.'

She looked at him closely. 'What for?'

He grinned, 'For being kind to me, understanding and everything. Will you still be friends when we're back with the others?'

Now she grinned. 'Of course I will. I told you we have a lot in common; neither of us fits into a crowd.'

'Can we go for a drink afterwards, just us?'

'That would be nice.'

They paused at the corner, looking into the small side street where the others waited. Emma and Chris were arguing about Simon.

He suddenly said, loudly, 'Oh fuck it. I've had enough. Sod the film, sod everyone. I don't need Lucy or the fucking weirdo on the camera. You coming with me, Emma?'

'I'm going to sort it out with Chris.' Neither man looked impressed.

Simon went on, 'Charlotte? Sally? Either of you fancy a run out in the car?'

Charlotte was too deeply into her phone; Sally shook her head. Simon moved to his car. Josh said, 'You shouldn't drive, Simon.'

Ignoring them all, Simon took off with a tyre squeal.

Puzzled at Simon's departure, William looked at his watch as he and Lucy crossed the road into the side one. He was excited, happy and relieved all at once. Lucy smiled at his boyish openness.

He told her, 'It's a new beginning for me, I really believe that, and it's all down to you ….Lucy, you.'

She gripped his hand, 'You always had strength of character within you, you'll do well now.'

'With your help?'

'This is your lucky day at last, William.'

He nodded, 'Yes, it really is.'

As they reached the middle of the road, Simon's car took William down, wrenching his hand out of Lucy's.

Simon stopped and leapt out, white and already shaking. Everyone stared, unable to even move for a moment.

If anybody had thought to film it, all of them gathered round an unconscious William half under Simon's car, a shocked Simon and Josh, Emma and Charlotte and a sobbing Lucy, it would have made a superb final shot.

And so to fade out.

# Judging Books

It was early in his first day that he suspected people generally didn't like him. There was a air of mistrust, despite the fact that he'd been sent to take charge of policing and security in the sector.

Misha was a fourth generation local – or at least near enough. He'd trained, served his probation at some pretty vile trouble-spots in other sectors. At his time of life – 39 – it was natural that he should look forward to being assigned a challenging but relatively peaceful area.

But during the first day in the office and on the streets as he walked out, he sniffed more than a sense of curiosity from citizens. They watched him with cold, angry eyes. Some were suspicious, yes, but many were outright hostile, leaning against walls or balanced on crutches.

As he'd dashed across a road of moving traffic, skilfully gliding between moving vehicles without disturbing any of the drivers at all, he heard two people in wheelchairs paused outside the main foodstore shout something that sounded like, 'disgraceful' and 'you should be ashamed of yourself.'

Misha ignored what he thought they said and simply waved a cheery greeting as he hastened on, enjoying surveying his new patch with a chance to stretch his legs after a lengthy journey cooped up in the slow-moving train all the way from the metropolis to the centre of the sector.

But it was in the evening that he was really brought up against the sheer hatred and loathing his very presence caused. He'd looked forward to the concert and had managed to get the timing of his placement to coincide with the one-off gig from The Paranodes, a group heavily into old-fashioned music played live by a drummer, three guitarists and two girl singers.

The management had saved him a seat, as they'd been asked, and he found it strange that he was positively hissed at as he took it during the gathering anticipation in the auditorium just before the music started. Hissed at him. He looked around and it dawned on him that he, though not especially tall, towered over the audience around and in front of him.

And, more importantly behind him. An old man snapped to his back and head, 'Oi, you AB, I can't see through you!' Misha turned to take in that the man had no legs and was perched on the front of his seat. Misha muttered apologies, but it wasn't his fault.

The lights flooded on in time with the opening chords. Misha had never seen a picture of them having only heard their music and was surprised that they all had degrees of various what he would call 'conditions'. Downs, Special Needs and physical challenges.

The opening number, *'Don't Let Them Get You Down'* was a particular favourite and stirred everyone. Misha pushed himself as low as possible into his seat in the hope that the old man behind would stop grumbling and calling him AB, which made no sense.

In the interval, Misha was glad to get up to look for refreshments. It was an idea, but the reality was that every aisle, each door, especially the toilet exits were clogged with wheelchairs, walking frames and crutches and a range of people nursing something that meant they were different from Misha.

In a sudden rush of impatience he jumped forward into a tiny space ahead with no body in it. His arm hit someone moving slowly out of a row of seats - he almost sent the man sprawling. A rash of hasty apologies and an attempt to help the man were brushed aside with shocking anger and deep loathing.

His return to his seat unleashed a further torrent of abuse from the old man and three of his neighbours. Misha longed for it to be over and it wasn't till the last number and the encore that he found himself caught up in the sheer joy of quality music.

The penultimate number was one of their own, a mixture of 'Delilah', 'Frankie and Johnny' and all the country ballads about a woman who done her man wrong that they could think of. With a twist. In this song, the wronged man didn't kill the bad woman, but killed everyone she cared about leaving her alive and alone in a life of hell.

It was moving, horrific and put Misha in mind of a girlfriend he'd once had. But he couldn't have killed anyone. He was a trainee cop then, after all.

Their finale, 'It's All the Others' was an emotional battle-cry for the afflicted, a confidence boosting hymn and Misha was on his feet applauding as the band reached the climax and took their bow.

That was what people did in theatres, sports events, churches, they stood to applaud to show that they'd enjoyed it.

Never mind anybody they blocked out. The audience was clapping and shouting but gradually Misha realised that he was standing alone, obscuring the view of several dozen people who were snarling and gesturing at him. 'Sit down, you selfish AB bastard' was the most clear to him.

For the first time he understood that he was the only person who could stand for more than a few moments without falling or feeling dizzy. Misha was alone in a world of what he would call the disabled, though he knew he was supposed to call them differently-abled.

Being the odd one out made him feel uncomfortable.

*********************************

'But I thought I'd have been told in the briefings to prepare me for this new job,' shouted Misha the morning of his second day at Tobin, his assigned assistant who was leaning against their office wall, her crutches parked beside her. Tobin said nothing.

'It's ridiculous. And why do they keep calling me AB?'

'That means Able Bodied. It's a derogatory term, you are able bodied in a world where we are all what we are. They dislike you; you make them feel angry at having to prove themselves. You are the freak here, guv,' Tobin explained.

Misha felt anything but comfortable with that. He looked at his desk, piled high with routine admin with the problem matters at the very bottom, to catch him out and test him. The door crashed opened and with a white stick feeling the way and tapping the cabinet and desk legs, in came Serin.

She was average height, late fifties, a little overweight and with an air of world-weariness he'd seen before in long serving officers.

'Boss?' she asked, as much to ask permission to speak as to make sure he was in the room. 'I'm here and pleased to meet you. I'm Misha.'

'Yeah, I'm Serin, how do you do and all that. Boss, double murder has been reported. A male, 46, in one house and a boy, 11, in the next door house. The father of the boy is being held on the settee in his house, shaking. A gun was taken from him. The mother is in hysterics.'

'Let's go!' yelled Misha, delighted to have something to do that required his skills. 'Tobin, call in whoever we need and get me a car!'

As they went, Serin keeping up surprisingly well, she filled in some more details, so by the time they'd bundled into a car and a driver had been instructed to set off to the location by sign language, Misha had a picture.

The dead man, Jaydon, and the man who had apparently killed him, Liffen, had originally been very friendly neighbours. Over the years they'd fallen out big time and had had confrontation incidents necessitating police attendance on several occasions.

Matters had clearly come to some terrible head if Liffen had killed Jaydon and his own son, Slode.

'Well, we mustn't judge it till we've got all the facts,' Misha muttered, speaking his thought out and glancing behind to see that two other cars were following, filled with other officers.

*********************************

A motorised buggy blocked the only sensible parking space outside the house, so an irritated Misha ordered the driver to stop in the road. 'Why hasn't somebody moved that vehicle?'

'Oh that's the Professor's, boss. Chief scene of crime officer. We call him the Professor because he's brilliant at reading scenes, at finding the fragments of DNA that the villains didn't expect to turn up.'

Misha decided to keep further comment to himself. He'd judge the man when he saw his work on this case. But how the hell had he got there before them in that contraption?

Misha was directed through the little crowd of neighbours and the cordon to Jaydon's house where forensics were already at work, filming, sifting, taking swabs and nosing around thoroughly.

Jaydon was lying on the kitchen floor, parallel to the cooking facilities and on his back staring lifelessly at the ceiling. Misha studied him a long time, feeling that Jaydon had a hint of anger on his white face. Two shots to his chest from close range had smashed out much of his upper torso.

'Shotgun, boss,' offered Tobin. 'Where is Jaydon's wife?' Serin asked and a junior at the door told her she was at the hospital, acute shock. She hadn't found the body. The police had done that when they had received Liffen's call saying what he'd done.

Misha looked at Serin, wondering momentarily, a) what she was doing here as she couldn't see anything and b) how she could contribute to the search of the house. But he thought it better to say nothing; his team seemed to be generally competent and doing things by the book.

He nodded and said, 'let's go next door.' As they made to move, the Professor came in on crutches and nodded to Misha. 'The Professor, I presume?' Misha said with a grimace and offered his hand.

The Professor took it, inadvertently letting his right hand crutch clatter to the floor. Misha picked it up for him and said, 'First thoughts?'

'Oh, I'd say at this stage, Misha – and by the way we have looked forward to you taking over control of this area; we haven't had an AB in charge since I was a young man. No, here, it appears to be as described by the suspect, Liffen.'

Misha waited. 'Liffen, in a rage, shot his neighbour for reasons we don't yet know and then, still angry, went home and shot the boy upstairs.'

'His son, Slode.'

'He shot the boy, Slode. He rang the police and confessed. But things may not be quite as they seem, Misha. We shouldn't judge a book by its cover. The back page is the time to judge.'

Unable to think of anything further to say or ask, Misha nodded. 'Right. We'll leave you to it, Professor.'

The house next door, a carbon copy of Jaydon's, was busier, though most of the forensics had yet to make a start. The boy, Slode, was in his bedroom, lying at an awkward angle across his tablet and what looked school work. He had been shot once through the chest as he turned to look up, presumably at Liffen. His face showed surprise.

He was dressed in Saturday casuals, the room was warm, slightly fuggy and needing the curtains open to bring in light. But perhaps not. Misha had seen dead children before, but not like this. Not butchered in cold blood.

The wife and mother, Moison, was at the kitchen table, sobbing on the shoulder of a one-armed female police officer.

Misha waited a moment but all he could make out was something approximating to 'It's all my fault', so decided to wait awhile to question her.

Jaydon was on the settee in his living room, two police officers, one with a prosthetic arm and the other very small, so small that Misha took a moment to locate her. Jaydon was doing nothing beyond staring at the space in front of him, his eyes filled with hatred, his fists clenched.

Misha had an uneasy feeling he'd seen the man before, but couldn't place him. A shotgun in a roll of clear plastic lay across the armchair, safely away from Liffen. Misha took the man in. 'Shotgun legal?'

Serin answered. 'Yes, boss. He has a hunting permit.'

'Liffen?' The man showed no indication of hearing Misha, who positioned himself in a crouch directly in front. 'Liffen?' he repeated. Still no response. He was either in deep shock or was a very good actor. As Misha moved away, he noticed a crumpled ticket to the Paranodes' event of last night.

And then Misha recognised the man he'd knocked into.

Misha decided Liffen should be moved. 'Liffen, we are taking you to the police station while my officers continue their work here and at your next door neighbour's.' At the mention of next door, Liffen snapped to life, growled and struggled to raise himself.

All officers made a rush to contain him, but Liffen was a spent force. His movements were uncoordinated and clumsy. The officers took hold of him and helped him towards the door. The man had special needs at the best of times; now he had a whole lot more.

Misha didn't feel that Liffen had recognised him and also that the man's clear rage was far more deep seated than some small incident at a concert.

**********************************

At the station, Misha had looked forward to leading the interrogation, but the burdens of command were quickly apparent. The pile of papers had increased. Tobin told him the local press wanted to talk to him.

He knew goodwill was vital, so agreed that he'd see them early on. He freshened up and made sure his hair was tidy. They'd surely want a picture as well as some comforting words about his mission in maintaining confident law and order in this sector.

The pair of journos who'd been sent were unpromising— one was so old she could barely hold her body upright and the other was a victim of motor-neurone disease, speaking via a muscle-device attached to a portable screen on the arm of his massive wheelchair.

They wanted to film him, yes, but the interview was about him being AB in general and in particular his crass insensitivity last night at the Paranodes' gig of standing up and blocking the view of 'three quarters' of the audience.

Misha was taken aback at this lesson in the way the media works. Something to criticise is always more newsworthy than something to praise, because that makes people jealous and aware of their own inadequacies.

Misha put on a brave front and blustered and huffed about not being fully briefed, unaware and apologising profusely. It took forever and he was quite pleased with his salvage operation until he saw the result on the news later.

But first, he wanted to catch up on the double murder. Tobin reported that they'd interviewed Liffen and he'd confessed and signed the paperwork. He refused to say why he'd murdered his neighbour and son. Junior officers were interviewing Slode's mother, Moison.

Her story was that she was to blame for it all, so the general consensus in the team was that she and Jaydon had been rather too close and Slode was Jaydon's son, not Liffen's. Open and shut case.

Jaydon's widow had been interviewed at the hospital and then sent off to stay with a relative. She had nothing to add, never really understanding what her husband and Liffen had fallen out about, much less why he stormed in to their house this morning with a shotgun.

*****************************************

The Professor's call had brightened Misha's day a little. There was something he needed to see.

Misha called for a car to take him to the lab, but found he wasn't allowed to make the journey alone. He had to be driven with Tobin and Serin aboard and a back-up car behind them.

The Professor kept them waiting ten minutes while he finished cutting up a manic depressive who'd hanged himself off the footbridge over their main road. 'Not like the movies, hey, Misha, where the focus is on just one case and everyone is suddenly free to tackle it!!'

Misha mumbled his thanks for the Professor's time as they were all shown into Lab 4B. Small, clinical and heavy with disinfectant, the chilly chamber had Jaydon and Slode stretched out on adjacent metal tables.

Parking one crutch, the Professor flung off the cloth from one and then the other with what he thought was a flourish. 'Now, what do you see?'

Misha studied man and boy. Beyond their gaping chest wounds were the cuts made to remove key organs. 'Death by shotgun in both cases,' the Professor confirmed.

He wasn't sure what was extraordinary, why he was brought here. They had the confession, so it was quite straightforward. The Professor shook his head, sorry that the new Chief failed to see the obvious.

'Look at their feet.'

Jaydon had a pair of very small, high-arched, curled and hammer-toed and twisted, deformed feet with vicious calluses and corns on the balls and heels. Slode's feet were a younger version of them, slightly less pronounced.

'Father and son.'

Misha nodded. 'So that supports the view that Liffen found out about Jaydon having it off with his wife.'

'This confirms it. The condition they have is hereditary motor and sensory neuropathy. It's a genetic mutation, passed on by a sufferer in a one in two chance to each child that he or she has.

'So that's why Moison said it's all her fault. She had the relationship with Jaydon and passed the disease to her son who was raised by Jaydon till it became obvious that the boy had it and so wasn't his own.'

'And that's what must have triggered the falling out between them,' Tobin grinned, happy that it was all coming together in a nice speedy resolution.

The Professor eyed Misha closely. 'Happy, boss?'

'Oh yes, Professor. A result. We can file this one away and get Liffen in court. Job done.'

But he didn't fool the Professor.

Few things were what they seemed. But he stored it away. The day could come when he needed something over Misha.

And for his part, Misha wondered how long he had to serve before he could credibly apply for a transfer to somewhere where he wasn't the only AB in town.

Unless being here for long turned his brain so that eventually he fitted in perfectly.

# The Quiet Man

It was their seventh cruise. He'd added them up before they left, because one of the most frequent conversations that cruise passengers indulge in – 'and is this your first cruise?' - meant a high number reply would lead to instant camaraderie among the fellowship of cruisers.

Where have you been? How much did you pay? Which shipping lines? All vital information for the nosy holiday-maker, of course. The first person he replied to this year was a woman with a sun-gnarled face and wrinkly shoulders as they stood waiting on deck wearing lifejackets for the interminable evacuation rehearsal to be endured.

'Oh this is our seventh!' he cried with a small sense of achievement, suddenly thinking that the half night in a hotel with the 4am check in for 6am flight had been worth it. The tiredness would float away as the ship set sail in an hour or two. And he would feel calmer.

'Seventh this year?' she demanded, quite seriously. The serial cruiser deflated his moment. He reached out with both hands, grabbed her lifejacket and rigorously tightened it about her neck while lifting her feet off the ground as she struggled for air, her legs flailing pointlessly - he hung on till she was a lifeless rag.

In his mind.

James and Sally were occasional cruisers, when they'd saved up enough, they enjoyed one, as they'd done every year or so since their children had stopped holidaying with them.

But James was a serial killer. He'd murdered, slaughtered, butchered, annihilated, taken out, offed, done away with and revenged himself in the most barbaric, gruesome, merciless and savage ways on more human beings than anyone else in history.

In his mind.

Outwardly people called him The Quiet Man; inwardly he seethed, raged, boiled, loathed and hit back with mafia-like retaliation as he'd done most of his life. He had what some styled 'an enigmatic personality', others an 'enigmatic personality disorder.'

Teens, university, places where he'd worked, his town, most roads he'd driven on, most queues in shops, many officials, hundreds of places they'd visited were littered with the corpses of people who'd offended, harassed, crossed, slighted, angered, thwarted, humiliated, ignored or wronged him.

He felt instantly better for it every time and as far as he knew, he'd never actually done it. He had various tests in his earlier life when he raised adults' concerns by his anger and occasional outbursts, but was never actually and visibly violent. He was just short-fused with a pathological desire to imagine people dealt with, graphically.

To take one recurring scene of his assassinations – supermarkets. People who block aisles while mindlessly chattering to people they probably saw last week or even live next door to. People who distract the cashier and then suddenly are surprised that they have to pay so fumble around for money. People generally.

Over the years his ire began to include people who were not present, but still got under his skin – all those with tattoos who thought they were being 'different' when they were merely conforming, those who spoke in an Estuary accent with an Australia uplift question at the end of every sentence, those who used 'um' as a substitute for words.

He'd once thought of writing to his MP suggesting a new offence – criminal stupidity – with the penalty of amputation, tongue removal or being shredded alive. In public.

But his MP had been hung, drawn and quartered when she ran late to a public meeting he attended and failed to apologise sufficiently and in proportion to the Quiet Man's time she'd wasted.

He kept copious notebooks of all perpetrators against him. It was less a diary than a blueprint for a horror movie that he thought perhaps one of his kids could make when he was gone.

Students, colleagues, three former girlfriends who'd betrayed him before he met Sally, passers-by, people who outlived their friendship – all dead. And some of them several times over, often with a different form of execution.

He had beheaded, garrotted, gouged the eyes from, hanged, split from head to toe with axes scythes and chainsaws. He had fed poison, plague and fungus down people's throats, he had dismembered thousands; he had disposed of bodies in acid or in concrete foundations; thrown dozens in front of trains, lorries and planes, slapped to death and even fed his former sports teacher at school to an industrial salami slicer.

People didn't have to actually harm him. He had only to think or imagine they did. That was his variant of the vengeance syndrome he harboured.

Sally gave him a warning glance as she noticed his irritability rising with the woman in the lifejacket and prayed silently again that James would relax on this cruise. He usually did and the goodwill lasted for weeks. Once, and only once, they decided to keep in touch with a couple after the cruise.

Five months later James and Sally drove all the way to the Midlands in filthy weather for an hour of mindless chatter about their pointless lives and cruise highlights. The couples had nothing else in common.

James left them spread over their poncy garden, without legs, arms and heads. So Sally always gently avoided giving out contact details to anyone they got on with on board.

This cruise took in several Croatian, Greek and Italian ports in the Adriatic, including Corinth. They joined one of the bus excursions ashore to look at the sites of the ruins of Corinth.

Immediately he was taken with an exhibit in the little museum of artefacts discovered in the area – a line of headless statues. Apparently this was the remains of a factory where people had their own heads put on a flattering torso back in ancient times.

The statues were wonderful. James at once pictured appropriate heads on them, including one of the bar staff on the cruise who was asking for it with his annoying vocal traits, the woman in the cabin next to them who coughed for a hobby and would clearly be a night time problem and the patronising youth who had told him to 'sit there for me' as they queued to get on board.

And that was so far this cruise. James often felt he could supply murders to *Midsomer Murders*, the TV detective fantasy that specialised in usual butcherings. In his quieter moments he realised that he had a problem, while other people didn't spend their lives taking revenge on a stupid public he was forced to share earthly space with.

He looked at his long-suffering Sally – she was an angel, really, having coped with him for decades and stuck by him. She'd long since told him he should no longer drive or his road rages might become real and he'd accepted that.

He was, he told himself, a reasonable man. If only everybody else would cooperate.

He'd promised to make an effort this holiday and so he did. He allowed large numbers of his fellow passengers, several crew and almost everyone on the first couple of ports they stopped at to stay alive.

With the heat, the vast blue skies, near clear waters and on-demand food that was generally very agreeable and no shopping, washing up or clearing to do, James began to genuinely unwind and actually enjoy their holiday.

After a few days, they always felt that the cruise was the perfect holiday for them. When they wanted to socialise they could – and got dressed up for dinner in the restaurant. When they didn't, they ate in the cafeteria.

Conversations with others about the ship could be as long, short or humorous as people wanted.

Evening shows were generally fun, though the man allegedly in charge of entertainment had a weird walk, a strange distorted way of inverting his vocal pitches and a tone that implied everyone was a primary child. James coped by thinking of something else whenever that particular moron was invading his space.

So, it was a good holiday. Another week to look forward to with a different set of ports and time in the sun on deck and lounging around. Some lectures, some films, some people-watching... it was fine and by half way through, James was fully acclimatised to his new moderation.

Sally was fully relaxed, less on guard about him and able to talk to people, alone or as a couple, to have a laugh and to get the most from the opportunities of foreign travel, albeit with 1000 other British passengers.

It wasn't till the second week when most went home and new passengers arrived that James found himself challenged again. They spotted the suitcase among a pile at the end of their cabin corridor. New arrivals' luggage prior to being delivered to individual cabins.

They didn't recognise the name, but the address was clear enough. These new arrivals were from their town. It had happened before and had passed off without any problems. This time would be different.

James hurried Sally away and they carried on going down to dinner in the lift. As they made their way into the theatre for the evening show, James waited to be hailed by the people who lived but half a mile from their own house.

It was the next morning, a day at sea, as they walked the deck that Al and Marianne made themselves known. Older than James and Sally, but sporting the unmistakable local accent and pleased to have encountered James and Sally. Marianne and Sally knew each other from years back when Marianne had been a senior teacher and Sally a junior one in the same school.

James and Al made small talk. It took some doing to get away to finish their walk without agreeing to meet up with the older pair at a given time. But on a medium sized cruise ship it's hard to avoid certain people. Chance encounters in corridors, lifts, meal places, the gangway going on and off, coach trips out, queuing for the gents, sitting in the library or on any deck are frequent.

And so it was that Al talked a lot and James listened a lot, despite Al being a dead man several times over. Neither a bullet in the centre of his forehead nor being minced in the ships' propellers stopped old Al from bending James' ear.

James had worked at one point for the local authority in the department dealing with business development. Al had been a fisherman, a part time life-boatman and an all round busy man over his long years. He and some of his local old boys had ten years ago gathered a few quid to invest in an off-shore provisions company.

They'd applied to the council for some assistance – a business rates reduction, help with technology, a loan for equipment and a grant for training staff. Anything. They applied for it all.

And despite applications, assessments, meetings and support from other businesses in the supply chain, Al's consortium never achieved any local authority aid at all. They never really got off the ground; they lost all their money.

Now Al didn't hold James individually responsible, of course. But somebody in James' department had put the evil eye on them and while Al himself hadn't been charged with the negotiations, he'd worked hard for his money and to make a go of it and he'd lost the lot.

James recalled the case vaguely and knew that he personally had not made the decision and hadn't even studied the paperwork at the time. Al suddenly said he needed to go to the toilet – in their cabin as he preferred the privacy -and when he came back he'd bring James and Sally a drink.

James said that the last few living deck flunkies walked about frequently, so he could get a drink then, but Al insisted.

When he returned with a tray of drinks, he handed glasses to Sally and Marianne and made sure that James took the beer glass nearest to him. He sipped and thanked Al, who brushed aside the thanks and set off again.

James abandoned hope of reading in peace when Al re-opened discussion by repeating verbatim what he'd said before he went for drinks – that he didn't hold James individually responsible, of course, but somebody in James' department had put the evil eye on them and while Al himself hadn't been charged with the negotiations, he had worked hard for his money and to make a go of it and he'd lost the lot.

James sighed and put what he thought might be a sympathetic face on. 'That must have been a hard time, Al, I understand, I really do, but they had a set of government criteria to fill on start-up assistance and the cost benefit analyses were pretty stringent.'

Al smiled grimly at James as they lay side by side on a deck lounger, both couples having enjoyed a day ashore in Montenegro and were now soaking up some afternoon sun before the sail-away. 'No, James, but you see, here I am a working man after 45 years of grafting with my hands affording a week's cruise with no more in sight and you on your seventh this year.'

James opened his mouth to correct Al but there was no stopping the man, even when James picked up a steel hawser and forced it down the old man's chicken-neck throat. 'You see, James, I know that a sum of money was, shall we say, bunged to some big-shot in your department and when we didn't get what we needed, we heard it wasn't enough.'

James stopped reaching for a machine gun to fill the man with bullets and his jaw dropped. A bung? Bribery in that department? Impossible, wasn't it? Surely James would've heard or suspected something, especially if it didn't work! He racked his brains to think who would have taken money from an applicant company.

'You see, I can't help think that everyone in that department must have done two things, James. First, they had a share out of the money so that everyone was guilty, all tainted. And second, everyone must have had a good laugh at us because we were just little men who couldn't say anything as bribery was illegal.'

James was at a loss for a sensible word. It must have been the second in charge – Carmichael – a cretin who'd fallen foul of James many times and was dead and buried long ago. Literally this time. He had no reason to think Al had made it up, so Carmichael must have taken money.

And not delivered! Certainly no share went round to anybody else. James was innocent; he knew that and tried to tell Al so.

But his mouth refused to open. Their wives' voices droned in a muffled distance. Al relieved him of the beer glass as his arms dropped and he was in danger of spilling the remainder.

And in his dying moments James knew three things. Al had poisoned him. Al had brought poison on the ship to deal with anybody he found who needed punishing. Al was deep in the same, but stronger, condition as James himself was.

And when they returned home Al would have to check out James' widow Sally and see if she was living in better comfort than she should've been. Sally would have to suffer a million times for a crime James didn't commit but Al assumed he did.

In his mind.

# The Representative

It'd been a tough surgery. Most were these days with the government now out of its honeymoon period and the real difficulties stacking up. And then some.

Will Clements made himself available every other Saturday morning in different places about his constituency. He was there for all and everyone to queue and see him privately to talk, moan, ask, complain, get upset, take the piss or be in genuine, sometimes desperate, need.

It took all sorts. Clements had done it ever since he was first returned at the general election before last following the path his predecessor had trod - he had followed the exact same pattern. Many colleagues did fewer surgeries; some had appointments only so that a few of the cranks and persistent attendees were filtered out.

But Will Clements took them all. Council problems, health and social security, consumer affairs, tax matters, criminal defences, deaths, births and marriages – the full gamut of human life, including those issues that should have been dealt with by local councillors if people only understood the system better.

He was their representative. Their voice in the dark corridors of power and in being available he was living his life's dream. Now, with two election wins under his belt he felt he was sitting reasonably pretty, but never took anything for granted.

It had been a bit of a strain lately. Things at home were officially marvellous. But there were some issues to sort out.

He pinched his nose at the top, took a deep breath and waited for the next to come in. But the queue had gone. He was free.

Free to gather his papers, lock the council office, exchange a few pleasantries with the bobby at the outer door and drive home for a late and rapid lunch before the autumn fete to open this afternoon. At least he'd have his wife, Stella, and kids with him.

They'd struck a deal. In exchange for next weekend (their October half term) he'd agreed no functions so they could go to CenterParcs. They had just to go with him to the fete today and Church tomorrow. Job done. People liked to see him with his young family.

He recalled the discussion with a smile. Stella had presented a case for the break on the grounds that their lives were under scrutiny, were hard, were difficult for the children, were challenging for her who never asked to marry into public life and a forced rest amongst strangers and ordinary people would do him good.

Improve his temper, was what she'd meant. He resisted rising to that bait and accepted that they'd enjoy some family time.

His smile vanished as he walked towards his car. On his windscreen, flapping in the gathering breeze, was a tatty page torn from a lined exercise book. He'd had several like it already in the past few weeks.

'We know.' Written in biro, ragged lettering – could be a kid, could be a middle aged person. Whoever it was had been trying to panic him into some sort of response. Letters to his Westminster office, to his home address and to his party offices in the main town.

He'd numbered, dated and bagged each one. Time to tell the police. He turned back to the local cop to mention it, but he'd shuffled off. If the officer had seen anybody put the note on his car, he hadn't thought anything of it. And Will knew he shouldn't either.

But it was disturbing. What did they know? Who were they? Where were they? What did they want? It was like something out of a corny horror film, slowly building up the tension of a terror plot. But why him? He had nothing to be afraid of, he was pretty certain there were no nasty skeletons.

But, the sick dread that such notes created and fed was real enough. Whoever was doing this was a master of psychology. Anybody would start to wonder if there wasn't something after all.

And was it time to share the information with his agent, Ralph? And where the hell was Ralph this morning? Time was when an agent was expected to turn up to surgeries to help out the MP, to smooth the arrangements, organise coffee and generally make him or herself useful.

But not Ralph Barrow. Oh, no he thought himself too busy and above such menial tasks. He would have to move on soon, Will decided. He had served his purpose and was now becoming a real liability.

********************************

The remainder of the weekend went off fairly smoothly. At least there were no more notes. He mentioned to Stella as they cleared the snack lunch and the children played to avoid having to get ready to leave that there'd been another message on the windscreen and she made a sympathetic face and gripped his arm affectionately.

'You'll have to go to the police, Will. And what about sharing them now with Ralph?'

'Ralph was nowhere to be seen this morning.' She raised her eyebrows to show surprise but it didn't shake Will's feeling that she knew he wasn't or wouldn't be there. 'Well, it wasn't Ralph who put it on the car, then!' she smiled.

When he'd told her about the notes after the second one, they had discussed possibilities and what on earth was 'known' by somebody. Ralph was on Will's list of suspects, which didn't sit well with Stella, which in turn confirmed to Will that Ralph was indeed in the frame.

The fete was duly opened, Church was attended next morning and the whole family was happy enough, even though there was a sense of fulfilling a pact in order to be rewarded next week.

He himself had gone to a Party supper on the Saturday night; Stella feigned a headache. So, he arrived, bought enough raffle tickets to guarantee a win statistically, knowing that he'd be expected to put any prizes back in again. He quite often won the House of Commons bottle of whisky he'd donated, which several members found endlessly comical.

He circulated, sat at the top table and ate an indifferent meal. He'd stood and made his speech, a variant of the one he'd done last weekend with a couple of new points about the misguided opposition they'd faced this past week. He'd drawn the endless raffle, put back a box of bath scents and kept a box of chocolates for the kids.

The evening raised money, it made members feel part of his great machine – they were the ones who knocked on doors and delivered for and with him. They were his eyes and ears on the ground when he was in London.

And he was their representative. Of course, he represented all, but those who were his party members felt a special pride in having their own member among them. And again, where on earth was Ralph bloody Barrow? Agents surely went to functions whether the MP was present or not?

'Oh, he's hurt his foot on one of his long distance marches, apparently,' Stella explained when Will got home. She was sitting up in bed, reading, her face freshly moisturised, grateful to have missed yet another function. Will stood by the en suite door and considered it. 'You've seen him?'

'He hobbled round earlier to say he was sorry he missed your surgery, but he had to go to A&E and tonight he just couldn't face the standing around.'

'He could walk to his car to come round here but not to his car to drive to the surgery or the supper tonight?'

'I think he was in quite a lot of pain, actually.' She looked at her book again.

'He didn't think to ring me, leave a message or something?'

'I can't read his mind, Will, I'm just the messenger. It's a pity he couldn't hang on because you could have asked him yourself.'

'He's only just left?' She looked at him, unsure of his tone. 'What time did he come round?'

'I don't know exactly. I didn't record the time but I would have done if I'd known I was to be cross-examined. He waited till I'd got the children to bed as he didn't want to disturb them.'

'I bet he didn't.'

'Meaning?'

'Did he tell you about his application to be a candidate for the European Parliament?'

'I knew that ages ago.'

'Well, I declined to endorse it, this week, earlier. He didn't take it well.'

'Well of course he didn't. Why did you do that?'

'I don't trust him.'

'You still think he's leaving you childish notes and sending you weird anonymous letters?'

'I'm certain of it. I just can't trust him with anything important any more'

She was astounded, dropping her book and leaning forward. 'You don't trust Ralph Barrow, your own agent?'

*******************************

It hadn't always been like that. When Ralph first arrived, a mature agent with experience, he and Will had bonded well, enjoyed each other's company, engaged in banter but shared common purpose and hard work, particularly at the last election.

Ralph Barrow had been married but was alone and looking to make a fresh start. He was efficient with the admin, encouraged volunteers to run the
socials and political activities, raise funds, find more members and generally he supported Will, claiming he was happy working long, anti-social hours.

He was naturally funny, made people feel at ease when he was on form, worked a room better than Will did, and basked in people's approval and enjoyment of his company.

He'd like to have been an MP himself, but had missed a single chance years back. Will thought they'd have been friends in the House in that case, but Ralph said he was happy as an agent and besides, he thought there was a better chance of finding the right woman if he was in one community, rather than Westminster, the notorious hothouse and destroyer of marriages.

Will later realised that Ralph harboured little grudges and desires behind the surface of his affability. He clung to them as they festered in his mind. If anybody, paid or volunteer, mucked something up, Ralph had no more time for them.

His dreams of finding a woman were dashed after a relationship with the wife of an independent councillor turned sour last year. The fall out was not pretty with high octane rows, public slanging and some adjustments to everybody's social calendar.

It was after that when Will first noticed Ralph being especially attentive to Stella at events, often being round theirs with messages or to kick a ball in the garden with the kids or bring a book or some music for Stella.

After a time Will mentioned it to her, but she brushed it aside with a laugh and said she valued her family life too much to do anything with anybody, 'however appealing they were.'

That was the phrase that stuck in Will's mind and troubled him enormously. And it was shortly after that when the anonymous threats began to arrive.

**************************************

Will's reaction to the note on Monday morning was Oscar-worthy – he showed any passers-by that it rocked him.

'We know what you did, where you did it and how you covered it up...'

It was on his car parked on his drive outside. He lived reasonably well, but not ostentatiously so. The house and small garden were in full view. Anybody could have placed the note last night, perhaps a dog walker or jogger.

Pocketing it, he waved back at Stella on the front step. The kids were already in school, counting the days till next weekend. She was free beyond a visit to an old housebound couple that Will had asked her to do for him.

She'd seen him remove the paper and knew that the problem was not going to go away but would only get worse. For the hundredth time she dismissed two thoughts as she watched him drive off: she couldn't imagine Will doing something so bad nor Ralph writing those notes.

Clements drove to the offices of a small engineering company ten miles away to make a visit, talk to the directors and selected staff members before heading back to Westminster late afternoon.

Once the visit was done and the spotty youth on some Government training scheme he paid to do his photos had shot several of the MP on the shop floor, talking with expansive gestures, pointing meaningfully into the distance and getting into his car, Clements decided he had time to look in on his agent.

He found a parking space with some difficulty and got caught in a long conversation with an elderly couple moaning about the Post Office being moved into a large shop 100 yards away.

The office secretary was clearly not expecting him judging by her face as he breezed in with, 'Morning Joanne, all well? Ralph busy? He shoved open the inner office door without knocking to discover Ralph frantically folding away the *Daily Telegraph* and sliding a pile of documents in front of him.

'Morning, Ralph. Hear you've hurt your foot?' He was delighted to see that Ralph wasn't entertaining Stella on the desk, at least.

Ralph spluttered, 'Yes, I have, look,' and swung his leg out from behind the desk to reveal a foot swathed in a ludicrously over-size bandage out of a comedy film. 'Sorry, I was chasing around a bit on Saturday. All OK with the surgery? And the supper? Sorry.'

'You walked round to mine to talk to Stella, though, Ralph, how did you do that? Come to think of it, how did you know Stella wouldn't be coming with me to the supper?'

'I didn't. I was going to put a note in your door, but I saw the light on and she answered and invited me in for a glass and a chat. Call it lucky, I think.'

'Mmm,' replied Will with a grunt, looking at his watch, suddenly bored by this agent and his lies and plans, so naked, so inappropriate, so small. ''You could have stuck the note on my windscreen, Ralph, instead of going in to see Stella.'

Ralph pretended surprise. 'I could have. But I was glad to chat with her, haven't seen her for ages.' Will didn't respond.

The two men stared at each other, both aware of the chill between them that had not been so blatant before. 'Not lucky in my politics, though, Will…'

'I was asked to endorse your candidacy for the Euro elections, Ralph. You know I had previously come out big for both Mary and Simon from the west of the county, months ago. I could hardly swing against them and support my own agent.'

'You could have done whatever you chose, Will. You're the MP. I think I'd make a good MEP. It wouldn't tread on your toes, in any way.'

'I'll have a word up the line to area office, Ralph. See if it's too late.' Ralph nodded, playing along, though he knew it was too late, he'd already had the letter of rejection.

As Will looked again at his watch and moved to the door, Ralph studied him. How unfair that Will Clements, an ordinary, local, unremarkable man had got lucky and landed the MP vacancy and subsequent elections at just the right time. A beautiful wife he didn't appreciate enough and two great children. And he wouldn't even help his own agent up the ladder.

Ralph knew he needed another job in a different part of the country. Perhaps he could get a seat elsewhere, find a wife like Stella and enjoy some overdue success. He was two years older than Will Clements and in better shape. Why shouldn't he enjoy some of the good life, too?

\*\*\*\*\*\*\*\*\*\*\*\*\*\*\*\*\*\*\*\*\*\*\*\*\*\*\*\*\*\*\*\*\*\*\*\*\*\*

As Will drove, he cursed that he hadn't updated his music disks for this week's journeys. Oh well. He didn't particularly want last week's selection, but the silence gave him time to think about the notes and what was really going on.

The journey was uneventful until a near-hit on a pedestrian crossing as he drove along the river, approaching the Palace of Westminster, his second home. As he swept into the gates, acknowledging the nod and wave of recognition of the two officers at the gate, stopped to have his car searched underneath with mirrors before going down the ramp to the car park, he decided it was time to bring in the police.

He had to go down three levels to find a space, but every time he did it he was grateful to have the most secure carpark in London at his disposal, despite thinking of the IRA blowing Airey Neave up on that ramp all those years ago.

He hung his coat in the Member's cloakroom on his named hanger with its loop of ribbon for him to park his sword that he was not allowed to take into the Chamber. He loved the old traditions. Carrying just his briefcase, he trudged upstairs to the lobby of the Chamber, without getting out of breath.

At 45 he was still fairly fit though on the last check-up the Commons doctor had prescribed more exercise on top of his daily routine and losing some of that belly that was beginning to overgrow his trouser belt. He found PC Adkins, one of those who hung around the lobby, watching, managing and being available for advice and ensuring no Strangers entered.

Clements had got to know him a little, being the sort of MP who valued contacts at all levels of society and none, knowing that nothing was ever wasted. He told Adkins he had a little problem with some anonymous letters, but hadn't had time to raise them with his own police force's Special Branch, which would have been the normal way.

Adkins listened, watching Clements closely but saying nothing till he was done. 'Leave it with me, sir.' The two parted leaving Clements to go to the basement to find his secretary and make a start on the notes from the surgery and the pile of around 100 letters that would have arrived since last Thursday night when he'd left to return to his constituency.

*******************************************

The senior detective was brisk, efficient but not unsympathetic. He reached across the table in the cubby hole room and took the notes from Clements. 'That was helpful, to bag them all, like this, Mr Clements,' he observed.

Will Clements nodded and waited to hear the expert's opinion. 'We'll see if there are finger prints on them. I'll be in touch. This remains a confidential matter at this time. If there is any further action we need to take, we'll let you know, going forward.'

Clements hid his dislike of the pointless expression 'going forward' that seemed to be everywhere and thanked the man as he stood to leave and return to dictating letters to his secretary before heading upstairs to serve some time on a Standing Committee.

He reflected that the detective had shown no interest in what Clements may or may not have done, only that a public order offence may have been committed. And that it could foreshadow more serious threats to come.

The Committee Room corridor was packed, people coming to and fro, members, public and witnesses. There were several Standing Committees on Bills and a few Select Committees carrying out enquiries into current burning issues.

It was harder not to be in attendance on Select enquiries, but if a Member was on the Standing Committee of a long-running Bill, he or she could sit on a little bench outside the room during endless speeches and/or prevarication/filibustering by the opposition on a single clause.

Some dictated into little machines while working though correspondence; others did it directly to secretaries. When a division was called in the particular room, the Member had a minute and a few steps to get back inside to participate in that stage of democracy, a vote on a clause or amendment.

Among the tortuous case of an old boy fighting for his riparian rights on a stretch of riverside, the case of a single father he'd met at the surgery who said he hadn't enough to feed himself this week as the child support people had taken everything he earned this month and the case of a child tipped off a bus because she was two pence short of the fare after school, was another anonymous note.

Normally, his secretary, Anne, a senior and well-experienced lady who'd worked for Members since he was a boy, kept all the anonymous letters and envelopes and gave them to him in a mass every week or so. This one was on its own. He recognised it at once; Anne had put it in a clear plastic wallet.

He raised an eyebrow at her as he read it twice. 'We know all about it. How can you sleep at night?' She nodded, 'I had a call from security asking me to let you see any anons at once. This came today.' So much for it remaining a confidential matter, Clements thought as he began to feel this could slip beyond his control.

***********************************************

However, over the next few months, he was informed only that there were no prints on the notes except his own when he opened them and would he keep on gathering them in plastic wallets and to let them know if anything changed or escalated? Such as phone calls, notes in different handwriting, an actual encounter or anything apparent to one of his family?

Of course he would. And so the pile of notes grew with no escalation or change. Whatever he was supposed to have done remained unexpanded with no explanation at all. Whoever it was must be in the constituency.

Until he wasn't.

Sitting in the Chamber one day waiting to be called in a debate of prime importance on a change in employment law affecting hundreds of his constituents, a Badge Messenger tapped a folded note on the wooden edge of the bench.

Messengers did that to attract Members' attention when they were in the Chamber. They wouldn't pass a note along the rows; the Member had to take it. It was only for urgent notes from the lobby which was as far as visitors got. It was a request to come out and talk, often from people hopeful of a few minutes though it was not pre-arranged.

Clements scooted along the green leather, took the note with a quiet thank you. The Messenger muttered that they'd found the note on the floor, so apologies for the delay getting it in. He then stood impassively, waiting for Will to nod or scribble a response on it which would be taken straight back to the visitor.

The handwriting was all too familiar. It was the 'we-know-what-you-did' anonymous person! The opposition Member speaking sounded as if she was coming to the end of her tedious and predictable lambasting of the Government; Clements thought he might be next to be called.

He scribbled a quick reply on the request – 'Sorry, in Chamber waiting to speak, can't leave.' He returned it to the Badge Messenger with a second thought that he ought to abandon his attempt to speak, but then the lure of resulting local publicity won out, even over his curiosity.

He was called next and as he rose he put aside the problem and spoke for nine minutes taking one intervention and making a fairly good job of it, he thought. Among the twenty Members present, few agreed. The front benches looked bored witless and most other Members were only there waiting their turn to be called.

The convention was that after being called to speak, a Member should sit and listen to the next speech, regardless of what it said, in case that Member responded to anything that had been said previously.

It was a good half hour before Clements was able to leave the Chamber and get to the lobby to ask the duty police officer about any visitors for him. There were none and no staff could remember noticing one asking to see Will Clements and sitting waiting before giving up.

Will described Ralph Barrow to them, including that he had a massive bandage and must have walked with a limp, but they all shook their heads. The caller was a mystery. One of the staff wondered privately about this particular MP's well-being.

He wouldn't be the first Honourable Member to be off his chump. Or the last.

Will rang the detective he'd talked to and told him the visitor had come but vanished, and the Badge Messengers still had the request note. Will said he recognised the handwriting.

The police officer told him calmly that they'd look into it.

\*\*\*\*\*\*\*\*\*\*\*\*\*\*\*\*\*\*\*\*\*\*\*\*\*\*\*\*\*\*\*\*\*\*

Looking back much later, Will thought that that weekend and the week after it were the turning point in his mind and the moment at which his descent into hell started.

Others have pinpointed various political and economic circumstances that set in train the loss of the next general election and the return of a massively grown opposition. But Will Clements thought only personally.

His subsequent loss of the seat was as if there'd been a death. He had died to the work and very nearly to himself.

At that weekend, looking at Stella and at Ralph he was convinced with a certainty which fed on earlier fleeting suspicions, that his wife and his agent were cheating on him behind his back.

The election was not wanted – it was just that legal time ran out and although the party machine kicked in and ran a competent campaign and everybody worked very hard, genuinely fearing the damage the opposition would do if they took power, the media had decided. It was the opposition's hour.

By the end of the second week of five, Will knew he was a dead man walking. Gradually his daily team of volunteers dwindled. The urgent crowds he had deployed in his previous two forays didn't show up to canvas, swarm round him in the street, swamp the public meetings or ask helpful questions.

In the final days, even Anne his Commons secretary employed to handle correspondence during the election period went off sick, clearly not expecting him to be back. In the constituency, he was driven round in a borrowed van - a mile apart from the shiny minibus he'd had last time.

His rota of drivers dwindled to just two, one of whom used the opportunity to run his own business while out and about. Ralph found no end to do in the office, though Will failed to imagine what it might be.

Stella was distant most of the time, unable to handle the domestic tension and keeping the kids safe and well. Why Ralph had to go and see her to discuss the campaign while he was on the road was another mystery.

With one week to go, what in political game-play is called 'wobble Thursday', when all parties have private doubts about everything to do with strategy, policies, people and events, a handwritten note on A2 paper was stuck on the office door.

It was from a pile of paper off their printer, so Will knew it was an inside job.

'Resign now. You mustn't win. It would not be fair on your family. Don't let the truth about you get out.'

It was the longest so far. Shockingly, it was seen by several citizens so it was soon in the local media. Local police were asked to investigate. Will made a statement to regional TV news teams saying that it was the work of either a crank or the opposition.

This provoked a furious row with his opponent stating that he was so confident of defeating Clements that he was hardly wasting time playing childish games. It was probably kids having a laugh.

The strain began to show on Will's face, in his voice as his tolerance levels drained. He barked and snapped at people. He was vitriolic as he tried to cope with rising conviction of political death and a sense of failure and as Stella observed, of a small thing he may have done long ago that somebody was blowing out of all proportion.

She began to find talking to Ralph about the campaign or about Will's shortcomings as Ralph pointed them out to be unbearable. She started avoiding Ralph and deliberately stepped up the visible support for her husband.

The incident became a small footnote in the story of the election that unseated Will Clements, triggered Ralph Barrow's departure for pastures new and allowed Stella and Will time to rebuild their lives and particularly their strained relationship.

Will chose to believe that Stella had been duped by Ralph; she was the innocent victim of his machinations.

*******************************

Election day dawned just in time. Much longer and their marriage would have collapsed. His mind might have tipped over the edge. Now he could spend time with family and find new friends. He could appreciate what Stella had done for him and far from being tempted to stray, was his bedrock.

All the constituency case notes and files, all the projects half dealt with, Will handed over to his successor. He wrote hundreds of thank you letters and as soon as he could he took the family abroad for a good holiday.

He feared that teachers would be unkind to his children and that the redundancy payment would hardly last forever. There is nothing more ex than an ex-MP, so who would employ him, along with dozens of his former colleagues?

Funnily enough, the one thing he never worried about was the secret the notes had threatened to reveal about him getting out. Not even when he and Stella talked about it and she came to believe it was his opponent, now MP.

And not even when they had the clear-out of all clear-outs of stuff accumulated over the years, and she produced a pair of padded builders' gloves that had the fingers of the right hand part stuffed with foam pieces and asked him about them.

He could hardly say they were the gloves he'd used to write the threat notes to himself with disguised handwriting because he wanted her to think that Ralph had something unpleasant on him and she'd go off him.

Nor could he say how he had cleverly palmed a request note from the desk in the Commons' foyer and dropped it as he passed the time of day with the bobby that day he needed to be 'visited' by his tormentor.

So he lied and said he thought Ralph had done it all to incriminate Will.

Stella nodded, as if she thought he was more than capable of that. Will was very satisfied with that, if not his life now.

# Things to Do Before You Die, 2060

L4/0987.2.Swan swallowed the pill with water. Bit of a luxury that, water. But why not, it was only one mouthful. And it was his last pill, ever.

It'd been something of a medical miracle when he started taking it in the late teens of the last century. All people aged 25 and above had been offered the chance to tackle directly the effects of natural aging, the diseases of years and the losses of their basic faculties. He was among the first to volunteer.

The little pill, the 'old man's friend' they'd dubbed it, had worked on his system for forty years now, giving him the same effect as if he'd had a severe diet. He just had to keep up the daily exercise regime and had been fit and healthy throughout all those years.

He vaguely understood how the chemical worked on his metabolism to suppress or alter his genes to stop the curvature of the spine that had plagued his forefathers from emerging in his body, except for a slight twist and curl.

The little monthly pill had allowed Swan, though his official handle was as strong in his mind as it was on the chip in his head that identified him, to grow old gracefully without the frustrations of frailty. He still recalled with a shudder watching his old, deaf, partially blind, immobile grandmother struggle as an invalid for years before her release. And his dad, twisted and clutching for air with his lungs squeezed by his bent rib cage, still in his forties.

Swan had signed a Lifetime Agreement and Understanding that he'd stop at an agreed date and then in the second month, with no further pill, the natural body decay would take over in an accelerated process and he'd be dead in days. Some people, he'd heard, slipped away in hours.

Quite dramatic, really. You hold off diseases; then at the agreed time they all crash in at once and bam! You're gone. Time to make space on the planet.

And in your final two months? Well, sit back and enjoy. There'll be food and drink; as much mindless entertainment on screen as you can stand and even the opportunity to meet and talk with other people, if you ask for it. At least the first month will be great, because your body has the drug to keep it going well. When you don't it take any more, well, then your body gets less comfortable.

But that was the price you agreed to pay. A pact with destiny for a relatively healthy life.

It's a time of reflection. What have you done with your years? Who will remember you after you're gone? The answer nowadays is that nobody will and you will have contributed little or nothing. But Swan was from that generation that did contribute, at least when they were young, which wanted to do something with their lives; make a difference if not change the whole world.

What do you actually want to do in your final days before you leave? He started to think.

*****************************

Back in 2020, Swan, just struggling with the loss of his independence from the compulsory chip implant to 'combat

80

terrorism and criminal activity', aged 25, qualified to try the new drugs that would fight the aging process, that would hold back a long and miserable slide into old senility and painful passing.

'Yes, yes', he cried in delight as the medic, at that point on the cusp of being a 'Doctor' which meant he/she covered everything from physical to mental impairments and sometimes did all for you, explained it to him.

'This drug will hold off your inherited disease until you stop taking the tablets. Your supply will end when you are 65, a little later than some of our patients and earlier than many others. But the fact of your spine weakness means we need to see how 65 works... you understand?'

Again, the excited Swan was itching to sign the document and get started. If the hideous deformity and breathing nightmare was not going to happen to him till he was 65... then Faye would be his!

'When the medication stops, you will have around one month during which the effects will hold off the disease and old age illnesses, but then when you don't take it, you will experience rapid onset of illness, physical and dementia and you will die quickly'.

The doctor passed him a little device which he touched with his thumb, forefinger, ear and top lip. He let it scan his eyes and link the data to what the system already had on him. He became officially part of the Full Life Medication program with the label L4/0987.2.

Then he went outside to meet up with Faye, tell her the good news and get her to agree to apply for a license to have a baby of their own, knowing that his problem would be held back, and by the time their child was grown, who knows what medicine could do?

\*\*\*\*\*\*\*\*\*\*\*\*\*\*\*\*\*\*\*\*\*\*\*\*\*\*\*

Across the sustainable eco-city, in the area that was created for doctors to maximise the assets of the population for a greater, undefined good, AA/1102.4.Serina looked at her personal technology.

An update on her own health status was fairly reassuring. She worked in health and drug treatment research but in her younger days had sometimes neglected her own well-being. But since applying for a procreation license (intellectual/academic), she'd been more aware of her own fitness and general health. She was a single-sexed being and wanted to meet a similar single-sexer but from the opposite lists.

AA/1102.4.Serina resumed her work. Occasionally she had a moment of wonder what it would be like to be a manual or domestic. Someone she knew had applied for an intellectual/academic variation license to procreate with a domestic, but that had been turned down.

She refocused on her task. The city showrooms were calling her, and she needed to make her selection of participants in the new memory recall stuff, what was it called? Oh yes, the Human Memory Bank.

She needed to get on with it now. She'd set her heart on visiting a new clothing showroom, and could virtually try on any number of tempting delicacies before ordering for delivery to the residence.

Of course she had to travel a bit, but her personal program gave a simple route via Overhead, public taxipod and a short walk to minimise the journey. No, the prospect of her outing was getting too strong, so she just pressed auto select and sent a message to the random choice.

And then she got out to spend credit to make herself look and feel better.

***********************************

L4/0987.2.Swan received the message and noted it in his head. It broke into his thoughts about his last month of life ahead and what he would really like to do as the voice droned on in that officialese-confidence speaking that made any sort of protest virtually pointless. He'd been expecting it. It was coming up to the agreed time, and the Full Life program would send for him to prepare for his departure.

'You have been selected to make a real contribution to society ... we note you are on your final Full Life Medication, and when it has worked through you will be leaving us ... make a difference .... sign up now to donate your key organs when the time comes....'

Swan came out of his reverie instantly, looked at the screen and demanded a repeat. Alarm bells began ringing in his mind. Donating key organs? Hadn't there been every kind of scandal about that throughout his life?

Didn't they encourage organ donation and then there was a big row when it was found they were taking organs from the living on demand? Didn't they take executed convicts' organs till it was discovered they were executing certain people for their compatible vitals? Weren't they then caught breeding people with particular genetic strengths/weaknesses on demand?

Didn't it all go very quiet on the transplant program years ago? Was this the same thing come back? And why had they selected him? Hadn't he signed up to organ donation from the outset of the Full Life Medication program anyway?

He sat staring at the screen while he tried to think of how to respond, completely unaware that his response had already been recorded, noted and analysed.

His consent was a given.

\*\*\*\*\*\*\*\*\*\*\*\*\*\*\*\*\*\*\*\*\*\*\*\*\*\*\*\*\*\*\*\*\*\*\*\*\*\*\*\*\*\*

They came for him while he was resting, naturally. Wasn't there an old adage that torture victims were always tackled at night so they'd be more disorientated? It may be that as he was on the countdown to the end he was more conscious of remembering his past. He was beginning to feel there should be a record of some of his experiences.

And that was what was being said to him. He peered around in the darkness, just making out a number of people and machines. If he shut his eyes there was no difference between them.

A voice was saying, "So Swan, we want to use your past experiences, your memory, for our new civilisation memory bank'.

Another voice chipped in, more authoritatively.' You have been proud of staying as a single-sexer, you had a procreation license. You are of the age when people did things differently, thought in different ways from now. We are aware of the dangers of losing the past. '.

'I am the past?' he responded. 'I suppose I am'.

AA/1102.4.Serina came fully into the light around the bed on which he was strapped and smiled at him, her eyes searching his face. 'Swan, we need to tap into your memory bank to help us teach the young people their roots, their origins....'

He laughed. 'You have to go back thousands of generations to do that!'

'We can go back as far as you can. Your generation was told a lot about the distant past.'

For some niggling reason he began to feel the pressure was unnecessary. He didn't want to be strapped down, he didn't want to be lower than this woman, he didn't want to co-operate with these anonymous, smooth sounding people. 'I thought you wanted my organs!'

Now they all laughed, and Swan realised the room around him was full. 'Oh we'll take them anyway, Swan ..."

He said, a fragment of doubt clouding his mind, 'You are the Full Life Medication program, aren't you?

He got an official, vague reply, 'We work closely with all official health programs. It's all the same; our only concern is the well-being of every single person'.

Another said, 'You see L4/0987.2, we want you to spend your remaining time answering questions, filling in knowledge blanks, describing things you remember, so we can know the living past...'

Swan persisted, 'But why don't you just make it up if the past is suddenly so important after all this time of willfully destroying it?'

Nobody answered at first, but then Serina did, mechanically while admiring her new garment under the white coat and hoping that good-looking trainee opposite would also appreciate it. 'We want to be open and honest with people, whatever happened in the past. There are tough decisions ahead, and even our medical technology is insufficient to make life immortal and to feed the world we will have in the next few years. We want an informed, intellectual population to solve the problems and give us the solutions and decide who's worth living and who's not.'

'You want to play God?' Swan hooted. Nobody spoke. 'You want to tell people things they are denied now in the hope of what exactly?'

'That they will make selfless, informed decisions for the greater good.' Another added, 'we may lower the agreed age for departure....'

Swan snorted, 'but that's just a version of crowd-sourcing popular in the early days of the digital revolution. Why don't you just cull people at 55, or 40 or whatever you damned well want? There was a film when they went at 30, I think.....' Again there was no response.

Doctor M5/1009.8.Banks said, 'You are now part of a new program, the Human Memory Bank. It's the final service society will ask of you before you depart. Your organs will naturally be donated as your Full Life Medication program ends, but tapping into your human memories is a new idea that we are working on. You're chosen to donate your final month plus however many days before the diseases come on and take you...'

'But I was going to do -'

'No, that's too selfish. Society has a greater need than you completing some personal list of things to do before you slip away. We need your past. And everybody else on the final month, we need their past, yours has been a collective past in a way that today's lives are not, ours are more on screens. You're not alone in this'.

'Bucket list, they used to call it. Things to do before you kicked the bucket...'

Some of them looked at each other and Serina said, 'You see why it's important we reconnect with old words. What's a bucket that you kick?'

Swan just shook his head. He was suddenly faced with an understanding of the sheer scale of what he'd seen, done, tasted, tried, laughed and cried about in sixty five years, and now they wanted him to remember it all.

'And if I run out of time in just over a month?'

Someone in a white coat came forward to him. 'I am Doctor M5/1009.8.Banks, Swan. If you run out of time we will give you another pill to give you a further month.

'And if I refuse to do it?'

Banks didn't hesitate, 'If you refuse to assist, we will give you another pill to give you a further month, but this one will not have the gene mutation element within, so your back problem will come on fast, and you will be gasping for breath for as many months as it takes to finish your memories'.

*************************************

The message to L4/0987.2.Swan from AA/1102.4.Serina was anything but random. It had been made inevitable by the actions of Doctor M5/1009.8.Banks. He'd watched this case for a long time, taking an obsessively personal interest in it. In Swan.

'What have we got on this one, Serina?'

'Well, it's all here, Dr Banks. Quite a lot. He was not totally unique, what with his physical problems and his emotional ones. But he did meet a lot of the criteria for the experiment.'

Banks was thoughtful for a moment. 'We need him to come face to face with those closed areas in his mind. It's important to squeeze every last drop out of him'.

Serina shrugged, 'why is this one so important...?'

'The Full Life Medication Program,' replied Banks firmly, 'is yesterday's contribution. Its leaders are yesterday. We must move forward building a civilised society and that means making our program work. Human Memory is the ultimate untapped resource.'

'Do you know the leaders of Full Life?' asked Serina.

'I'm not old enough to know the pioneers of Full Life, obviously, but the second generation... well, shall we say I knew one of them.'

*******************************

What Swan didn't know because he'd been taken so he didn't see it, was that he received a later message from the Full Life Medication program itself.

What only Doctor M5/1009.8.Banks knew was they'd actually snatched him from Full Life to do their own Human Memory program. Full Life was still very active, and had indeed come up with new medication that would prolong Swan's life by holding back the aging and illnesses for a further indefinite time.

They wanted to try it out on him. His inherited disease on top of his advanced 65 years made him an interesting case.

When Full Life saw from the monitor that Swan wasn't at home, they sent a team for him. They found nobody in, only the message from Human Memory. They called it in, back to Full Life control centre.

It was the first that Doctor RS/6577.5.Rhodes knew about the Human Memory program. She was not happy. They'd taken her patient. How unprofessional.

She was downright furious when she asked the system and discovered that Human Memory was being run by Doctor M5/1009.8.Banks. She and Dr Banks went back a long way. She'd hoped it was long enough to forget him, but clearly not. Bad news sticks around or comes back.

*******************************

The treatment area was more relaxing and brighter. Swan was not strapped, but invited to sit on a lounger, lie back and take in the myriad screens in front of him. Silent staff busied themselves with attaching scanner tips to his head, checking his temperature, connecting him to a urine-holder and urging him to drink a cool, colourless liquid to 'relax him'.

They showed him what they'd gathered, films/simulations from other oldies now gone. Once familiar towns, cities,

89

schools, clothes and transport returned to life before his eyes. He stopped it all each time there was something that didn't ring true or he remembered additional angles about.

The hours flew by. He became absorbed in games of childhood especially those played in the streets and playgrounds, in schools, their food, music and clothes. Attitudes that seemed natural and familiar had grown strange and distant over the years. By this process they came back into focus and he relearned a sense of tradition and value for things that'd long since passed away.

He never seemed to return to his residence or do anything he'd done for the past several years. The recent era seemed unimportant. All that mattered was the deep past. That past became the reality of now.

He dreamed back his little dog, Sammie, who'd been his constant boyhood companion. He was glad the dog had expired before the cull of all domestic animals because of the increasing infections crossing over into human beings. And then commercial animals, and then virtually anything that moved was a potential threat. What birds survived the pollution were hunted down.

It was a global madness that failed, because no way could every other species but human be wiped out. In lots of places animals escaped or were kept alive secretly. But it was what the authorities did. It was a fact of life he recalled lots of detail about.

And his family. He wept afresh at how his father, grandmother and older sister suffered with their bad, twisted backs. He laughed again with Faye, when he first met her and when they knew each other well. He cried all over again when she said she couldn't contemplate a life with him and that genetic time-bomb ticking away in his body.

Faye told him she loved him too much to stay with him. He had a procreation licence; he should use it with another. That's how much he loved her.

Suddenly after about three weeks it didn't seem right. No, something was decidedly wrong, out of kilter and then some.

They stopped the process, and some white-coats gathered round. Flapping at him, trying to see from his face what was wrong.

A voice behind the assistants asked him, 'What is wrong? What about Faye, Swan?'

\*\*\*\*\*\*\*\*\*\*\*\*\*\*\*\*\*\*\*\*\*\*\*\*\*\*\*\*\*\*\*\*\*\*

After a session, while Swan was allowed to sleep listening repeatedly to two tracks of music popular in his teenage angst period, the doctors discussed progress. Dr Banks held the floor, enjoying himself.

'The old, largely discredited sodium pentothal was a rapid depressant and relaxant that was used not to harm, but to relax so that during interrogation, the patient found his or her resolve to withhold uncomfortable information was weakened drastically'.

Several nodded and made brushing motions with their arms. That was old technology. Banks indicated he wasn't finished.

'We have drugs which can mimic that, of course. We have drugs that can fool anybody into believing anything at all. How else are we holding people in prisons? By and large by laser projections and tricking their minds through drugs into believing they're in cells.'

He went on, 'What we are going to try with L4/0987.2.Swan is give him a shot of water in his arm which makes him believe he has been given a truth serum and then achieve the same effect as if he had. Then he will remember everything. The boundaries of medicine of mind and body go onwards.'

He waited and after a moment the staff got up and went back to their work.

\*\*\*\*\*\*\*\*\*\*\*\*\*\*\*\*\*\*\*\*\*\*\*\*\*\*\*\*\*\*\*\*\*\*\*\*\*

It was an hour later that the attack began.

Over the years, the Full Life Medication program had acquired its own enforcement units because occasionally, some patients had tried to protest as their pills were ended and they started their final countdowns. Some had got violent and attempt to steal more.

The enforcement unit was equipped to enter places. The centre of the Human Memory Bank was not well secured and the team crashed in and made medical staff and patients alike gather on the floor in the main reception area.

They quickly identified L4/0987.2.Swan and bundled him away leaving puzzled Human Memory people posing unanswerable questions of each other. They were familiar with memories of movies that many patients had dredged up for them, so some wondered if they were in one of those.

Doctor M5/1009.8.Banks knew that the enforcers were from Full Life, and he had expected that people there would want to monitor Swan closely in his final hours, given everything about him. But why would they want to snatch him back? He was a dead man, his organs would still be used and what harm was there in a rival program just making use of him till then?

Banks slipped out and to his own office space to interrogate the system. He quite quickly realised that somebody he really had forgotten about as she was so insignificant was behind this. Doctor RS/6577.5.Rhodes.

Swan, however, while remaining confused, also wondered about movies and if some living simulation was being made to assist his recall processes. They gave him a small tube and forced him to suck the contents down. It was sickly sweet, and he almost immediately felt quite relaxed, but just curious, as if viewing the scene from a distance.

However, the journey was real enough. The Overhead was crammed with travellers, but his guards pushed into a unit and made space. One literally threw out the door a couple of innocent people before the thing slid off. Nobody looked at them; all avoided any eye contact with the enforcers or Swan.

He felt his voice asking what was happening, but received no response.

********************************

The whole scene in the Human Memory Bank was watched by Doctor RS/6577.5.Rhodes. This wasn't how she'd planned it, and ordinarily, her patience being what it was, she'd have just let it go. But L4/0987.2.Swan was an important patient.

He had to depart as planned, his organs removed just before the agreed date when he didn't expect it. Indeed, it would save him any suffering at all. That was one of the tweaks to the Full Life program that she was most proud of. Nobody suffered, because there was no lead into death.

It was sudden and effective. Job done.

Just as important was that there was a new drug and new thinking. Swan could have his life extended for decades yet, so they could see how long an inherited disease could be held off.

More importantly still, L4/0987.2.Swan had to be recovered to Full Life because it was her old adversary Doctor M5/1009.8.Banks who'd taken him.

\*\*\*\*\*\*\*\*\*\*\*\*\*\*\*\*\*\*\*\*\*\*\*\*\*\*\*\*\*\*\*\*\*\*

Banks was notorious in Full Life at the start of his career. He'd made all the right noises, smoothed the right people and fluttered his eyes at his young colleague, Doctor Rhodes. They were both fully signed up to the doctrines of Full Life. Spare the suffering, plan your end and make a final contribution to others just as you depart.

That was back twenty odd years ago. Or was it more? Earlier generations might've called it a romantic attachment. At the time it was more cerebral than physical. At least that's what most colleagues surmised.

When Banks and Rhodes fell out, it caused quite a stir in the department and was put down to professional differences.

She'd told him, 'I believe in what we're doing, and I am prepared to devote my life to it. I've started on a course of pills that will last until I'm 80. I'm not prepared to sidetrack myself and experiment in the weird and risk all that we have here'.

He'd replied, 'My love, you must do what you will. Or vice versa. I have a destiny that means I must break boundaries and I refuse to spend the rest of my career here staving off the illnesses as people grow old just so they can die quickly.'

'And without suffering.'

'No, they can make a much bigger contribution to society before they go ...

'You mean give up their vital organs? That could happen legally in the future...

'No, more than that. I want to know what's in their minds. That way lies ultimate power.'

She'd sighed, 'then you'll have to go without me down that road.'

'I will,' he nodded. 'I will never forget you and what we've shared.'

Neither knew then that the idea of tapping people's historical memory to acquire knowledge and understanding to control the present and ultimately the past, was born in Dr Banks.

Neither also knew that an author, George Orwell, had made a story out of that very premise back in the pre-history of 1948. Banks learned it later when interrogating an old-timer.

*********************************

Banks took charge of the operation as he realised that Full Life were sending out security to grab Swan back. He had the archive of old movies searched to predict a number of possible outcomes of a pursuit.

He decided that if she wanted to play cat and mouse, then he was ready. He ordered his people to divide into two teams, one with the patient and the other to grab a random man looking as close to him as possible. Then each group was to take a public taxipod to double back on themselves.

Rhodes' team at the base soon accessed the tracking systems, so realised what he was doing. She ordered another team to get out of uniform and put on workaday clothes, taking a stab at where both Full Life teams would go.

She hit them simultaneously as they switched to the Overhead and set off small explosions that stunned everybody within a sizeable circle.

Swan was grabbed along with the unfortunate decoy. She had some of hers hold the man at the steps to the Overhead, weapons at the ready and wait. The rest took Swan on another tortuous circuit of the Overhead.

Rhodes felt she had the upper hand, and simply sat waiting for Banks' team to approach. They came from above by swinging off the Overhead and dropping down, firing laser weapons indiscriminately. Members of the public were caught up in an instant hail of crossfire.

The street Crime and Security robo-officers emerged in a big sweep to investigate and an automatic fleet of drones was launched to watch, report and regain order. The hapless look-alike was crushed by flying debris when another personal bomb exploded near him.

Rhodes and Banks faced each other through their respective screens. She looked tense but determined. He smiled with that hint of arrogance that she remembered so well.

'Dr Banks, you seem to be under the misapprehension that patient L4/0987.2.Swan is under your professional care'.

'And so he is, Dr Rhodes,' he responded.

'He signed with the Full Life Medication program forty years ago, as you know. That hasn't changed and I demand that you return him to me so that he can be prepared for his final day and his organs harvested'

Banks laughed unpleasantly. 'You have no idea what you're dealing with here. The Human Memory Bank is a far more important project, it takes precedence over an old program to give a false sense of last-days security to patients, and gives them a real sense of contributing something as well as their organs.'

'Their memories?' She stared at him hard.

'Exactly. Worth far more to society. Knowledge is power, my dear.'

Her lip curled, 'Don't patronise me, Banks. You...' And she started rehearsing their old arguments as if the intervening years amounted to nothing. Flaws in each other's personalities were bandied about like insults again.

This childish verbal skirmish afforded precious time for both sides to get the
Crime and Security robo-officers to back off, re-arm and re-group strategically and to check that Swan was still alive.

When he was located, hiding in the supporting pillar area beneath a large public tower block, Rhodes and Banks could see him on camera. And talk to him.

'Michael, Michael Swan, this is Dr Banks... it's alright, we are coming for you and will be bringing you safely back to finish the project...'

Rhodes interrupted, 'Swan, my name is Dr Rhodes and your name is Swan, not Michael Swan. I am with the Full Life Medication program, not the Human Memory Bank project. I understand that you long to spend your final days doing what you want, and as was agreed all those years ago....'

Banks cut in with, 'Remember Michael Swan, we can just prolong your life, with or without the gene therapies, so it's your choice. Remember the twisted spines and rib cages...

'You don't have to be threatened, Swan, we'll look after you...'

The assistants of both were frantically tracking him down and dispatching recovery teams and redirecting guards to fight off the opposition.

Swan suddenly spoke to the screen. 'Faye... I want Faye'.

Both Banks and Rhodes were initially puzzled. 'Faye?'

Swan cleared his throat and came closer to the screen. He was bleeding from a shoulder wound and was in some pain.

'Get Faye to me, you know who Faye is, get her to me on screen and then to me in person and whichever of you does it first, I will come with'.

Both started to protest/argue/persuade. 'Do it or I'll let myself bleed to death before you get here...' He showed them that the injury was greater than they'd thought.

********************************

Both sides had expertise enough to call up Faye's records, see what the connection with Swan was, the procreation business and what happened to her. She was long dead. She'd opted for suicide by organ donation three years after she and Swan had talked and he went into the Full Life program.

It was a matter of seconds to conjure up avatars of Faye from the known information. Banks opted for an aged one, as old as she would be if she'd been alive. Rhodes went for the younger version that Swan would have remembered best.

Even in his pain and with dry mouth he laughed to see the competing visualisations of Faye. He shook his head sadly. 'Alright, now bring her to me. You know where I am, you've traced me by now.'

It was then a race to get their people in place, surround the area, secure it fully and be ready for whatever the other side threw at them.

By luck or judgment, Swan found a spot that was not camera-covered. He made a mighty effort to gather enough strength to seize an unsuspecting innocent walker past off the moving pavement and beat him into a near-coma with his bare hands. He dragged the unfortunate man to the uncovered spot and waited.

Nobody raised any alarm or comment. Thoughts were kept to themselves, the legacy of the early part of the 21st century when most people could commit crimes inadvertently that they stopped doing much except mind their own business.

Swan didn't have to wait long before he realised he and the beaten man were surrounded.

He'd thought they'd waste time dealing with the injured man while he could check if either side really had got Faye in any form at all.

In a split second, the battle for Swan entered its climax. Opposing teams started shooting. The hurt man was wiped at once. There was no Faye. He knew it really, but had just wanted to see her one more time. She was top of his bucket list, after all.

He staggered up and walked into the crazy cross firing, holding his hands up, blood still running from his shoulder. He stumbled but stayed upright. They all stopped firing and positioned themselves better to grab him.

Rhodes spoke to her team in their earpieces. 'Make sure you take him alive'.

Banks spoke into his team's ears, 'On my countdown, take him out. 3, 2 ...'

In the final seconds of his final day in his final month L4/0987.2.Swan remembered that Faye loved him and he loved her. But there was no time to tell Doctor M5/1009.8.Banks.

And there was no time for Doctor RS/6577.5.Rhodes to harvest his organs.

Nobody benefitted from his departure.

Banks told Rhodes through their screen, 'The operation was a success, but the patient died'.

Rhodes replied to Banks, 'Nothing changes really. Meet up for a drink and a talk? We need to discuss the future of the pharmaceutical industry in the next fifty years'.

Banks smiled and gave a single nod.

# Private Asylum

It's a common habit among creatives to raid their own back catalogues for ideas and materials to refashion, reshape and reinvent.

Other people's catalogues, too, of course. In fact anything that may be useful is manna from heaven for the creative person.

Felicity was one such inventive creative. At least she had been. Jo, her daughter, liked to think so as she sat at the bed, watching her mother for outward signs of life, any life. Even recycled life.

'Slug?'

It was Jo, saying something she hoped would get through. It didn't.

Jo would gladly take any twisting, misremembering and downright lying about the past stuff in her mum's catalogue that would indicate the possibility of a future. Jo knew enough of her mother's life by now to feel an immense sadness that she'd never fulfilled her potential.

Felicity was incarcerated in her own private asylum, locked in. This was fifty years ago, long before dementia and the like became fashionable. Jo, in her early twenties, wondered if the same would happen to her in the next few years, but there was nothing she could do about it.

*******************************

The family used to joke that Mum was lazy. She'd lounge about the house after breakfast in a baggy dressing gown, even as she dished the kids and her father Nathan their breakfast. Off they went to school and Nathan to his labouring job on a succession of small scale building sites.

As far as they all knew Felicity stayed in her bed attire all day and sometimes was still like that when everyone got in for their tea. Very rarely was Mum dressed and 'normal' by that time.

At weekends and school holidays it was the same but when there was no school to go to the kids were packed off to the recreation ground or the station to watch other people being busy or the bridge which lifted and fell to allow boats through from the harbour upriver to the shipyards and warehouses.

Such was the freedom they enjoyed, then. And still Mum was 'lazy' going back to bed as soon as everyone was out the house. Felicity never once corrected them or told them what was going on. Even when they were all grown up, she never said a word.

One day, Jo recalled as her mother stirred - but it was a physical reaction, not mental activity, curiosity or boredom driving her towards life - an event that amused them all even more as they learned to accept her as she was.

Jo had been given some school homework to find something in the *Book of Proverbs* that would inspire a painting and/or a poem. She didn't have time to read them all from start to end, so flipped through, hoping something would hit her. Psalm 26 verse 15 did just that.

*'The sluggard buries his hand in the dish; it wears him out to bring it back to his mouth.'*

Hilarious! Somebody who was so tired that he stuck his hand in his food but couldn't be bothered to pull it out to feed himself! That was Mother exactly.

Except, of course, it wasn't. She kept house and home, fed, clothed and disciplined them, she ironed, washed, cleaned, shopped and produced wonderful Christmas surprises and made birthdays special.

It was just one of those family nicknames that took hold. Over time the sluggard in it became a she and put her head not her hand in the food bowl. 'Slug' was the affectionate nickname Mum came to answer to.

*******************************

One of those occasionally resurrected family history tales was that Mum had been creative as a child. She'd danced, painted, played piano to performance standard and recited poems and Bible passages at the drop of a hat.

None of them ever got beyond that – how marvellous Felicity's future was, but why wasn't it ever fulfilled? Why were they all living in a basic house, too small for them and with quite modest means?

In her teens, Jo began to think it was because she met Nathan and became pregnant with her older brother, Paul. One day she put it to Felicity but was shut down sharpish. 'That's nasty, Jo. I loved your dad and I love him still. He works very hard for all of us. Don't try to judge me or your father.'

'So why don't you work hard too, Mum?' Jo had asked, aware she was entering new territory.

'You don't think looking after all of you is hard work?'

'Well, yes, but you know what I mean... in your dressing gown...' Jo looked at her mother's eyes, suddenly a little afraid to probe, yet really wanting to know now. She wasn't planning to judge, only to understand better.

Mum wiped the table and replied, keeping her head down, no longer looking at Jo. 'I like to wear my dressing gown in the mornings and yes, I do have to spend more time than most mums you know lying in bed, but we are getting on fine. Just fine.'

There was finality about that response and Jo let it go, knowing that there was more. Mum was covering something up.

*********************************

It was in her mid teens, not long before she made the decision to stay on at school after the compulsory years and hopefully avoid the office or nursing careers that seemed to be all that was offered to girls who didn't want to settle as wives and mothers at the earliest opportunity.

Jo was sent home from school with a headache. She'd spent an hour and a half lying in the medical room suffering a migraine of flashing lights and feeling sick. As her vision cleared, leaving a hammering somewhere in the centre of her head, it coincided with fresh calls on the room.

A playground fight had led to a nasty boy being gingerly draped on the camp bed with a bloody nose, a shiner swelling across his cheek and a sore wrist. Another little kid was removed from his classroom after vomiting profusely over his desk and two other students, so Jo was hastily dispatched home.

No calls home first from the office in those days. Off she went, walking slowly to let her head travel with her. The journey went calmly until she reached the top of her road. All was quiet at this time of afternoon with most men working, kids at school and the mums finished their cleaning and shopping and not yet preparing the teas.

Felicity'd told them she sometimes had half an hour after all her work before they got back from school, half an hour to herself. Did she read? If so, what? Did she draw, sing, play an instrument? No signs of any of it in their home.

A man Jo did not know was knocking on her door. He seemed in a hurry, looking up and down the street but she was too far away to register in his quick glance. The door opened and he scooted in.

As she closed the gap to her house, Jo's mind raced. Who was he? What was he doing there? Did Dad know about it? Should she use her key and go in as normal? Mum wasn't expecting her yet. Would she find the man and Mum sitting at the kitchen table over a mug of tea?

As far as she knew, nothing in the house needed mending. She was positive she'd never seen the man before, a casually dressed average sort, perhaps in his forties. He'd come on foot, as there was no car outside.

Not that everyone had a car – they didn't – but Jo realised that more and more people did, so not having a car was unusual. Something stopped her finishing the steps to her door.

Feigning interest in a few gardens, Jo retreated, and went back as far as the little corner shop. She had no money and nothing she needed anyway, so she stood and read the postcards on the board in the window by the door. Piano lessons, cleaning offered and some bargain child clothes and toys for sale.

She spun it out as long as she could and turned back again towards home. The man left and dashed off in the other direction. Jo was none the wiser, except now perhaps she could go home, certain she hadn't imagined it.

If Felicity was more than surprised that Jo was home so early, she didn't let on. She raised an eyebrow and listened to Jo's symptoms. 'You'd better lie down, Jo. You'll feel better in a bit.'

And that was that. No explanation, no hysterics, no nothing. Just her mother's suggestion she went to bed to rest, with no opening for Jo to ask about the stranger.

*******************************

Over the next few weeks, Jo made a point of listening more to her mother, particularly when she was talking to Dad. Her gradually formed belief that they were neither close nor particularly happy was borne out. They kissed with a meaningless peck when he left for work, again when he came home.

Jo didn't think there was any affection there. In fact, watching one day, she felt there was sadness, as if Felicity's life was a disappointment that dare not be acknowledged and Nathan's world was narrow and little understood.

Felicity caught Jo staring at them one morning, and just snapped, 'Don't judge me, Jo, and don't judge us.' This embarrassed the girl, as if her mother could see right through her and into what she was thinking.

Jo had a look round her parents' bedroom when Mum was hanging washing on the line, but found nothing untoward. Nothing in the drawers or under the bed. She decided to check the loft when she could, but it wouldn't be easy.

Several times, off and on, the question 'who was he?' was on the tip of her tongue. It remained unasked. In those days, people didn't often open up to each other – the brutal heart-searching honesty of later years was not commonplace, even between mother and only daughter facing her own adulthood.

Her brother Paul now used home as mere accommodation - approaching the end of his apprenticeship at the boatyard nearest to them, he was courting and had neither time nor interest in his family. Her other siblings were too young to confide in.

So, Jo let it ferment in her mind. What was Felicity up to? She had committed a crime and was being investigated? She had seen a crime and was being interviewed as a witness? The man had come to collect the payments on their black and white TV or the washing machine?

She thought she'd imagined him. Or perhaps he was her long lost brother that Mum didn't want to tell them about? Or a previous husband she didn't want Nathan to know about?

She kicked each possibility around her imagination, adding other people and situations until each was believable. But none was certain and factual unless and until Felicity confirmed it.

Jo determined that she'd find time, somehow, to ask her, once and for all. The opportunity arose almost as soon as she settled it to corner her mother. It was a Saturday morning. Dad was off with little Tommy playing football, which would last all morning. Susan was doing her first Saturday job at the hairdressers and would be gone all day.

She herself was supposed to be going to her part time job at the branch library, a bus ride away, but she crept out early to the telephone call box at the end of the street and rang in sick. As she walked back to the house another man, a different one was knocking on their door and looking round furtively.

Then Jo clicked, just what her mother was up to. She ran in tears to the recreation ground.

**********************************

The chance vanished to ask about it and talk it through. The opportunity slipped by to try to share some of what was incomprehensible to her with a woman who had never been close but was nonetheless her mother.

When Nathan and Tommy came home they found Felicity in bed, awake but staring at the ceiling unable to speak or move. In a panic, Nathan rushed to the call box to ring for help.

So it was Tommy who told Jo that Mum was upstairs behaving strangely. She was alarmed thinking she'd been caught with the man in the bed, but when she went up, angry and determined to challenge her, Mum was incapable of any communication at all.

The doctor arrived after two hours and following a cursory examination of the patient, declared she'd had some sort of stroke or fit. He wasn't sure which, but they'd take her in for tests and let everyone know.

The arrival of the ambulance and Felicity being stretchered out enlivened what was otherwise a humdrum morning for the street and those who were not at home later regretted missing it.

Dad went in the ambulance with her like a scared rabbit to the hospital leaving Jo in charge of the house and kids. Once it was all quiet and Tommy started to be afraid and want his mum back, Jo allowed herself one outburst of rage.

She crashed through the kitchen door, rattling the frosted glass dangerously, into their tiny, scrub of a garden, kicked at a few nondescript shrubs, yanked the washing line, threw the bin over, smashed a clay pot and swore with angry, ugly words she'd heard at school but not used herself.

Till now. Then she calmed. Wiping the tears from her face, she drew Tommy to her, sat him at the table and made him cheese on toast. She looked in the fridge to decide what to make for tea. She waited.

Nathan came home mid evening to report that her mum had had a stroke and was not likely to speak again. Jo stared at him. 'She's in a private asylum now, Jo. Her own private asylum, where nobody can touch her.'

So now the questions would never be answered and the burden of knowing what she knew was firmly attached to her young shoulders, pulling her to the ground. With a single wail that woke Tommy, she slumped in the lounge while Nathan did his awkward best to put an arm round her.

*********************************

The family took it in turns to visit her in hospital. She was there so long that plans were made to bring her home where she could be cared for. Jo saw her life's course being changed for ever as her father seemed incapable of making any decisions or having a sensible discussion about her.

While Jo wondered if he knew what his wife'd been doing, it slipped to the rear of her mind and then down into the back catalogue of memories which may or may not be dredged up years later.

Felicity passed away almost two years later, never having spoken again nor given any hint that she knew what was happening around her. Jo abandoned her plans for further education; made sure that Dad managed the house and helped get the kids grown up.

All the promising creative sides to her personality gradually disappeared. She grew into her early twenties and with a very small social circle was happy to take up former school friend Jim Bennett's offer of a night out, the pictures, a meal and soon they were regarded as an item.

Nathan was relieved. He didn't want Jo an old maid, blaming him for Felicity's mishaps and departure. Besides, he had a lady friend he visited from time when funds allowed and her husband was out.

Soon Jo was pregnant and then happy to take up Jim Bennett's further offer of a wedding ring and a police house that would come his way with a wife, even before he made sergeant.

*********************************

Within that awesome yet often awful cycle of life, Jo forgot most of her early years. They had two children to raise - Ashley was a sickly boy who never grew into full strength either physically or mentally; Louise from an early age was drawn to the creative side and showed such promise that they dared to hope she'd make it.

She was a close runner-up in the semi-final of a national televised singing competition and Jo talked about her constantly to whoever would listen. Even those who wouldn't for long.

Once Nathan passed away, Jo took all the papers and junk from the house as none of her siblings cared. She found Felicity's little red book, a cash file that had cost a shilling from Woolworths, its faded price label still on the cover.

The first half was devoted to men's names – Joe, Bill 1 and Bill 2, William, John. Alan, Michael, Patrick, L, J, O and S – when they visited and how much they paid her. In the back were listed their monies as a running sum deducted from a massive total of three hundred and eighty pounds, eleven shillings and four pence.

That was labelled 'Nathan's Debt'.

With no Nathan to ask, she hunted afresh through what documents they'd left behind. She found letters and an address of a solicitor in town. She bussed to see him, but found he was long dead and his son was in a joint practice miles away.

But Jo didn't give up. She rang and secured an appointment with this legal person who took pity on her after hearing her story and promised to look in his father's archives which his sister was currently ploughing through to write a book about the late lawyer.

To her surprise, he was true to his word and eventually wrote to Jo with an explanation of her father's debt her mother was paying off. Nathan had been married to a woman who'd dropped and lost their child and because he couldn't cope with that, had simply left the woman after she'd been put in a public mental asylum.

Nathan had started a new life and met and married Felicity, entertaining high hopes his fortune would turn with her. In a sense it did, but Nathan was blackmailed by his best friend to keep quite.

The solicitor reckoned that Nathan and Felicity had somehow come up with an unknown scheme to make money to pay him off, because it all went very quiet.

So Jo concluded that Nathan had known what his wife was doing all those years. It was the price they agreed to pay for the life they had, such as it was in Jo's mind.

And when Louise was old enough to ask about her grandparents on her mother's side, Jo had the dilemma of telling her the truth she'd discovered or not. She wondered if she should fudge it all.

But then, Louise was a gifted creative in a very public arena and could probably use those details from the family back catalogue to useful purpose in her young creative life.

# The Spiral Escape

Above, the sky was perfectly clear and bright. Nobody looked up to admire it, though because it was the same every day.

There were no seasons. There was no spare space; Green-Metro 109 went on indefinitely. At least as far as most people were permitted to know. Overhead travel cars, the silent lifts and moving walkways transported people to where they needed to go at their appointed hours. There was no free choice.

Huge, strategically placed screens reported through image and commentary how food was grown in vats of constantly recycled chemicals, how waste was disposed of for the greatest good, how air was cleaned and recycled and how the plastex from which everything was made was endlessly reshaped as needed.

The screens informed viewers of how the cameras and automatic forces of law and order watched over everybody's well-being. And how everything was free – food on demand and clothes.

Of course people had to work according to a program compiled by the government; so some were builders, recyclers, carers, medics, educators or entertainers. Twelve hours of work; twelve hours of rest and play.

The wonderful government was described as the ultimate caring democracy – though anyone bothering to watch and think would've been hard pressed to remember when they last had an election.

When the sequence ended, it restarted. Absolutely nobody stood to watch; they glanced as they passed, but it had always been there, so the screens were part of the environment, like the floors or the sky.

Informative government propaganda was shown between announcements and entertainment repeats. Trailers for future fun were endlessly recycled.

If anyone had had enough information to wonder, they may have marvelled that the technology available when Green-Metro 109 was built was as far as it went. There was no development of later technologies. In that sense, it was a time warp, or bubble. But people only knew the time they were told it was.

************************************

As nobody expected to see a crowd gathered in the approach to a dormitory area, nobody saw it.

On a buzzer signal, this particular collection of people filed past a scanner into the building and straight through to a narrow alley between two identical buildings, through another door and down an escalator, guided by lights and further buzzers.

Every step was monitored and nobody except those selected moved this way. None of the group looked up at the sky at any point. Yet they were here to be briefed on a plan to escape through that sky.

************************************

The lecture area was full, the doors sealed. Low-level muttering was silenced as a voiced emerged from the wall.

'Citizens, you know your purpose here; you've been informed and trained. It's almost time. As you know, you were selected carefully for this honour, this challenge and we're all grateful. *Our city is in danger.*'

Images of their city exploded onto screens lining the walls, pockets of building decay, people lying sick, food uneaten. Danger was a word they had become used to hearing on their training, yet it was not common vocabulary elsewhere in this city which was run harmoniously with everything planned meticulously by the government.

'Our food supplies are no longer providing all people's needs on demand. There is a physical and mental weariness in many sick people we do not understand and cannot treat. We cannot continue like this, so as we are a caring, compassionate and far-seeing Government, we will solve our problem. *You* will solve our problem.'

\*\*\*\*\*\*\*\*\*\*\*\*\*\*\*\*\*\*\*\*\*\*\*\*\*\*\*\*\*\*\*\*\*\*\*\*\*\*

Across the city on a link area of walkways, a different voice addressed other citizens. This one was emerging from an actual human being and the message was partly similar. 'Our city is dying, we are overpopulated, our economy is failing and our Government doesn't care ...''

The audience were not held; most drifted off, as if fearful that hearing this would harm them. The young woman, agitated and constantly looking around and behind, was stood on a box made of the rigid material that characterised the whole city – plastex.

Brushing her hair from her face repeatedly, she raised her voice to a higher pitch. 'The government must go if we are to survive. It's us or them. Do you want to live or are you happy to die slowly?'

The crowd was never static; people came and went. She needed to hold them. 'Everything is free – we have whatever we need, but the supplies are no longer sustainable, recycling is not enough.'

A louder, stronger voice suddenly cut across her from speakers on the edges of the walkway.' You will not stand and listen to the revolutionary; go to where you are required to be. Go now, go quickly. Do not listen to her. Do not believe her.'

Conditioned obedience cleared the area in seconds leaving her and a small, rather less attractive woman. 'Aytee, let it go, we don't want to be arrested.'

But Aytee had one more go at a man walking past who'd not heard her earlier. ''If you obey the Government as you have always done, you are trapped, not free ...' He hurried away, eyes downwards.

The girl helped Aytee off the box. 'Let's get away. I don't know why Zena wants us to do these street talks, they achieve nothing.'

Acknowledging it as she picked up the box, Aytee replied, 'You're right, Jui, but we might find one or two more helpers.'

They were joined by a morose-looking, heavy-set man, more body than brain. 'What now, Aytee?' he grunted.

Handing him the box she said, 'Meet later as planned, Stone. Zena will be there.' Stone blinked to acknowledge his instruction, amazing Aytee afresh that a man so programmed to obey the voice commands of the government was so smitten with Zena he'd joined their rebel activists.

Jui and Aytee walked side by side talking, drawing the attention of the surveillance cameras if not any of the citizens they wanted to rescue.

********************************

The chosen people in the lecture area received a summary of their training. 'You were selected for this pilot project to see if it's possible for the whole city to escape. Upwards, to the sky. You've been put into three carefully balanced teams and have trained together. The adjustments are done. The teams are ready. *You are ready.*'

An old woman appeared on the platform, rather surprising them. 'My friends, thank you for volunteering.' There had been little choice. 'Green-Metro 109 was built about 100 years ago, a brand new safe city, self-sufficient and separated from other communities to escape pollution and corruption.'

As she spoke about the dangers of revolutionary thought and rebellious action that had seeped into their society, her eyes travelled along the rows of trainees. Each face was unique, yet there was a similarity, a sense of identical, obedient, young citizens trained in a common purpose.

'We know there were other domed cities built like ours. As pollution got beyond humanity, these places of safety controlled temperature, daylight, drawing energy from beyond the dome through wind and water. Our food has been specially balanced to provide what we need; we have made our own fuel.'

This was repeated stuff, but it was necessary to ensure they understood the enormity of the risk they were beginning.

'We don't know what has happened to them because we've gradually lost contact. It doesn't matter. What matters, is that you fly up to the dome, spiral through it and find us somewhere safe above, in the skies.'

**************************************

Down a flight of old stairs, long abandoned, a workshop used to build the city originally. So there were no cameras watching. This was the nearest thing to secrecy the liberationalists could find.

People filled the room where material was once shaped, sat on the stairs in the murk, no extra lights possible. Aytee and Jui shared a stair, saying nothing, waiting as the hubbub continued. Suddenly it stopped.

Zena appeared. Neither young nor old, neither attractive nor dour, she was dark-haired, smooth-skinned with a penetrating gaze from blue eyes that weighed people up in seconds. She led the rebels because she had an inner drive and had once been the mistress of some bigshot government official. Nobody ever asked her about that. They generally felt compelled to follow her.

From him she'd witnessed the sheer extent of corruption across the city and decided that power is what mattered and through the ramshackle group of discontented people she'd gathered so far, she was working to fashion a force that would escape this lifestyle and see her achieve the power she deserved.

Several, including Aytee, reported on their failed attempts to harangue people in the walkways. Zena nodded, 'I've heard. It's time to do more. Citizens are moved away from us by the automatic police through their cameras. We will destroy some cameras.'

The call for direct action went down well.

*******************************

In a tiny monitoring station Disli sat before a panel of screens, one focused from above on Zena addressing her would-be revolutionaries.

On another, the trainees' lecture was continuing.

He could see both escape plans being worked out in front of him and with this illegal equipment he could follow both until he could see clearly which one was the better to support, which side would win.

*******************************

Before the lecture finished, the old woman who hadn't introduced herself told them, 'In view of the fact that one or two of our citizens have become infected with an illness which makes them resist what we enjoy in Green-Metro 109, it's possible they may find out about the rockets.'

This was shocking. An official admitting to the existence of rebels who had only been the subject of whispered rumours! 'If you are ever challenged by anybody, do not admit that you are trying our three spiral rockets to see if they can penetrate the layers of our sky and find a new place for us.'

She went on, grim faced. 'You will return. Then the senior members of our government will go through the holes in the sky and set up a new city so that all citizens will leave on the next phase of rockets to be built. Everyone will be welcomed by the government.'

The question of what unimaginable horrors might pour through the holes hadn't been addressed. Neither had the idea that the rockets might only get through twice and the government would not let anybody else escape.

The monitors of screens concluded that all trainees were happy, honoured to have been chosen. Nothing could go wrong with a plan dreamed up by their caring government.

*********************************

Disli left his cubby hole and merged with ordinary people on the walkways. He looked as if was one of them; he wasn't. He held extraordinary power, not because he'd been appointed to it, but by what was called chance in the previous world.

He loved making things – gadgets, machines, tools, weapons, anything he could get the precious materials for. On one of his forages around the forgotten nooks of the city, he'd discovered a small cache of now rarely used metals, enjoying the smell, the feel of cold metal, but mainly worked expertly in plastex.

On another exploration, focusing on what was hidden behind wall panels, which were often put up quickly to cover a variety of things no longer needed and a new batch of cameras, he happened upon an early monitoring unit.

He'd been caught by the local security woman one day, but had glibly talked his way out of being reported by trading a replica of the official fusion gun he had made from stolen materials. Disli demonstrated how the gun could fuse anything in a tangled mass of plastex, human flesh or both by a single shot.

The guard was delighted. She went from the monitoring unit to try it on a person she'd taken a dislike to but was seen by several who screamed her description into an automatic police monitor.

The woman asked Disli to hide her and the gun for awhile, so she took up residence in the old unit, an outlaw effectively. He enabled her hiding, in return for all she knew about security.

Once she'd told him everything, Disli asked, 'Anything else?' The woman shook her head, 'you know all I know', which was the signal for Disli to smile and say, 'in that case your troubles are over.'

In a single burst the woman's legs melted. Her screams went no further than the thick walls. Slowly, smiling Disli raised the weapon and fired again, taking her head out.

Once he'd cleared up her remains he knew nobody could touch him now. As he walked along he realised he had the power to obliterate from the security system all trace of this walk, any search and everything else he did whenever he chose.

************************************

From the lecture area it was a lengthy walk through corridors and down a long lift ride to the area containing the rockets. A vast area reminiscent of an old industrial facility – though nobody knew that – was silent, the automatic arms of the construction machines idle, their construction done.

Corkscrew noses stood sharp and proud on the top of each rocket.

They were ordered to find their assigned places inside each rocket now the teams were complete. Silence and secrecy were impressed on each volunteer again, and they sat in their allotted places, getting a feel for it, imagining the take-off and how their training would kick in.

*****************************************

On his way to meet Zena, Disli stopped for a drink. He wanted to feel completely at ease when he met the woman in charge of the undesirables.

Perching on a vacant bar stool, he pressed a button from the mini battery in front of him. Juice 3. A hygienic straw emerged and he sucked till he was sated, looking at the notice above - 'All refreshment is free - your government looks after you.'

Disli thought back- how easy it'd been to track Zena and her minions down and when he'd contacted her, they'd agreed to meet him, despite not knowing anything about him or his motives.

They were very naive and inexperienced compared with the government. On the other hand they were hungry while the government was heavily weary.

The domestic block that was currently in use by Zena – one of four she instinctively rotated round – was a short walk. The uncouth henchman by the door pretending to be casual stopped him and waited.

'Automatic policemen looking very lifelike!' Disli joked, enjoying a feeling of superiority. Crunch. His back was rammed into the shiny wall. Crunk. His head jerked upwards from the fist and as he managed, 'I've come to see Zena' he felt disadvantaged with his strangled voice.

'Put him down, Stone', was ordered from behind. It was Zena. She was impatient. She was not the smiling, dreaming Zena of the monitor shots, but a business-like leader bothered with trivialities.

Stone released him enough for a muttered. 'I'm Disli.'

She looked Disli up and down and moved Stone aside with a nod. 'What do you want, Disli?'

Dropping his voice to force Zena to move closer to him, Disli said, 'I have information you may find useful.' She was very close. He could have hurt her with his bare hands. But she smelt of something he dimly remembered. Dreams of sex? But he couldn't recall it fully.

'It's not safe to talk here,' she snapped.

'No cameras in this zone. Upstairs yes, outside yes.' She knew that; how did he? 'Go on, Disli.'

He told her that he knew she was escalating her campaign and as he possessed security data that would be invaluable, she could make her execution list –

'My what?' she demanded, intrigued.

'I assume when you take over, you'll have a list of people to be removed, those who'll be a threat to you.'

As she thought it through, he held her stare. 'I will prove that I have the information.'

'What's your price, Disli?'

'Everything is free from the government, isn't it?'

'Not when we take over, no.'

'Oh I'm sure you'll find a way to repay me, later.' Stone showed him out and the two men locked eyes for a moment. Disli never forgot grievances nor slights. Stone's days were numbered.

*******************************

As they left the rocket bay, the volunteers were advised to enjoy entertainment and rest, 'tomorrow is a big day.'

None of them noticed a large, old woman – Blid - standing in the gantry above, watching them, clinging to the railing for support, her straggly grey hair hanging limply off her head.

She smiled, approvingly. Turning back to her two assistants she said in a surprisingly high voice for such a large body, 'We have thought of everything, I trust.'

The assistants heartily agreed. That was their job – to agree.

*******************************

Zena asked Stone to fetch her refreshment. She wasn't hungry; she just wanted time to think. Her self image was of a ruthless, determined and focused woman. But was she?

She toyed with the composite that Stone delivered in a bowl. 'Send Jui in.'

Stone obeyed without a flinch. 'Jui, draw up a death list. All those who've hindered us, who've ever betrayed us. All the government. And any others.'

Jui nodded acquiescence, blinking as she took in what she had just been asked to do. 'Don't worry, Jui. This is for after we're in full control.'

'I'm not worried, Zena, you know what you're doing.'

\***********************************

Ray and Malk set a fair pace on the walkway, demonstrating their lean fitness, if anyone had noticed. 'How do you really think they chose us, Ray?'

'I suppose they pressed buttons on their machines; names came out. Not our department, is it, Malk?'

Malk, late twenties, tall, sandy hair cropped short as required, thought it through. He was looking forward to their challenge and hadn't entertained any doubts. Ray, a year or two younger, slower of body, shorter, fleeter of mind, had experienced doubt.

'The spirals may not work. Or they may only work once. Have you thought about that?'

Malk hadn't and didn't wish to.

Blid rolled around the rocket bays, down from the gantry, her assistants still agreeing. The rockets stood so proud, so hopeful. What an achievement for the government and sadly, one they couldn't boast about.

To have plundered all the old records of technology and amass the necessary mechanics and plastex to make three working rockets without anybody outside the government was an achievement they could be proud of.

If they knew, the rebels would certainly be stopped in their tracks.

High above them in a control box accessible by a sequence of plastex ladders behind the walls and screens, Disli watched and activated microphones so he could hear Blid. 'You can see why I was proud to take charge of this exciting project. Green-Metro 109 is doomed, but some of our expertise will survive. It's the culmination of my life's work.'

The trio paused to look up at a spiral. 'The perfect spiral. You coil up, you coil down. You save the city. Simple and perfect.'

As the nodders nodded, Disli was less than happy. If Blid was sure it would work, should he go with them and not the rebels? The rockets certainly looked impressive and the explanation of escaping upwards sounded plausible.

He pressed the loudspeakers he had relayed from the current control station, 'Citizen Blid, there is a man to see you called Disli. He has information for you. The government will be grateful if you see him.'

He'd heard this kind of pompous command and response between government staff. Blid and assistants moved unquestioning towards the exit. Disli leaped up, raced down the ladders to arrive at the foyer entrance as they left the bays.

'Disli, is it?' barked Blid. 'I'm Citizen Blid. If you have information, you should tell me.' Disli feigned excitement, 'Citizen Blid, may I first say what an honour it is to meet you ...'

He'd also heard this kind of drivel used elsewhere, but she cut him off. 'What do you know?'

'Through a friend with a contact who overheard something, I ... you must appreciate ... well, I believe the rebels know about the rockets and want to sabotage them.'

She stared at him through the heavy hoods of her eyelids. 'Are they common knowledge, the rockets?'

'Oh, only to the leaders I hear, not the riff raff.' Blid laughed, ripples passing through copious flesh. Her assistants dutifully joined in but Disli was confused.

'If they attack here, they will be destroyed. Once the rockets are up, it's too late anyway. Thank you, Disli. Your loyalty is appreciated. What reward can we offer?'

'To serve is reward enough, Blid.' She nodded as if expecting nothing less. One of the assistants watched Disli closely, 'Excuse me, Citizen, back in a moment.' He went to the security area behind the main walls and set up a verbal security alert of 'Disli' and asked for it to be fed to him later.

This was Kre, Bild's assistant employed both to boost her and spy on her. What Kre couldn't know was that his request had been both anticipated and sidetracked to Disli's private area.

*************************************

A small gaggle of rebels edged along the walls of the walkway, clutching a ragbag of grip tools, some found, most stolen from a maintenance bay.

Zena checked others approaching Aytee from one side; she and Jui came from the opposite. Ready to give the signal to attack the cameras staring at them, she caught sight of Disli rushing towards them.

'Stop, Zena. Don't do anything!'

'Why not?' demanded Zena, bewildered by his action and trying to think how he knew what they were planning to do.

'I've just heard from my friend that they know about you –'

'Nothing new, Disli. If that's the best you can say –'

'No, it isn't. I have news. They are planning... ', and he moved closer to her, lowering his voice. 'The government is planning to escape the city, all the senior people.' Jui came closer to hear it too.

'What?'

He nodded. 'They have built spiral rockets, volunteers will spiral them through the sky dome and find a place of safety and the rockets will come back to take up the government and then ordinary citizens ...'

It was too ridiculous to be true. Yet too desperate not to be. It would also explain a lot of secret work going on that they'd not been able to find out about.

*********************************

Ray and Malk walking despite being on a moving walkway looked up at the sky, thinking ahead. 'You know what gives me the shivers, Malk? How they just turn day and night on and off. Of all the things we don't know ...'

Malk didn't see the point his friend was making, but was only focused on tomorrow. 'Tell you what, Ray, if we're going to get entertainment in Block F, you stay on this and I'll race you by running the other way ...'

He was already off and Ray waved him on. No doubt all the others were larking about in high spirits; Ray was more reflective. There were so many gaps in their knowledge of the last century that Ray worried they might be missing something important.

He looked over towards an unusual noise – shouting – to the right, so he leaped across a barrier and made for it.

Noises were coming from citizens shrieking in alarm while Zena and friends bashed at cameras with their assorted tools, savagely, desperately, madly, making little headway, but the sight was unsettling to everyone.

Zena's face glowed. This was more like it. This'd make them realise she meant business. In fact, the official response surprised them all.

The security voice boomed out across a swathe of the city. 'Citizens, hurry to walkway 301. Some of you stand in Square

ZB and some in ZC. Rebels are destroying cameras we put there for all your security. Stop them. Citizens, hurry to walkway 301 ...' The loop went on and on.

Ray pushed through the crowd who had taken to shouting derisively at the rebels from the sides and the higher walkway. En masse they were slowly advancing.

Zena couldn't hear the command, only the shouting. She beamed – at last, here was a response! She tucked her metal away and opened her arms to welcome all. Then she grasped they were abusing her, closing on her.

The rebels stood back to back, in a rough circle. Those citizens were ugly, angry. Suddenly panels slid aside and hoses released white foam from the sides and above. Aimed at the rebels it drenched everybody in a large circle.

It was an anti-riot system installed when Green Metro 109 was built and unused for decades. It enveloped people, rendering movement and shouting impossible.

It started to evaporate quickly and by then, the activity was over. Citizens took themselves away, clothes clinging to them; as keen to escape as they'd been to arrive. When somebody fell, others were pulled down and a panic grew with anyone falling bringing more down.

Zena stood alone where they'd been, dripping wet, tears streaming down her face. Tears of rage, frustration and hatred. 'The bastards.'

***********************************

Aytee got away, terrified, mixed up. She fell over Ray's foot as he moved to avoid somebody on the ground. He helped her up, she muttered thanks and was off – only to be sent flying by a large, panicky man. Ray stood her up and moved her out of the flow.

'You're wet, you know', he said inanely.

'So are you,' she grinned, beginning to relax in his presence. 'I'm cold as well.'

Ray checked the area was clearing. A refreshment bay was close so he led her towards it. She selected hot food and a hot drink – Juice 15. She stood by
an air blower to eat.

'Which way are you going?' he asked.

''Who wants to know?' she responded as if joking, but actually serious. 'Which way are *you* going?'

'Who wants to know?' he smiled back. 'I'm not from security.'

Talk stopped while she dried off and sat to finish her food. 'Did you see what was going on?'

She looked at him. 'Did you?'

'No, I arrived just as the foam stuff hit. How close were you?'

After a moment's thought, she decided to shake him out of his citizenship superiority. 'If you want to know, I was at the heart of it. Some of us were destroying cameras, we're sick of being watched and controlled.'

He didn't respond. He was taken aback. He was actually

listening to a rebel! She took his silence for a kind of approval, so told him more. It was the only way to spread the word and this was more amenable than standing on a box trying to draw a hostile crowd.

She shared their unofficial manifesto, to be rid of the government and put ordinary people in charge who would make the place freer with real choice.

'You do know that Green-Metro 109 is dying, food is running out, recycling is not enough, people are ill, there is a stagnation, a nothingness ...'

He stopped smiling. 'Do you know what you're saying?' She nodded.

''This city is doomed. We've seen with our own eyes, human eyes, and as there is no escape out, we must escape within. Some of us –'

'Us? Who are us?'

'Are you sure you're not security?' He shook his head. 'I am Aytee. I am helping to free Green-Metro 109,' at which she stood and spat onto the lens of one of the obvious cameras watching them at the side.

Ray stood and left the area without a word. Aytee ran after him, clung to his arm, 'I'm sorry if that offends your obedience training, but you need to know. Let's talk about philosophy, medicine, recycling, anything, let's talk...'

They approached a man stood waiting for Ray. Malk laughed, 'I told you I'd beat you here, Ray. You didn't say you had something to pick up on the way!'

Ray snapped at Malk to shut it. Aytee said, 'So, you're Ray. I'm Aytee.'

'And I'm Malk. Nice to meet you.'

A moment of awkward silence hung in the air before Malk suggested, 'hey, why don't you bring a friend and meet us at Leisure Block Mech tonight.' Ray was appalled; Aytee nodded acceptance.

*******************************

Disli caught up on the recordings of the rebel trouble, enjoying the spectacle. He then followed the bulk of them who went straight back to their current base without thinking and Aytee with her encounter with Ray. He flinched when she spat at the camera leaving the slime to obscure future views and noted they met up with another unknown man called Malk.

He sat back. Violence escalating; the rockets leaving tomorrow. How was all this going to work out?

*******************************

Aytee grabbed a steam shower in the domestic block and stood reflecting on whether the event had been a success or not. Certainly she quite liked Ray, so that was something.

Lo was waiting her turn in the shower. 'Ah, Lo, doing anything tonight?' Lo said she wasn't, a bit wary as to what Aytee was going to suggest. Lo wasn't wildly adventurous.

'I met two interesting men, and I have a date with one and we need someone to come too ...at the Leisure Block Mech?'

'Isn't that where they have all those boring scientific and progress-in-the city shows?'

'I don't know, is it? Well I don't suppose we'll spend too long watching the shows.'

\*\*\*\*\*\*\*\*\*\*\*\*\*\*\*\*\*\*\*\*\*\*\*\*\*\*\*\*\*\*\*\*\*\*\*\*\*

The evening was full of a sequence of separate events which made it difficult for Disli to keep up.

Citizen Blid ate, squashed into a booth, her fat elbows on the table, with Kre and Slir, her appointed assistants. Her main concern was why their security reports were coming in a bit later than 'as they happened'. It made no sense.

They were joined by Disli who had no good reason for knowing where Blid would be eating, but warned her that the rebels proposed to attack the rockets first thing, before take-off and that what was different now was they had acquired actual or replica fusion guns.

Blid thanked him politely for his information and he left, smiling. He would only know that Kre followed him when he later checked back over the recordings.

In Leisure Block Mech Malk paid close attention to Aytee, leaving Lo with Ray, but they found each other's company awkward. After lots of food and drink, Malk wanted privacy and despite Ray's horrified protests, Malk said he knew a secret place.

Disli trudged to Zena again and was treated to Stone's neck assault before he was able to tell Zena two vital things – one, the location of the government meetings and two, that he had acquired some fusion guns. The rebels had never seen one of these fearsome weapons up close and examined the single one Disli produced from his tunic with interest and genuine curiosity.

He was sent to get more, followed by a suspicious Stone to do the heavy carrying. He loaded up the grim-faced thug and thought of shooting him as he walked away, but he needed Zena to be armed in the increasingly bizarre game he was playing.

Malk was able to identify himself to the door camera, push Ray in front of it and they entered, keeping the girls low. Easy. As was simply following their earlier training routes into the rocket bays to the changing areas where he settled with Aytee on a massage bed, normally used for relaxing muscles.

This left Ray to wander into the bays, thinking only of the journey ahead. Lo followed him and so discovered the spiral plans. She dashed back to alert Aytee and so the secret was truly open.

Of course, it was all recorded anyway. Well, it was for Disli's benefit. Blid sat with Kre and Slir and wondered about who Disli was. He seemed to have no records at all on their system, which comprised simple names and residences manually entered.

The rockets stunned the girls and Malk, carried away with a desire to show off, told them too much about the purpose of the strange spirals on the noses. Ray was livid with Malk but then turned on Aytee just for being there and because he may have been a little jealous. Lo was of no interest to him.

Disli had crept back into his rocket bay control area, followed by Kre, but not close enough to allow him to access the area where Disli was locked. Kre spoke into his hand-held gadget to warn Blid what was afoot, that the entire rocket team may have to be sacrificed and Disli couldn't be trusted.

It went no further than Disli's control panel, but Kre couldn't know that.

********************************

As the next day dawned across the dome, Kre woke Blid – annoyed at losing sleep – to say he'd heard nothing of his recommendation to sacrifice the teams … She was horrified as he recounted what he'd seen.

Zena woke to the pleasure of seeing a pile of fusion guns in her room. Unbelievable. Now they could do anything.

Ray refused to speak to Malk once they'd arrived back in the rocket bays with all the other volunteers and started routine exercising.

The government met in emergency session and Blid reported what she knew. If any outsider had seen the government, he or she may have been struck by the fact that they were all old and all women. They were the second or third generation of the founders of Green-Metro 109. They knew their world was crumbling.

They endorsed Blid's plan to let the launches go ahead and to liquidate the rebels by force in the rocket area.

******************************************

The battle began as the crews moved to their rockets. Disli released the doors so Zena and her small army rushed straight through, fusion guns in hand.

Simultaneously, Disli opened other doors for a squad of security guards, equally armed to swarm in to face the rebels. It was a short battle but ferocious.

Not used to firing or the vicious effects of the fusion guns, the rebels wasted a lot of shots. The guards were well drilled and more effective.

But in that space, with lights that Disli had kept dim, the screams and howls of people injured beyond repair, chaos was all that could be described.

The outcome was that some scrambled aboard the rockets; anywhere to get away from the hideous death. Nobody knew anything accurate any more. The final burst of conflict centred on one of the rockets which got damaged in several places, with huge gaping holes from the fusion guns.

The government had decided to sit in permanent session given the imminent launch of the rockets and the worrying security situation.

It was there that Zena's fired-up fans found them, following advice from Disli. The fat old slugs looked in open-mouthed astonishment as they were ripped to coagulated shreds of skin, bones, muscles and clothes one by one. Even their bewildered security guards were destroyed as they fumbled to respond to a situation beyond them.

The revolution had begun. From small beginnings often come big upheavals. Their tragedy was that this one would be very short-lived.

***********************************

The launch was not the well-planned affair everyone had rehearsed. It was messy, hurried and a rather desperate attempt to escape the carnage in the bays. Ray checked every panel. Where was Malk?

He looked through the camera into the deck below. Aytee had made it. She had no business on the rocket but everything was changed now. The remainder of the people on board seemed to be the regular crew, or rather some of them who had survived

Two men met in the bay; Ray knew neither, one was Disli, the other Stone. When he looked again a few moments later, both had gone. Ray was getting anxious to be off now; nobody seemed to be in charge in the control box.

With one final look outside he saw Stone lying in a mangled heap of mutilation, fresh from a shot. The rocket registered a person had just boarded, so Ray sealed the doors. As a fresh cohort of security guards rushed in to the bay, the leader beckoned him to get out of the rocket, Ray set to ignition.

A voice boomed from the control. It was one of Zena's assistants, 'Where is Zena? We haven't found her anywhere. She must be on one of those rockets.'

'Not this one, we're full,' snapped Ray as lift off began. The fumes from the tail stripped the remaining lining from the bay. Ray noticed the second rocket was also on lift off.

Concentrating, Ray nonetheless heard laughter from below. He glanced at the screen. It was Aytee laughing with Malk! He was battered and bruised, but alive. After a moment, Malk broke away from her and climbed up to Ray.

Suddenly the rocket stopped with a jerk that crashed Ray into the panel, sent Malk flying down and violently threw others about. Aytee hurt her arm badly; others started muttering and cursing.

Equally as suddenly the rocket restarted and lifted. The ceiling section slid open and they rose with gathering speed, closely followed by the second rocket.

As they rose above Green-Metro 109, nobody obviously looked up. Life went on as normal. The automatic instructions played as normal.

What was different was the government was dead and the security system in meltdown. But ordinary people didn't know that.

\*\*\*\*\*\*\*\*\*\*\*\*\*\*\*\*\*\*\*\*\*\*\*\*\*\*\*\*\*

They'd been taught that it wouldn't be a long journey. In terms of the size of the city it was probably twice as high as it was broad. A few minutes, that's all.

It was enough time for Ray to begin to digest what had happened and how quickly everything he knew had ended. Was he right to launch? What would happen now? And would they come back?

The remains of the ground control crew sat at their stations watching the progress on screen. Disli's voice came from behind them, reassuring, calm. Whatever they'd experienced prior to launch was now under control.

Outside, inexplicably, some of the food points appeared to have dried up. People moved on and looked elsewhere but queues formed quickly. The first cracks in the fabric of Green-Metro 109's society were showing.

Jui had taken control of the rebels and was beginning to put the execution list into effect. She gave orders in a way that showed she had taken on a new authority – no more the sidekick. She roamed, discovering areas she hadn't seen before and some where it was 'forbidden' to enter.

She was found by Kre and some guards near one of the food vat areas and cornered. 'Well, look what this is!' he cried to his mates, who stood close to her. 'It's a shame she's so ugly, but never mind, we can improve her. Strip her.'

They blinked, but did as he ordered. She fought back but was rapidly stood shivering, naked against the vat. 'Up the ladder.' They moved Jui up to the platform.

'Punishment time for rebellion. Either I use this gun on your limbs one at a time or you jump in this and swim...' She looked down at the liquid; no chance of surviving in that, but she had seen what the guns did to human flesh. Her eyes darted looking for some means of escape.

Kre smiled. He raised the gun and fingered the trigger. She jumped.

The splash hit the guards but Kre had stepped back. By the time Kre stopped laughing, Jui was drowned.


*********************************

Ray slowed the engine. The dome was approaching, still going upwards but now in slow motion. 10, 9, 8, 7 ... He slowed even more, and then got the jolt as the nose hit the dome and bounced back. A quick thrust of engine repeated the process, this time he went back further.

Finally, Ray got it right and he locked to the inner dome surface. Everyone on board held their breath. This was the critical moment. He set the blades swirling and they bit, to everybody's relief.

Slowly, nobody near him, Ray drilled into the surface, the discarded waste spewing out of the blades and falling on the city. They had done tests on the dome at the city boundary over a long time, so this part was as expected.

Footsteps up the ladder brought Malk, Aytee and then – Zena! Everyone was surprised, not aware she'd been below all this time.

'I am Zena. I had to get away for reasons which I think you can guess. We have to start a new world up here.'

There was no time to argue about this statement from someone clearly deranged as the note of the spiral had changed – they were cutting through a different material. The rocket stopped.

They were stuck. 'Go on, Ray, keep going,' shouted Malk.

'No, look, we're off-centre and going in twisted.' One of the trained crew came up to give an opinion. 'Looks like we're overweight, Ray.' She went back down and head counted. She shouted up, 'Too many.'

Zena suggested coming out and trying again. Ray shook his head, 'no, we've used our thrust. If we wind out we just drop down to the earth.'

'We will have to drop someone out of the base doors to lighten the load, 'Ray said grimly.

'We'll draw lots,' chirped Aytee, confident in her own luck.

By now several citizens found things not quite as normal. Bits of bodies lay scattered; more food areas ran dry and in one zone the lights failed. The timings for these failures had been programmed by Disli, but none knew that.

Two rockets half hanging out of the sky above was a terrible vision, a sense that all was not well in their universe, that a power was set on destroying them and a panic set in that rose to unstoppable heights. When many were covered with flakes of the dome, several were convinced the end was nigh.

Intermittent rioting broke out with somebody, anybody, the scapegoat.

Above them, an argument was triggered after Zena said that if there were building a new world, a man should be dropped out as they needed all the women they could get for a future.

Malk named one of the men below and went down to throw him out. Ray stood at the top of the ladder and shouted down, 'Malk, be a man and go yourself. We don't need this.'

Everyone was surprised at his anger over Malk. 'He started it by bringing those rebels into the rocket area. Without that, we'd be doing what we planned with the right number on board.'

Malk climbed back up and went for Ray, furious as that was just the sort of thing that could take hold of the rest leading to Malk being jettisoned. It was a silly, childish, confined punch up, with neither winning as they were evenly matched.

It was Zena who realised a small fusion gun was clipped to the control bench, took it and stepped between the men. There was a shriek, white faces and open mouths of agony.

Malk was almost dead, so Zena grabbed him and dragged him down the stairs with no fuss, noticing the sign for 'drop doors'. 'Open them,' she barked at one of the crew who obliged. Malk's remains fell to earth – a further example of some supernatural evil over their city to those who witnessed it.

**********************************

The rocket restarted itself. Nobody said anything. Everything recent had been too terrible and shocking to make any sense from. Another ten minutes and the note changed again. The spiral was through but kept turning.

Around them was pitch black. One of the women below shouted that the other rocket was ahead of them, its tail disappeared. Their machine indicated further stress in the engine as they powered upwards.

'We're still overweight!' Zena said.

'That noise now is because we're off-centre. It's the tail fin scraping against the hole in the dome. It will cause friction.'

'And we will burn,' said Ray. They still travelled upwards but the noise was louder. Then suddenly they were free and rising more rapidly.

Now they seemed to be out of danger, Aytee was bored and went below to see if anything amused her. There was one door she couldn't open which made her both curious and irritated. It was a store, of course, but something heavy seemed propped against it on the inside.

The impression in the top deck was that outside was getting less dark and murky. And then suddenly the rocket broke into bright light – daylight – and dropped onto its side.

'It looks like water!' several cried in amazement, using knowledge from the training footage they had watched and what they had seen of water in the city.

They were floating on a mass of water. 'They built Green-Metro 109 under this water!' said Zena, understanding. 'I believe this is a sea.'

\*\*\*\*\*\*\*\*\*\*\*\*\*\*\*\*\*\*\*\*\*\*\*\*\*\*\*\*\*\*\*\*\*\*\*\*

The first stream of ocean poured through the hole, followed by a trickle from the other one. It hit the city with a huge splash and bounced up before falling to run along sidewalks.

It was not a massive torrent, but a steady flow. And it just kept coming.

Even obedient citizens couldn't ignore this. Quite quickly walkways were underwater and stopped moving. Buildings began to flood. Some lights flickered and went out. This was so far from experience or explanation that terror gripped people.

\*\*\*\*\*\*\*\*\*\*\*\*\*\*\*\*\*\*\*\*\*\*\*\*\*\*\*\*\*\*\*\*\*\*

Ray set the engine going again. 'What are you doing?'

'We need to move from here. There is pressure from the holes pulling us back; we have to be free of it. Their partner rocket was some distance ahead.

They said nothing, each thinking of what must be happening below. 'The water will pour down; air bubbles will rise up and through the holes. The dome will stand the pressure, but it will be filled,' said Zena, sadly, latching on to what was a possible outcome, though nobody really knew.

*****************************

Citizens dashed about, desperate to escape the rising water and shrieks of manic and fear, trying to scrabble upwards. The lifts stopped. The deafening sound of falling cold water drowned words. And to make matters worse, the city's night time switched in and the darkness heightened their fear greater.

Some were trapped in rooms as water kept doors closed. Many slipped and fell, and being unable to swim well – their municipal pools were quite limited – many drowned.

There was nowhere to run.

*****************************

Ray switched off the engine, letting the rocket float. Their partner rocket was drifting away from them. No means of contacting them, no way of knowing who was on board and alive.

****************************

There was a brief equilibrium, a balance between water coming in and the air inside.

Tops of buildings held fewer citizens now, clinging on, pointlessly.

Before long, there was only the roof on the once tallest building in Green-Metro 109 on which clung fifteen adults and 6 youngsters. They were fighting as one of the men was trying to strangle a child in order to stand on her body to raise himself above the surface. It was a futile gesture, but the moment of final abandonment of hope wasn't there yet.

******************************

In front of them they saw a vast replica of their city.

'It's Green-Metro 109!'

'No, it's a city, but not ours.'

The rocket floated closer. They could make out people, hundreds of them lining the water's edge looking at them.

'What's that line?' asked Aytee.

''It is the water line! It shows that all that water has dropped into our dome.'

People looked curious, some hostile. The rocket was headed to a lower decking area. 'They don't look like they'll welcome us with open arms...' warned Ray.

147

The rocket stopped and bumped against the edge of the land and water. 'Let's get whatever we might need to defend ourselves,' Zena suggested with an order.

Quickly they searched the lockers and found as much as they could carry. One of the men got the mystery door open. On the inside was the body of Disli which rather alarmed everyone.

'There's our overweight explanation.'

'He must have crept on board having covered his tracks and fallen and broken his neck when we hit the dome first time,' concluded Ray, already weary with death. His head was tight with trying to make sense of the day's events. The thought of an unknown future was too much at the moment.

******************************

Nobody lived. The water rose to the top over a period of time.

Green-Metro 109 was no more, though the dome and the day/night mechanism would be there for decades yet.

******************************

They had no choice but to go ashore, so one of the men got the side hatch open, reached across and held the rocket as close to the side as he could.

People moved back from them.

'We won't need the rocket anymore,' pronounced Zena. 'There are buildings here, let's see what we can find and I'm getting hungry.''

They walked together into the city, a space in the crowd perpetually around them. They got no answers, people only mumbled to each other. Cameras watched their progress and all concluded they were why nobody would talk.

Zena decided to make some progress. 'I am Zena,' she shouted. 'We are from Green-Metro 109, which we now know was built under the water, not far from you and your city. Can you help us? Show us to the authorities?'

Rich coming from the rebel, but nobody appreciated the irony and sensible in this situation. Nobody answered, though some older people gave the impression of understanding her words, but didn't attempt to reply They moved on, Zena slightly ahead.

They came to a post, a loudspeaker on top and a board on the side. Zena walked round it, listened a moment and called over to Ray. 'What exactly is a spiral?'

'A coiled round shape, a going round in a circle, like we have just used to get here … why?'

'Come and look at this.'

They joined her and stood reading the board which was being voiced by a mechanical sounding person through the loudspeaker, over and over.

''Citizens, it has been no secret for some time that with the ending of pollution on our planet, other problems have arisen. We need volunteers to be trained to fly rockets upwards, beyond the sky, to find a new world and come back and lead us there to a new life. Be the first to volunteer to escape for us all... Citizens...'

It repeated over and over.

And so the visitors understood there was no escape, spiral or otherwise. And they were all alone in an overcrowded world.

# Travelling

Only a few signed up for her first evening class in 'Confidence' which included public speaking, drama therapy and a bit of amateur psychology on the way.

There was Fred Ingham with weary eyes, a stooped back, little hair, a school teacher aged about fifty but feeling like seventy as he came to the end of all he could cope with as a teacher.

Rod Down, an artist in his 30s, looked wild and cultivated a bohemian image but supported views about the place of women that later came to be socially outlawed. Jennie Summers, a professional dancer who just couldn't get through auditions, had passion for her art but lacked a sense of self-belief.

Nigel Starmer was in his 40s and needed to make a father-of-the-bride speech next year. He ran a small woodyard where he and the two men he employed made a living supplying builders and DIY enthusiasts.

And then there was Malcolm, Curator 14 at the local museum, thin and hollow-eyed. Nobody was sure what he wanted from the sessions since he'd rarely speak except about the work he did guarding artefacts in the museum.

Oh, and there was me. There because Vanessa and I were going out and I wanted to support her in this enterprise to broaden her CV and earn some extra cash so we could have a holiday together. Somewhere nice.

A typical evening launched with Vanessa encouraging all to join in a mildly controversial debate followed by basic, untaxing

151

physical exercises, along the lines of what Third Years in a secondary school drama lesson would do.

This she followed up with some individual mime work. 'Hold the position. You are hungry, but there is nothing to eat. Using your eyes only, look around and find something to your left. When I say 'release' you will go for it. Remember you are a savage person, a brute who is unreasonable, hungry... release!'

And off we all went, role playing and enjoying it immensely. That sort of build up to an aggressive piece of simple mime and roleplay was always a great icebreaker among what was a motley crew. Vanessa buttressed her work with several favourite catchphrases – 'the biggest journey starts with the smallest step' and 'however small steps you travel, inside your mind it may be a very long journey indeed.'

For some, inside our heads was both a long journey and a weird one, too.

**********************************

We shared as much or as little of our lives as we wanted to. Vanessa had this idea that we could imagine a film of our lives and describe a single shot, a panned moment in some situation which showed us at less than our best, perhaps at a point where we needed to develop it.

Of course, within the church hall we met in and the group that we were, there soon grew confidence and acceptance. We shared things; we acted things out in front of each other.

To do it in front of a large audience, especially strangers, was a taller order. Vanessa asked me to start the ball rolling, and my first thought was to describe the scene in our bedroom two nights ago which had been particularly pleasurable, if not exactly typical.

That wouldn't do, so I came up with a moment in my work – I am a trainee accountant and have been learning longer than most of my contemporaries as I just can't pass the exams. It was a typical day in the office with me struggling with phone calls, piles of paper and a boss who kept watching me from her glass booth.

Jennie described a dancing audition where she'd go along, queue for hours, perform a good dance piece but fell to pieces when she had to talk about herself or do some acting to go with it. Nigel with some hesitation and embarrassment gave us the horrors of an injury at work where two lads he previously employed had been pratting about and one had caught his hand in a machine.

Fred Ingham couldn't bear to talk about his school, so found a moment when he'd gone to a travel agent and asked about a fortnight's holiday for his wife and himself on a gas platform out in the North Sea. The girl behind the desk was dumbfounded.

'A holiday on *what*?'

Ingham explained, 'Being of an educational mind, I'd like to learn something. They have working farm, historical mine experiences so I wondered if they have that experience out in the North Sea?'

'I see,' replied the girl. She didn't. 'I'll ask.'

This one amused and puzzled the group, but it confirmed that Fred was losing it, if he ever had it in the first place. Vanessa told of a scene in her childhood where she was upset over the death of her granddad which I knew she'd told me ages ago wasn't true, but she used it to demonstrate emotion-memory when she introduced Stanislavski in drama lessons.

Rod Down, a true artist, painted us a moment in his studio above a garage, with Maria, his long-suffering muse lying in front of him.

'You're not special, Maria, but you are the only model I can bear to look at for long. There is a wild beauty in your eyes which I'm buggered if I can capture but I will, don't you worry, although sometimes you remind me of a cat and as you know I hate cats but when I'm painting I come alive but deep within is a sickness a burning desire....'

Maria had yawned, apparently. The verbal stream of consciousness rambled on, making us all wonder about Rod's stability and how he'd ever achieve his aim, 'to relate better with people, especially idiots.'

Malcolm was last to share his moment.

Curator 14 sits on a chair facing the large painting of *The Journey of the Eyes* by Claudia Frankel - a green blank face on a block head and huge, cavernous eyes that fix on the viewer. Not like the Mona Lisa, more a mix of Picasso, Dali and Munch rolled into one survivor of a nightmare.

The eyes seem to be hoping for something; hoping for something from the viewer in return for staring at him/her.

***************************

Vanessa was unhappy about the exercise, as she shared at length on our way home afterwards and for the remainder of the evening. She returned to it the next morning. She should have kept to drama, or drama therapy or confident speaking.

She was over her head with these people; they were all fruitcakes. I agreed with that part but did my best to persuade her that it was going well.

Everyone was enjoying themselves and for an evening class in a grim winter, that was an important achievement. She wasn't going to take that. She needed to feel more success for her own self confidence. It hung over us most of the week.

The next session Vanessa opened with a discussion about the exercise from last week and everyone seemed happy with it. Malcolm said nothing. She'd prepared a handful of roleplay exercises of asking a 'stranger' for directions, to borrow money, to buy something, to help in an accident.

The session went off well enough after that. She had them reading short extracts from famous speeches – Martin Luther King, Churchill, Abraham Lincoln and, with an apology for no women in the list, Mahatma Gandhi.

As we had a few minutes before the end, she asked them to give us another film clip from their lives. They happily obliged: Nigel recounted the sacking of both lads from his yard; Jennie told how she practised in front of a mirror, hour after hour but that her basic problem was that she didn't love what she looked like.

Fred talked about when he went back to the travel agent and kicked up a fuss – these office people are just jumped up teenagers in a workplace. 'I told them what was what. No holidays on platforms? Why not?' He was asked to leave the shop.

Rod Down had done tons of painting this week. He'd had some money from his endlessly sympathetic mother and had put a naked Maria on a carpet. 'You lie there Maria with your hypnotic oven wide open to me and your legs calling me but I can't you see what your mushroom hours are doing to my eight circles here I have nature is perfect you are showing me but you bore me horribly I don't even like you....'

Maria had yawned again, apparently. Vanessa, although reluctant to question the group's images too closely, asked him what he was actually putting on canvas as it clearly wasn't a nude woman. No, it was circles, colliding dots.

Curator 14 had sat on the bus, leaving work behind for another day. He had to sit upstairs, which he disliked, especially as there were several young people making a lot of noise, silly laughter and banging on the widows to people in the street as they passed.

He'd looked at one girl in particular. Her eyes carried a demented look, a window on a soul that was far away in a world of its own. It reminded him of the painting, his painting that he guarded so carefully day after day.

\*\*\*\*\*\*\*\*\*\*\*\*\*\*\*\*\*\*\*\*\*\*\*\*\*\*\*\*\*

The evening class was scheduled for just the winter term, nine weeks. Vanessa had not pulled in enough paying punters to be given an extension in the summer, so she made the most of it. Of all the participants, it was Malcolm who fascinated her the most.

The next week she didn't do any film clip imagination scenes and to our amazement, Jennie asked for it as the session ended. Nigel, Fred and Rod nodded enthusiastically. So they had one, making the session go on till the caretaker rattled his keys outside the door.

'Maria, I'm the poor idiot holding the brushes and paint while you smile there like the sphinx and I try to extract meaning and honesty from your situation and smile and I know I can't do it justice but what does a fool do but try and try and don't go too far away from me or I can't catch you up where are you going?'

Maria had yawned, obviously. She was tired. She'd had a busy week at school and there was a lot of pressure with exams coming up. She'd have to stop these sessions with Rod soon anyway, as she thought her dad suspected it was more than just 'helping the artist.' And she was only 16 anyway.

Fred Ingham and his good wife of almost thirty years had discussed one particular day at school. One of his colleagues was under the impression that the second and third years showed promise, that their bad behaviour was temporary and they just needed encouragement.

Fred had replied that the only promise they showed was as future inmates of asylums or prisons or both and that really, when some of the teachers were only a little older than the kids, it was time he called it a day. His wife pointed out that he wouldn't get his pension for another decade and if he wanted to holiday somewhere every single year ...

Curator 14 had walked the last leg to his bedsit from the bus stop. As he reached the end of his road he saw a face at a window. Steps led up to the front door of the big old, once grand, house. A woman's face was pressed to the glass above him. She was sitting or kneeling because he could only see her head.

She was old, with grey wispy hair. Her eyes stared out unblinking at the dark street. He had been so taken with her that he stopped a moment to stare. This was not what he did normally. Those lessons in the evenings must be having an effect. He was drawn to the face, to her eyes. She was dead.

That was the turning point for Vanessa and the group. She abandoned any confident speaking and the drama games and therapy. Just getting them opening up about fragments of their lives was therapy enough. What a way they had travelled. She was excited now and I felt better that she was happier; briefly we were closer.

Jennie recreated a precise moment when she had this week phoned for an audition, fairly boldly, knowing it was above her ability and outside her experience. But she hadn't had a gig in months and waiting tables in a ghastly bistro was soul-destroying.

She led the way in adding a second snapshot scene now, which I found interesting and told Vanessa so later. Jennie did her audition and was invited back on a recall, which in itself added to her confidence. The dancing was quite good and she knew she could learn the routines.

The speech wasn't bad either. She felt able to act out something of the character – a woman betrayed by a feckless man and left holding a baby that was too sick to live without a miracle. The director's assistant asked her to wait in a side-room off the green room while her main rival performed. He was full of himself, as so many were and told her the director was his best friend.

If he hadn't come on to Jennie so strongly she'd have assumed he was gay, as so many in the business were. But he was all too straight. He made it clear as he pressed himself onto her on the table that if she played ball with him, the role was hers.

Kneeing him in the balls was not the playing he had in mind, but she realised how far she'd come in personal confidence. She marched straight out of the green room and interrupted her rival to tell the director what had happened. She got the part.

Nigel had been offered an opportunity to merge with a rival yard that sold timber to the public sector, which would open up new business opportunities and secure his future. It was a golden chance, but would involve longer hours and was a risk. Their house needed serious updating and decorating – they'd bought it for a song years back but had no money since to maintain it.

He had to convince the directors of the other firm through directly speaking and presenting. His wife asked him as he wrestled with the dilemma – 'what would your friends at the confident club advise?' He smiled. 'Go for it!' On that basis he was a happy man. He was going to go for it.

Rod had taken it badly that Maria wanted to end their sessions – at least till she'd done her exams. 'One egg becomes two becomes four becomes sixteen the perfection of creation and the universe Maria I am just understanding that I have to paint in smaller circles and you tell me you want to leave me let me down to a solo miserable existence do you know how hard it is to find a willing and beautiful young model without the perv brigade getting their knickers in a twist?'

She was clearly a generous-hearted girl who felt bad so promised him she'd come back in the summer and would keep helping him out till Easter, at least, it was just the exam time that would be difficult. He felt such gratitude that he stopped painting to express it.

Fred had been in the staffroom surrounded by colleagues and in conversation with Miss Greene, the number three PE teacher in a department of five. Why on earth they needed so many teachers to supervise sport was beyond him when his

English department was understaffed and struggling to teach the basics of our native tongue.

She, still young enough to remember her training, offered to welcome him to observe a PE lesson so he could see how they handled discipline in the gym and on the field. His own concentration camp-like experiences of PE as a child flashed before his eyes and who the hell did this girl think she was?

She looked at him, all keen, all enthusiastic and all sporty. And he opened his mind. 'That would be lovely, thanks, I'll let you know when I keep a free period,' which surprised them both. And he loved it! The bullying he remembered was still there but it was tempered with encouragement and co-operation and those kids who loathed the whole business were gradually caught up in the competitive atmosphere.

Jennie had to leave the class as she got the role and was off rehearsing night after night while the production was made ready. She was a different woman.

Curator 14 sat in his bedsit, his meal for one on the table at his side, and stared ahead. On the wall in front of him was a small reproduction of *The Journey of the Eyes*, that same painting he looked after in the museum.

************************************

And so it went on. Everyone told more and more each week. Vanessa explained moments from her training in drama, her college days, her school days, her first boyfriend, her day job, her parents, meeting me. I dredged my memory for some interesting stories, not in the event wanting to be outdone.

Some I exaggerated and two I made up entirely convincing me I should have gone into the arts, not finance. Nigel was preparing his presentations in a lively way but we got some incredibly honest revelation about his daughter who was to be married, how he knew she was not his as he'd known his wife had got pregnant just before they met.

The fact that he'd kept quiet and brought the girl up as if she was his own made him seem a head taller than most of them. Rod scoffed at such naivety and shared how he'd found a friend of Maria's who would do just as well as a model for a few months. A tall, willowy kid with a lousy, relationship-poor homelife.

She accepted Rod's haven of artistic peace though she took time to adjust to the smell of the paints and was streetwise enough to know that old Rod Down just needed to make believe he was an artist with basic needs. 'Sophie you just lie there and look as if you don't understand any of it but you do your eyes reveal the truth and it's that truth that I am capturing here now...'

He painted ever smaller dots, some with a magnifying glass, his nose almost on the canvas.

Curator 14 sat in the museum in front of the painting when he wasn't directed to patrol other locations, which was not often. Managers seemed to let Malcolm just do whatever he thought appropriate to fill his day.

He sat on the bus, watching people and finding common links with the world in which he lived. Sometimes it was a long journey with traffic, with the unbearable disruptions from passengers.

He sat at home staring at the reproduction. He had no family as far as he knew. He was complete. He'd been uncharacteristically bold to sign up for the evening class but now it had become too heavy with everyone sharing so much that should not be spoken aloud. And those eyes, they just intrigued him.

********************************

After the course ended, it wasn't great for Vanessa and me. There was a sense that I'd somehow not risen to the challenge sufficiently.

We looked for other ways to supplement our income so we could travel. In the end I decided to put my studies on hold and take a year out but she wasn't cool with that. She said I still had to come to terms with my own failings and madness, however far I travelled.

'Look at Fred, Jennie, Nigel and Rod – they all made incredible travels. I'm not saying they were all down to me, but what we did helped them. I'm surprised it didn't help you.'

I was a bit hurt at that. I wasn't aware that I'd done the course to be helped; I did it to help her. But I could see in her eyes which reflected mine that we had come to the end of our joint road. Certainly in a week or so, we would.

'And what about Malcolm, Vanessa? He didn't travel very far, did he?'

'Oh come on, he travelled the furthest. Can't you see that?'

I couldn't.

But Curator 14 was in his bedsit in the evening, alone with his reproduction which now sat on his chair staring at him as he stood against the wall where it had been hanging.

# Saint Rosa, I Die

He liked the title and even as he was writing the new play, he knew it was great stuff. This was, after all, the late 1960s when almost anybody could write unbelievably meaningful poems, songs and plays about almost nothing.

Of course, even at the time many thought it was, like much that was written in that period, incredibly pretentious crap. It was a view he only came to as he started to sort through his archives prior to age-related downsizing decades later.

It was his fifth play broadly or entirely inspired by the then love of his life, Rosie. The others were *The Flower, Everything Is Rosie, Why We Wear Black* and *Your Moods* – all of which said something about the girl herself as he saw her. *The Flower* had survived four performances with a group of his friends and achieved comments ranging from, 'why is anger constantly pervading your work?' to 'you might as well throw paint on a wall' and 'why not do this play on the top of a bus?'

Rosie was a fireball of energy, laughter and craziness who'd captivated him. Short, blonde and a talented singer, she was the friend of a girl who had hurt him and they enjoyed things together in a fun, mad way. Five years younger and happy to go along with his embrace of the hippie stuff and performance he lived day and night in his London drama college and his home life in their small town.

But she knew all along that she wouldn't stay with him. She was going to make it big in the world of the stage. He may do the same but it wouldn't be a shared path. He needed different things from a life partner and at 16 she couldn't offer that.

By the time *Saint Rosa, I Die* was making headway, the relationship was on its last legs but he wasn't yet prepared to accept that. In any case, the fact is, looking back, that it was more like the whole hippie culture thing that inspired the plays anyway. She was the name and the obsession, but any one of a number of muses could have fitted the bill. Saint Jane, Saint Sheila, Saint Ruth, Saint Alison...

Once she'd read it, she slated it as 'not sure what to think of it. It's the same theme again – insanity and madhouses.' She crushed him with a simple off-the-cuff remark. She could have pretended it wasn't all bad. Only when it was famous and later notorious and he was riding high on his first 15 minutes of fame did she write to say, 'It's fabulous. It's us. Just us.' By then, he'd had enough of her own quest for the limelight.

Still, crap or not, *Saint Rosa, I Die* had received rave reviews and got sent to the finals of the *Sunday Times*/National Union of Students' Drama Festival in Manchester at the tail end of 1969. He'd pontificated that the aim of his piece was to show five 'variations of one human being, each part plays the other, man can only destroy himself.'

He came up with the names of the five asexual characters – Adapt, Basin, Incense, Rot and List. Brilliant! The set he envisioned as stepped rostra up to a high window, a cloth-draped table and nothing else to distract from the forced simplicity. Even the scenes were clever – and different – beginning with 'Scene the First.' Yes, clever.

He wanted to reveal the plot, such as it was, slowly and gradually. Tortuously, in fact. That's how he saw it, so clearly.

Adapt is found at the top of the rostrum, 'I feel as if I should be welcoming all of you from up here...'

Basin replies tartly, 'Instead of which, Adapt, we are welcoming you.'

The cleverness was even in the stage directions. 'Incense sits at table or would do if any chairs were there.'

They establish that they have 'plenty of time' as List tells them the weather will never be better as the winds were wrong on 21$^{st}$ March. Basin takes over and introduces the characters to Adapt so they can decide if he/she is suitable to be here.

Adapt protests, 'Suitable? But I didn't ask to come here,' at which Rot replies, 'No one does.' List helpfully informs Adapt, 'You can ask me anything you don't understand and if an answer exists I can give it to you. If it is indefinite, ask Incense. If that fails, there is no answer.' List asks if Adapt has unfulfilled ambitions, to which Adapt replies, 'I have been fulfilled about twice a week for all my grown-up life.'

List snaps back, 'I was not referring to your sex life.'

Now this was humour. Such inserts of mainly verbal joking throughout made the often turgid, rambling, sometimes declamatory prose more digestible and forced the audience think a bit. At least, that was his intention.

Meaning and explanation of where they are, is not forthcoming on the lines of 'never apologise, never explain.'

'You are here. We are here likewise. We must accept that but we don't have to like each other.' Adapt is interested in the window above but gets no explanation, 'it just looks out'. Later, he/she thought the window should be a mirror instead.

Adapt, in an attempt to be jovial with the others tells a story, 'I heard of a man who in walking through a public park one summer evening accidentally trod on the back of a man. The voice of a woman underneath the man said, 'thank you.' It got a small laugh at the time.

From out of the blue Basin demands, 'Has anyone seen Saint Rosa?' This is the first time there is a connection to the title. Adapt thinks there was an asylum called St Rosa, but they think it's more like a church, or a state of being, Santa Rosa.

Basin then recounts a tale of how, as students, several would travel on the tubes, Northern Line, Edgware branch. They carried rolled up newspapers under their arms and after a while would open them and hold them to their faces. People opposite would read the headlines, inevitably, but the students had cut small eyeholes beforehand so as people read they suddenly met eyes staring at them.

It made them feel uncomfortable; it made the students laugh. Performance theatre, indeed.

Rot's contribution to anecdotes and information is, 'I stood for Parliament,' which surprises them all. 'I loved making speeches. I tiraded, remonstrated and demonstrated, I wrote articles, was questioned, cross-examined, quoted and misquoted, attacked, abused and bustled and hustled. And in the end, I lost my deposit!'

They return to the topic of Saint Rosa and Adapt thinks now that St Rosa's ruins have been built on, 'a slave factory of automation and coloured glass. Where I was torn apart by vile animals, my blood on the ground strewed with rose petals, they have now built a vast communal latrine.'

Into Scene the Second, time has passed but they're still like souls in limbo. They talk of suicide. There is a rapid fire section when Rot wants to break out, sick of the game, but is told he/she is dead, is in hell, this is a nuthouse, a church, an institution where 'you drowned in your failure' and turned it into a fine art.

There is a deliberate sense of circularity, characters turning on asking questions and occupying scattered positions around the set.

It builds to a speech intoned by them all together, 'A writer always inspires fears in other people. They become very frightened indeed, never knowing when some hideous distortion of themselves is going to pop up in print.' List added the line that caused some offence to the Manchester audience, 'It's the only revenge a writer has for having to live amongst other people.'

The scene ends, transitioning into the next with the news that St Rosa is dead. How? 'She just died.' They decide to shut the window if she is dead, but can't do it, being distracted with talk of her being laid out while people sang an opera. They stand in a circle and half-heartedly try a séance which is ruined when Rot blows a giant raspberry, questioning the truth of the news.

This leads to a bundle which accelerates into a nasty fight which becomes comic as they attempt to throw one of them, any one of them, out the window. They mime or use symbolic utensils to eat and drink a lot of wine. Quickly becoming inebriated, they tell childish jokes and sing a version of *Ring-A-Ring-A-Roses* before collapsing in helpless mirth.

This is followed by ages more of introspection, frustration, puzzlement at their condition and some bouts of mutual loathing before Adapt admits to lying about Saint Rosa being dead.

Scene the Fourth opens with them taking off their differently multi-shaded baggy all-purpose tunics and in their under-slips stirring the costumes round in a swirl. They redress themselves in whatever tunic comes to hand. They are ready to receive imaginary guests coming through the window into a restaurant, guests they serve in a robotic, stylised fashion with Adapt talking too much and spilling the food.

There is a moment of nostalgia about a meal that Rot once had with somebody. But as they are all parts of the one person, they recall it differently. Sat on a little table; no, a big one. It was summer. It was winter. Steak and a bottle of rose. We called it love. Like madness. Like moths, they flit about, drawn to the window as the room darkened. A symbolic darkness while Incense responds to a prick of pain. Pregnant? Indigestion? Hunger? Constipation?

Scene the Fifth is the final, shorter leg of the journey. They're tired and begin winding down from 'not a bad performance at all' that they have just delivered. They've done it many times. The window beckons, but only one at a time may go through and then only after the nurses let them. They don't know if Saint Rosa will be there to hold them up. 'Saint Rosa is not God.'

There's further debate about going through and out, at which List rushes to the window to be first as the others chant about madness, death, sanity and mystery and a solution 'out there'. List turns as if with a broken neck, 'Saint Rosa, I Die'. This climax causes the others to subside slowly to the floor and lights fade leaving a rose projected on the back wall.

He tore the last page out of the heavy book he'd kept all these years. He wrote it in July 1969 and improvised around some parts with friends in the autumn with Rosie herself present for some sessions. In September it was presented at Norwich Arts Lab with him as a narrator in a rendition that lasted just over half an hour. He was pleased with the feedback and first responses. But they were the sort of audience that liked the off-beat and depressing.

Back at his drama college after the summer break, he submitted the play and himself as director to a competition to find an entry for the *Sunday Times*/NUS festival. He wasn't accepted; Graham got it. But Graham had no play in mind! He'd won the slot on his directing ideas alone.

They came together and discussed it before Graham said he'd like to direct it. After rewriting and making the characters all asexual, auditions were held at the college. There were 55 hopefuls for the five parts.

Two hours in a restaurant and then a long stint in a pub finally produced the cream of final year students – Lizzie (Adapt), Eve (List), Trisha (Incense), Ray (Basin) and Roger (Rot). These talented actors struggled with what sort of characters they were to be, but gradually within and among them a blend of ideas emerged.

Terrified of letting the opportunity of this show pass him by, he sent out invitations to press, TV, agents and anyone he could think of. He attended most rehearsals, enjoying the thrill of hearing his words brought to life. But at first, he made them nervous being there. On 22nd November with the set not quite finished, the first performance took place at the college.

The theatre was a separate, quite modern structure in the front grounds of the grander Ivy House, which had been built for the painter John Turner and was later owned by the dancer Anna Pavlova. The college was the former drama department of the Royal Academy of Music and in those days had not long been established. He loved it, the building, the people, the learning about performance.

It was packed out, students keen to support their homegrown attempt to get into the festival and a few relatives of the cast bravely turned up. Rosie herself deigned to come and sat next to him roaring out loud when there was anything she recalled from their relationship, thus ensuring that everyone knew she was the Saint Rosa in question.

It went off well, with a confidence that built as it progressed. There was near silence as people left, with one saying to the excited author, 'I enjoyed it, if that is the right word.' He was not so happy that he didn't realise the success was due to better direction from Graham than he could have given and acting of a very high order.

The next night was the adjudication performance in front of Clive Wolfe from *The Sunday Times*. The comedy worked better in a near-perfect run, the cast really enjoyed doing it and that showed and the audience was very lively and seemed to love it. Wolfe said in his address afterwards he'd never written so few notes. He was not there to judge the play but it was 'theatrical and entertaining.'

On 1st December the College received a telegram to say it was one of 14 productions in the finals. The college exploded with wild delight! He was unbearable with his joy. Graham appointed him publicity officer and got on with arranging for a team of 20 to take it up north.

It was an exciting Christmas for all of them, away at their family homes. When *The Sunday Times* rated them one of the three hot favourites to win, the BBC 2 programme *Review* called, wanting an excerpt filmed at the college, in colour which was just coming in. They also interviewed him and Graham and filmed the cast in discussion. In Manchester they shot the set being made and warm-up exercises and rehearsals. Heady days indeed.

At 7.30pm Monday 29 December 1969, the play was the opening event at the Renold Theatre, University of Manchester Institute of Science and Technology. It pulled in an audience of 500 students and a few older people on a cold, drizzly wet winter night in that rather depressing post-Christmas, no-man's land week when festivities are over but normality has not yet returned.

The cast were nervous, understandably, and there were some lighting errors. Everyone was in unfamiliar settings and with the pressure of the trip north, the expectations from local communities (he had press released all their local papers), it was always going to be a tough call. He knew as he watched that it didn't have that edge it had achieved in London at their college. Perhaps it was because it didn't translate to a big stage. Perhaps it was just over-hyped. Perhaps it just wasn't good enough.

There was a BBC televised mass discussion afterwards where he was attacked mercilessly. Phrases like 'abdicating meaning', 'failing to have humanity', 'insulting to the mentally subnormal', 'Sartre done by Noel Coward directed by Walt Disney', a 'Saturday afternoon suicide play' and 'rubbish, abysmally acted and produced' filled the air. It was *Waiting for Godot* via Sartre's *Huis Clos* (*Vicious Circle*).

Few voices spoke up for it. When people started arguing about it and his use of 'too many other plays' one said it was a perfect illustration of animals fighting, telling bad jokes - perfect human observation.' He was actually delighted at the time to have been the man of the moment. Only later did he realise that he hadn't exactly established his career.

It was labelled in the press as 'a torrent of words', 'a weird line of vicious circles' and 'a game for paranoics.' When the God-like Harold Hobson reviewed it in *The Sunday Times*, he proclaimed it would have been 'a kindness not to have taken it to Manchester.'

He still sent it to the ATV Network script department, along with a stack of other vaguely similar plays he'd put together. The script supervisor said in response it was a shame that a writer with his 'obvious talent and inventiveness' wrote what was 'self-indulgent and needlessly esoteric.' He concluded by expressing the hope that the young man would 'tackle a slightly more straight-forward subject once in a while.'

Well, he continued to write. Not till he went into drama teaching did his plays get put on with any regularity and audience-building way. That was when he did them at his schools. He hoped in his old age that all those teenagers who took part remembered them and him fondly and learned from the experiences.

Not till the advent of the digital age which made everyone a film director, a published author and a viral blogger did he grab the opportunity to start publishing novels that sold a few copies to old friends left alive and colleagues from his teaching days who'd thought he was long dead.

This play, and the other forty odd such outflows from his once inventive mind, they were of their time. Gone. You had to have been there. And he was. He smiled as he tore the play to shreds and put it in the recycling bin. Nobody understood these days. Why should they?

They were great times back then. Or at least they were seen through the memory glasses. And that is why a few months back he had found Rosie online. She'd done much with her life and been a successful performer. She'd been through a lot of relationships. He wondered if she ever wished she'd stuck it out with him, weird and wonderful as it may have been.

But then, his own later relationship had been far more fulfilling and deep-seated than Rosie would have been. So he'd written to her. Heard nothing. Of course.

Rosie. He sat musing as a cloud, a hint of a shadow, closed off some of the picture. He couldn't quite recall her surname just at that moment. What was it? Who was she? Was it Rosie or Josie? It'll come back to him. What was he trying to recall?

He thought there were voices in the hallway, through a door. Muffled voices. Was that his son or his grandson?

He listened hard from his chair. 'Since my grandmother passed away, my grandfather has quite lucid moments for long periods and it's easy to think he is just a normal old man reminiscing and chatting happily. Then it goes away. The black holes grow bigger.'

Who was that? Black holes? What was she running on about?

The door opened to a young woman showing a haggard old woman into the room. She hobbled close to him, leaned on a walking stick as she steadied herself and stared at him through smudgy spectacles, wheezing loudly. Her thin grey hair was partly encased beneath an absurd woollen hat.

The young woman indicated a chair but the old lady shook her head and looked a little closer at the once lively man in the chair.

'No, I must have been mistaken. I don't know this man,' she mumbled, shaking her head rigorously, as two old people stared at each other with watery eyes and memories so deep that they were irretrievable.

After a few moments what had once been Saint Rosa left him alone again, never to return now or then.

# 17 The Crescent

-1-

Stephen arrived at 17 The Crescent on a September 1967 Saturday, about 11. Coffee time. Anytime was coffee time but Len offered Stephen coffee to welcome him to the house. The circus, the rolling freak show that was number 17 in The Crescent, a quiet, curved road of ordinariness in suburban north London. And it was at that moment that Stephen decided he'd keep notes – Len and his house would be a rich source of material for a book one day.

He'd got a small, top floor room to one side, but that was fine. Len said a bigger one would soon be free. Stephen sipped the coffee and had a job to swallow the seaweed, nettle, unknown brew that was Len's very own. Len sat opposite, his grin showing his yellow teeth off. His eyes were a cold grey, staring through dirty, thick bifocals. He was in his late fifties, slightly overweight with wispy hair sprouting from a generally bald top, he looked slightly eccentric. That was a cover for barking madness, Stephen later discovered.

'You'll get to know people here. We're a friendly crowd. There are some music students – just your sort of thing. This is the lounge ...' Their eyes took in the ancient decrepit settee, the mismatched armchairs covered by grimy blankets, two walls of uneven shelves, a double glazed window looking into the hall while the remaining walls were pasted with foam tiles – soundproofing, Len explained. 'This is going to be a studio.'

Len was the world's best project starter. He also rarely threw anything away, hence the 1950s' record player, piles of albums, magazines and curling Christmas cards. Stephen was there to be accommodated for his three year course at a drama college only a mile away. Dirty, shabby, weird it was, but as he'd never lived away from home before, Stephen was content with it.

'I'm glad to have a little table and a lamp in my room where I can write.'

'Writing?' beamed Len.

'Yes. Nothing successful yet, but poems, a couple of plays and I want to write the great British novel.'

Len appeared excited. 'I might be able to help. In a cupboard somewhere, there are bits that might interest you. You'll find plenty to write about here. We are refugees from a repressive society.' Len's communication style was to stare at the person he was addressing; Stephen found it disconcerting at first.

As he settled in Stephen met the first of the characters who would people his domestic London life for the next few years. Hedda was of unspecified age, though rumour had it she was over 80. Bent and withered, her face a mass of wrinkle contours, tiny frame, twisted fingers, ill-fitting false teeth, sparse hair sometimes hidden under a poorly shaped wig. Hedda, a story in her own right, was of Germanic/Austrian origin, who'd once been a successful European opera singer and pianist. She'd fallen low in her old age.

She made delicious cheesecake that she gave out to those she liked, answered the phone with an abrupt 'allo' and said 'Na!' in almost every sentence she uttered. One early evening in the shared second floor kitchen. She took Stephen's hands in hers, 'Na! You have creative hands…'

Stephen threw himself into his long college days – usually 9am till 9pm with rehearsals on top. Len caught him occasionally and made fatuous conversation, often offering coffee, but Stephen didn't accept any more. He sometimes ate in the house, cooking for himself and then escaped to his room to write. He was still adjusting to life away from home.

Downstairs in the big room off the main entrance slept John S, a tall, gangly, fair-skinned man of about 30, a would-be pianist who periodically went off and practised architecture to earn money before coming back to music. John B upstairs was also tall, fair-haired with a straggly blonde beard, a student at the Royal Academy of Music studying clarinet and hailing from Norwich.

From the same town, indeed they'd been at school together, was Paul, a shorter man with a solid face, a violinist so Stephen felt comfortable with lots of East Anglian talk. Susan, also at the Academy, was a pianist, organist and singer with gorgeous long red hair. The house was frequently full of music practice. His drama world was not a million miles from it. These were the main players, but there was a large supporting cast to come of oddballs and freaks.

There was a daily milk delivery and each resident had a label attached to his or her own personal bottle. Food was stored in old metal cupboards in one kitchen. There was a cleaning rota. Things ran themselves, with Len occasionally appearing amongst them, staring and talking.

One Friday night he told Stephen about his belief in self-help. There was a little organisation he was part of, a group of people who helped each other to help themselves and others. Stephen politely nodded along and Len offered to find some literature in a drawer somewhere.

The next morning Len crept loudly into his room and shook him awake. 'Mrs Cropper is on the phone. She's at the building we have in Covent Garden and asks your help with a survey...' To his surprise, Stephen found himself taking the call, tubing into central London to the headquarters of what he realised was a sect, listening to nonsense about helping him with his past, being offered a preliminary course for a bargain fifty quid and what did he feel about how his mother had brought him up?

He politely endured it even as it became more intrusive, and got away with a bag of literature promising to return the following Saturday. He never did. But he was bombarded with weekly mailings, occasional phonecalls and lots of attempts by Len to interest him. It was material for his book, after all.

Outside Stephen's room was a tiny landing leading up to a loft extension with a sloping roof and a curtained area nicknamed the Hole and down a narrow staircase to the main body of the house. There was a phone extension on the landing that took calls in but calls out had to be made on the ground floor phone. One night he heard footsteps outside and thought it was Len, so sat tight, hoping Len would go.

There was a swishing, a rustling of material followed by a gurgling as if someone was being strangled. He squeezed past the two single beds but saw nobody. The sounds stopped. He went down to the main house; no practising anywhere, but he found Len and Hedda in the lounge. He was stuffing his face with a pile of mashed vegetables that Hedda had cooked him. He was a vegetarian, among other things. 'Na! You look like you see ghost, Stephen!' cried Hedda, with some delight.

He told them what he'd heard. Hedda said a woman had murdered her daughter years ago next door. Len sniffed, and said a friend of his had written a pamphlet about ghosts, he'd find it for Stephen. Sometimes Len did find odd papers and information for Stephen; mostly he forgot or couldn't find it amongst the debris. An article about Shakespeare's sex life and a letter from Her Majesty's Inspector of Taxes to say that Leonard Boyd was a philanthropist and should be regarded as a charity, were just a couple of examples.

Stephen gradually appreciated Len's crippling fear of authority, of being questioned and held to account. He was suspicious of almost everyone, took offence easily and refused to 'play their games', whether they were from the council, the Census, utilities, companies, the police or individuals.

**-2-**

Jim Sullivan was a tall, grinning Irishman in his early twenties, a photographer and an amateur opera singer. So he said. His actual job was wages clerk at some British Rail office south of Norwood. Len was suspicious why he'd work there and travel every day from north London. He moved in for a few weeks, despite Len's suspicions. Stephen happened to open the door when he first arrived. 'Hello there, I'm the new tenant!' he beamed; a ridiculous pork-pie hat perched on his head at what he thought was a jaunty angle.

'You'd better come in, then,' welcomed Stephen through gritted teeth. This man was to share with him, albeit in the large bedroom on the ground floor, John B currently away architecting. As he unpacked, Jim told Stephen about a hundred girls he'd had, most Stephen thought in his imagination. He asked about Len and the house, but kept returning to his conquests. As soon as he could, Stephen escaped to make coffee for him and found Len in the kitchen demanding what he was like, was he suspicious?

Stephen only said that he was boring, 'What do you mean, boring?' as if it was a profound observation. ''Keep your eyes on him, Stephen, there could be more to him than meets the eye.' Stephen did watch him, along with everyone else. All seemed to share a degree of eccentricity. Stephen put his transistor radio on in the room, but Jim babbled on and on.

The next night as Stephen came back from College, he was blinded by the glare from a battery of silver dishes and lanterns. 'Hurry up and get your supper down, Stephen, I'm taking some photies of ye...' The man was obviously hell-bent on annoying Stephen beyond endurance. Len gave grinning approval to proceedings from the corridor – he'd provided the lights and was going to turn the room into a studio. His own photo had already been taken.

With Len won over to a point by Jim, Stephen allowed a filthy headscarf to be put round his neck as a cravat and endured an hour of being shot. His head thumped, his eyes hurt. Jim's attempts to make Stephen smile fell flat and their session finally ended with Jim reprimanding him for not waking him that morning as he was late for work.

Stephen responded with irritation asking why he didn't live over there nearer to work and was told Jim was after a photographer assistant job in Golders Green. Jim launched into a tale of a wedding he'd helped at in Birmingham where he'd shagged a bridesmaid for an hour and a half. Len knocked and entered, blinking behind the dirty glasses and suggested that Hedda, Susan, John S and Paul should be photographed. Before he could move papers he didn't want trampled, Stephen found the room full and a party underway as they posed and Jim attempted to capture their best sides. Hedda particularly found him ridiculous as she worked her teeth behind her sunken cheeks.

It finally ended when Len, in an expansive mood, wondered if anyone 'fancied a coffee?' Nobody did, so Jim dismantled the equipment while Stephen tried to write an essay about Greek drama.

Jim went to the cellar which had four sections – one crammed with broken furniture and boxes, the debris of Len's sudden schemes; another held a rickety washing machine and the boiler. The other two contained a lopsided bench, tools, nails, brackets, a tiny bed, bits of cable, wood, five TV sets, four radios – the great etceteras of Len's life.

Len slept down there when the house was full, but now it was to be Jim's darkroom, despite the chinks of light that came from the upstairs and the fact that no laundry would be possible when Jim was developing. Later that evening the results were displayed. Stephen was in Susan's room trying to write a song with her, he spouting lyrics and her setting them to music.

Hedda said, 'Na!' and went to bed in disgust. Jim's photos consisted of one of Hedda and Len together looking like exhibits at Madam Tussaud's Chamber of Horrors and one of Stephen as if in an ad for a bad amdram show. Nobody mentioned the incident again, so Jim went back to being an opera singer while he looked for local work.

A week later as Stephen crept down to the washing machine, minding his own business, Len emerged from a shadow, 'Come and look at this, Stephen!' He led into the 'darkroom area' and surveyed the junk. 'Look at this mess,' cried Len as if he was a model of tidiness. 'I suppose he's lost interest in it,' muttered Stephen who had also lost interest.

Len whispered, 'I can't see where he's put the film he's taken of my papers.' Stephen looked puzzled. 'My private files, letters, personal information ...' Len was deadly serious; he thought Jim was sent to spy on him. 'He must have a microfilm, all this is just a cover.' Stephen was still puzzled.

'They gather information, proof of whatever they want and once they've got hold of you, they never let go.' Just like Len's self-helpers, Stephen thought. 'They don't always send obvious types...' Stephen had seen enough waifs and strays, odd-bods and weirdos to quite believe that much.

'Why let them into your house?' asked Stephen.

'If I didn't they'd know I'm onto them.' Stephen couldn't think of anything to add, just as John S strode down with an armful of clothes. 'Beat you!' he cried at Stephen, stuffing the machine and draining the last of that day's hot water. In their room, Jim was reading a porno mag, 'photographic art, this is'; Susan was out at a choir practice so Stephen went to see Hedda in her room and was rewarded with a slice of cheesecake.

'Na! This Irish monkey takes all your time and patience, my dear!' She looked at him with her pale, watery eyes and he was glad she understood. 'Len will throw him out soon, you watch. Then we have some peace.'

'Len thinks he's a spy!' Hedda nodded. Stephen thought that if he went along
with the spy theory and confirmed Len's fears, Len would kick Jim out sooner than later. And three nights later, he had his chance. Jim hogged the lounge, listening to Irish jig music on the half a stereo system Len had installed before he was distracted by another idea. Jim didn't see Stephen look through the window from the hall. Jim had his hand deep in a pile of Len's papers taken from the bottom drawer of a wonky filing cabinet behind the curtain.

There clearly *was* more to people than met the eye.

Len was in a filthy mood. That was not unusual but Susan was getting concerned. Her 21$^{st}$ birthday was approaching - in an earlier moment of bonhommerie he'd promised she could have friends round. Lately, though, he'd been unapproachable, rushing between the Hole, the cellar and the lounge on a new scheme to offer a historic bookbinding service from the house.

Susan rewrote the rota in heavy ink to make the place half presentable. That would wait. Stephen had a rare free afternoon off college to write three operas, six plays, 56 poems, a hundred letters, three essays and, if he had time, some background reading. Everyone out! Bliss. He sat with a cup of his own coffee when the door slammed below. His heart sank as his door crashed open and in came an incandescent Jim who'd been sacked on the spot, 'late too often.' He was not to be pacified, even for a cup of coffee and the tale had to be told three times, growing each telling.

When Stephen sighed, his patience evaporating, Jim set off on a diatribe about friends not waking him up which Stephen was having none of. Within seconds it escalated into an argument. Jim accused Stephen of being lazy, his head up his own arse and Stephen stated that Jim was lazy and a pain in the arse. Before it got to fisticuffs, Stephen went to the kitchen where Len was staring in expectation. Stephen began an explanation for the raised voices when Len cut him off. 'Stephen your room is big enough to make a ballet rehearsal room.'

As Stephen spluttered, Len enlightened him. "Wall mirrors and bars, light and pleasant room, charge by the hour...'

Len appeared perfectly serious. 'The floor dips in the middle,' he snapped. 'Oh, I'll re-board it. Got some planks in the cellar, somewhere. I'll put the furniture in Paul and John's room.' There were two beds, two wardrobes and a piano. But it seemed pointless to argue. A half-made ballet rehearsal room they'd get. 'And that Irishman will have to go.'

Stephen wondered whether to tell Len the man had been sacked but didn't.

Jim was informed immediately and kicked up a row. Susan went on a bit at Len as the party was to be in that room. Hedda rose from her thick-piled bed to see what all the noise was about. Stephen moved his things upstairs at once, claiming the better bed. Jim refused to speak to Stephen as he gathered his stuff, confining himself to hissing 'traitor' at him.

Stephen sat in his new space and wondered if he'd get any work done when Susan knocked and came in, distraught at her arrangements thrown awry as Len had just cancelled her party. Once she'd calmed down she told him John B was coming back; he told her about the ballet rehearsal idea. After a time, Stephen said, 'I think Len is going off to Northampton at the weekend...' In Northampton, his group owned a house where people went to do whatever they did in their peculiarity. She felt better then and went to try to persuade Len to honour his promise to her.

A few minutes later she was back to say it was all on again. Len would be away and she could have Gary there. He was her newish boyfriend, one she liked and thought she was ready to open up to, but whenever he came round Len made it obvious he thought Gary was at least an escaped lunatic.

Len spent a day converting the room, leaving the floor untouched. Jim crept up to the Hole and kept a low profile and as the dust and noise subsided, Molly and Neville Glass arrived en route for Northampton. He was in his early 40s and had been a teacher at one point; she was an attractive African girl in her early twenties. Their relationship was based on mutual need and they were both calm, relaxed, cheerful people, more or less normal but they enthused over Len's rehearsal room.

17 was transformed. Well, they did their best. Sweeping and polishing. Floors, windows, toilets and kitchens. Stephen helped and hung his oil painting for Susan on the door to dry. John B returned but not in time to do anything useful. Jim kept out of the way, but those who saw him reported a pasty face, black under the eyes, unshaven and still babbling about finding a job.

Friday evening, Len and the Glasses were leaving for Northampton when Shirley arrived. Five feet tall, large teeth, some missing on one side. Long, lank, dyed hair with receding waves. Age? Hard to say, perhaps fifty.

Jim said his goodbyes with a cock and bull story about being offered a singing villa in Italy as they gathered in the front hall mid-Saturday morning. As Shirley entered the hall, Stephen caught the flash between them. They knew each other. Stephen, in a moment of thought that Len would have been proud of, concluded that she was the next spy to replace Jim as he'd fouled up. Then Jim left, for good. He was instantly forgotten, although Stephen had him in his notebook.

Susan spent time nervously on the loo which Stephen refused to re-clean. Guests arrived. These were Susan's musician friends, so they were not the usual run of oddities. Only one – Linda - attracted Stephen, a willowy blonde also from Norfolk, but Paul fancied her. People moved all over the house, the half stereo belted music, but most would have preferred classical. Susan drank more and more wine and regaled all with tales of Len and the house.

Gary was alright, thought Stephen. Suited Susan quite well; Stephen wondered why Len had taken against him. There was some tension between Paul and Graham over being disturbed when he was showing Linda the half-made rehearsal room. Shirley appeared – she could hardly be left out – with obscenely red lips and a ridiculous kaftan. Susan pointedly ignored her. Hedda held court from a chair in the downstairs kitchen.

Just after 11, guests began to depart. Linda had to be found and it was not with Paul. Gary left without saying goodbye. He must have done, because he was never seen again, dead or alive.

**-4-**

Gary wasn't missed. From the Academy to practising somewhere or from a concert to women's beds, no suspicions were aroused. It took nine days for people to realise he hadn't been around. Even Susan was on cloud nine for a couple of days; her party had been successful. Stephen wondered if he'd been at the same event. When Len returned he didn't ask anything about it. Hedda gave him an account, particularly of 'that Shirley creature.'

Shirley herself was quite reasonable and disappeared most evenings to usher people into their seats at the local ABC Cinema. She didn't cross paths with Len, who was busy in the Hole with a rare record catalogue he was making. He went to Hedda's or the kitchen to get his yellow teeth round a vegetable mash once a day.

Stephen, busy at college, found little unusual to record for several days, until a fresh-faced bobby, aged 19, eager to make an impression as he'd only just made the five foot eleven inches required to join the force, rang the door-chimes. Len opened the door and gave away nothing behind his glasses. The bobby asked about Gary and Len sent him off with a flea in his ear saying the man wasn't welcome in this house and so couldn't be missing from here.

That set in motion the arrival of two heavyweight detectives. Hedda dragged herself down to answer the door as nobody else bothered. 'Good evening, ma'am. I wonder if you could shed any light on a Mr Gary Ericson.' The man had a bruiser of a face, embittered by years investigating the impossible. Hedda's ears were bunged with excessive cotton wool as they were bad today. 'No zank you,' and she made to close the door. The cop put his foot in, 'May we have a word with the gentleman of the house?'

Hedda heard nothing, so stared at them. The officer took her arm off the door and led his colleague inside. 'Detective Sergeant Mills,' he said, swiftly taking in the hall and staircase and window into the lounge. 'Is Mr Leonard Boyd at home?' demanded the other cop. Paul came in behind them, pocketing the key he didn't need. 'Good evening,' he nodded as he pushed past them, violin case swinging.

In the hall the police crept further in, without an invitation. John S's sudden hitting the piano keyboard in the lounge was a shock, but not as much as Len hurtling down the stairs towards them. Instinctively they knew this was their man. 'Mr Boyd?'

'Who wants him?' Len parried from long years of obstructing enquiries. 'Detective Sergeant Mills and this is Detective Constable Haines.'

'He isn't here,' said Len, deadpan.

'Do you know a Mr Gary Ericson?'

'No,' was the curt reply. It was repeated to questions about when he last saw him, was there a party here recently, did he attend and when would Mr Boyd return?

They could do no more than let Boyd win the tiny skirmish. 'Thank you for your help.' That was a bit subtle for Len as he'd been no help at all.

Each resident in turn got a garbled version from Hedda. Susan was upset about Gary's vanishing trick. Len took Stephen into the lounge as he didn't fancy a coffee but would have a digestive biscuit from Len's secret stash. 'They were pretending to look for Susan's friend, a clever move, but they won't fool me.' Stephen decided to share his thought about Shirley being the next spy after Jim. Len nodded expressionlessly. The phone rang and Len talked about a course at Northampton before returning as Stephen was filching another biscuit. 'Keep an eye on Shirley, if you will, Stephen.'

In fact Shirley appeared to be harmless. Her shrill Cockney voice was all over the house, bending any ears she found. So when Rundle arrived, Stephen knew this was the next spy. Rundle pretended to be odd, a bit unstable. At 56 years old, a biggish man, thin and greying hair, a granddad face and ruddy complexion, he fitted the archetypal unlikely suspect. A slight speech hesitation was the crowning touch to his role.

He took to Hedda and Susan and confided he'd been receiving treatment for his fears. Len was suspicious of him and the women kept from him the information about the treatment. He never answered to anything but Rundle.

He had a friend called Peter who called regularly, always in a grubby once-white raincoat, regardless of the weather. Peter and Rundle started long discussions with Len in the lounge, all nursing a cracked cup of the vile coffee. Len was told Rundle needed to go out for air and exercise for several hours a day, as if Len was going to organise it for him.

When Peter talked of Rundle's fear of the people he met in society, how he dreaded them hurting him, Len was on board and changed his mind about Rundle. Then a day or two later he decided it was an enemy masterstroke to plant a spy who was pretending to be affected by the same fears as Len. He told Peter that Rundle would have to leave. Peter struck a financial deal so Len eased back.

Len suddenly decided he needed an office so ordered Hedda to leave her little room and take the upstairs kitchen with box adjacent and the 'dining area' through it. Paul negotiated a special arrangement to eat with Hedda as he was her favourite. The downstairs kitchen would suffice for everyone else. The office would be the dining room. He worked like a man possessed for a day and a night, impervious to others' need to sleep.

The changes were simply absorbed as always in the pageant that was the house. Peter provided Rundle with a typewriter, which Stephen would have liked, but nobody could think what Rundle had to type. Occasionally there was desultory tapping from a single finger. It was unfortunate that when the police returned Rundle was going upstairs. He turned and opened the door and began to shake as soon as he saw Mills and Haines. When they asked for Boyd, Rundle stammered and went red.

John B came to his rescue. He told them Len was out, so they showed their credentials and asked if they could look round. John knew Len would throw a fit, so refused. They asked about Gary and John told them he'd been at the party but had taken his girl Mary to the bus stop so had no idea when Gary left. They knew they'd get no more so departed with a promise they'd come again. When Len got in John B reported the conversation.

Rundle stayed in his room, without eating but tapped more on his typewriter. Peter visited more frequently. Susan caught a glimpse as Peter went in one night of Rundle crying at the table. When she reported this, both Johns and Paul were upset, thinking him a rather pathetic creature. Hedda dismissed him as 'nozink.' Typing continued every night for a fortnight; Peter visited every evening.

The truth was that Rundle had been smuggled out for emergency treatment and the typing was on a reel-to-reel tape-recorder. He was brought back after the treatment and resumed his existence at number 17.

-5-

Len planned a major overall of the downstairs kitchen, but got waylaid by the price of bananas and milk. Ever since he started, Len had provided tenants with daily milk and sometimes fruit from his sister's greengrocers. She hadn't been for a while and Hedda was looking forward to some out-of-date fruit. But when she did come, Len hid all the produce. He also rationed the milk, but people swapped labels on bottles. The worst offenders were those between courses at Northampton and the one/two day visitors. Shirley's milk and label just vanished.

She accused everyone in turn, including Len but left Rundle till last. 'I don't remember,' was all he managed, which she took to be an admission of guilt. He was terribly confused and promised her money when Peter came. Shirley attacked Peter the moment he arrived the next evening - an ugly episode that Stephen witnessed as she left her room to deal with him and stopped the typing of Stephens' play that he was dictating as she put it straight onto stencils for him.

The typewriter Len picked up at a jumble sale and periodically Shirley'd shriek as a stiff key cut the wrong letter. Still, Stephen was pleased with his work. As to Shirley, well, he appreciated her help and concluded that while she was a royal pain in the butt, she wasn't evidently spying on them. Lonely, insecure yes, but not a threat. Then suddenly, he wasn't sure. Max moved in.

Max was a kid about 17, long greasy sideburns, pugnacious round face always chewing gum. Morose he was, a moron in a leather jacket who liked rock music and walked with a natural swagger. He was put in the tiny upstairs room with Stephen who found him a surly bugger. He asked a bit about everyone but exhausted his curiosity after discovering all the musicians were into classical stuff and Stephen was doing 'drama.' He soon secured a place in Stephen's notebook. They disliked each other, mistrusted each other.

Amazingly, one night Stephen woke to bed sounds. Max had someone with him! The bed shook rhythmically. Stephen lay still, glad that the lights were out. Max was an Essex version of Jim with his tales of birds he'd pulled, yet here he was, actually doing one in their room. When he'd finished he slapped her backside and whispered she had to go. She protested and Stephen's jaw dropped to his pillow – it was Shirley!

There was no accounting for people's taste. Stephen tried to stay awake after that in case the exercise was repeated. There was nothing and they didn't even look at each other about the house, Stephen noticed. He wondered if he hadn't dreamed it.

Two different police officers arrived to say they'd tracked Gary's last known movements to this house and if they didn't get answers soon everyone would be down the nick in cells having the crap beaten out of them. This threat addressed to a visitor from Northampton but meant for the whole house was lost against the clatter of Shirley's typing, Susan was listening to records, Hedda was with Paul practising his violin, John S was rehearsing a complex piano piece. And Len stayed in the Hole.

Stephen, going back to his room with Act 2 stencils in his hands, heard Max on the upstairs extension phone. 'Yeah, through the window, along the guttering, on the bay window top, along a bit to next door – it's empty. Naaah, don't worry. If you clump about they'll think you're a ghost or it's all in their fucking lunatic heads…' Stephen shared this with only Susan in confidence but when John B mentioned it, Stephen became suspicious of him.

A bunch of men in dark blue came through the said window while Mills and Haines entered the front waving a piece of paper they described as a 'warrant.' Rundle looked out and slammed the door shut. They looked Max up and down with loathing. Stephen followed the two cops through the house till they found Len. To Len's 'what the hell?' Mills waved the paper – or it could have been Haines. Stephen forgot which was which, like Rosencrantz and Guildenstern, except they weren't dead.

'Good evening Mr Boyd, I am Detective Sergeant Mills and we have a warrant, all legal, to search this house from top to bottom. And from bottom to top again if I don't find something.' He smiled.

Len stayed calm. 'Boyd is away, but let me see that paper.' He held it while Len made a show of reading it. 'I applied for this as you failed to co-operate with my enquiries, Mr Boyd.'

'I'll tell him when he comes back,' muttered Len, still playing the game. Every room was checked. Hedda made noisy fuss as she was ejected, and sat on the landing grinding her false teeth. Rehearsals stopped. Susan treated them to a superior look, but they continued looking. Rundle was invited to step out of his room; they knew all about him. A girl was found in John S's room. He may have had a practice tape playing too. The Glasses had returned and were moved aside.

The police carted away a series of random items, 'for fingerprints,' and as they were ready to leave, Mills asked them assembled in the hallway if anyone could shed any light on Gary Ericson. Susan fought back a tear. 'Mr Boyd?'

'I'll ask him when he gets back.' And they swept out, leaving uproar with everyone talking at once. Stephen went to his room expecting to see Max and Shirley at it but the boy was reading a comic on his bed, alone. They didn't speak. Stephen knew the boy had talked to the police.

Susan called him down to a meeting of the trusties in the lounge. Len realised that if they had a warrant, there was nothing he could do. Len listed the equipment they'd confiscated – all junk. Paul said, as a joke, 'perhaps they think Gary was poisoned!'

It was the first time the word was used. The first realisation that Gary must be dead. Hedda looked up at Max watching them through the window in the lounge and gave him a 'Na!'

-6-

Max left the next day without ceremony. Len compared notes with Stephen when it became obvious that the enemy were not just sending in another new tenant, but tried a different approach altogether. Stephen encountered it first, when he came home one lunch time to collect some props he'd forgotten. He was back in the big room downstairs with John S, nice and near the front door.

As he approached the house he felt someone was following him; when he opened the door a man appeared behind on the four foot path. 'Excuse me,' demanded a tallish man in his late 40s. A grey streaked beard covered half his face. 'I noticed you at the corner and I followed you, I hope you don't mind...'

Stephen was in a hurry and said nothing; just waited for the sell. 'My name is Cavendish, James Cavendish and I'm an artist, a painter.' He held out a hand, which Stephen ignored, so he continued. 'I'm working on a large Christ-figure and I noticed, well, your face, your hair ...' He made vague shapes in the air near Stephen's head. With regulation long student hair and a thin face, Stephen looked several parts, but Jesus was not one, he thought.

'I've got my sketch book here, I wonder, would you be so very kind and just let me make a quick sketch of you? It will take only a moment.' Cavendish wasn't pushing his way in but he was persuasive. Stephen often played baddie parts, so was curious. John S's bed was unmade and his breakfast remains adorned the piano top. Cavendish started sketching. Just as Stephen never went anywhere without a notebook, so Cavendish carried a sketchbook.

So far, so good. It was when he demanded Stephen take off his shirt so he could capture his frame to fit the head that Stephen heard alarm bells. 'No, that's not going to happen. Time for you to leave, please.' The man reluctantly allowed himself to be led out, asking for a phone number to let Stephen know when the painting was ready in his Camden studio and could he do some more sketches?

Only when he was out of sight, did Stephen breathe in relief. He shouldn't have even let the man in.

The second approach came the next day when Susan happened to be home. She was just back from organ practice. She fancied the organ master, and partly to get over Gary, she'd decided she'd accept the married master's suggestion of a weekend away after a visit to a clinic to 'fit herself up.' The chimes took her to the door where she saw a spotty youth in an ill-fitting suit clutching a fire extinguisher. 'Good afternoon, madam, I am from the Stinguish It Company and we are making a special offer to households in this area. This is an obvious product but I'd like to make an appointment this evening when your husband is home to talk about fire safety in the home...'

Susan blinked, looked at him closely and said, 'I have no husband. Not worth your time coming back. Good day.'

The youth was not a persistent seller and hadn't mastered the parrot script to push on. 'Come back when Mr Boyd the house owner is about.' He thanked her with an excess of nodding and backed away. It was only when telling several of them later and Stephen sharing the artist story they began to think these visitors were connected and suspect.

A man from the council rating department came to measure to check their rates. He got short shift from Len who said Mr Boyd was on holiday. The next day both gas and electricity men came to read their meters. Len cancelled a trip to Northampton – the house was under siege. Close questioning of other residents unearthed recent calls from two people looking for accommodation, three from Northampton and one from Covent Garden and someone who claimed to have lost a cat.

The day after, Len was convinced workmen were told to fracture a water pipe to maroon them for hours, giving Hedda plenty to grumble about. The telephone cable was severed by other workmen. The road was partially resurfaced. A beat up old van pulled up outside and three men unloaded an empty coffin for a 'young man who had died.' Len went whiter than usual. It must have been the police playing mind games with him.

Mills and Haines took to calling every day, at different times. Once Len let them ring the chimes for half an hour before Hedda shrieked for pity. John B remarked the strange coincidence of all the disruptions coming at once. John B was a definite suspect to Len, and possibly to Stephen too.

Gradually, Len felt confident enough to go out for short periods. In the lounge, a crowd around, Paul casually remarked that neither Rundle nor Peter had been seen lately. That typewriter was silent. Susan tried the door to look and returned to say Rundle's door was locked and no light. 'He's probably out.'

'Or asleep. Or dead.'

They dispersed, thoughtfully. On his return, Len was told by Susan that Rundle was not there. 'He's gone.'

'What do you mean, gone?' she wanted to know.

'I threw him out while the house was besieged by spies last week.' Len offered no more, so that was Rundle.

**-7-**

Susan always needed to be looking forward to something. She'd told the organ master she'd chickened out of going to a clinic and as the time approached she became quite agitated and stopped practising. Shirley wanted details but was rebuffed and Stephen stopped asking her to finish the final act of his play as she was wary of typing now.

Len was busy in Stephens' old tiny room, banging and crashing, brick dust on the landing, cement smell in the air. Hedda dragged upstairs with a bowl of mush and he ate it on the landing lathered in sweat, his shirt ripped. Rundle's old room was empty and Len advertised to fill it.

Stephen spent a couple of hours pulling together the strands of the Gary business and what had happened afterwards. Certainly he felt that Gary was murdered in the house, that night or later, and his body still here or cut up and dispersed. The police search had obviously found nothing, but then, it hadn't been thorough; it was more like a frightener visit.

Len was capable of killing, but Stephen doubted he murdered Gary. 17 housed a slow poisoner. It was a nagging thought, despite the absence of proof. Len stopped work in the attic room when the Glasses returned for another stint in the house with a van full of electronic bits for Len to play with. They became Stephen's preferred suspects. Hedda was convinced that Len had a thing for Molly Glass way back, but looking at her, Stephen couldn't see it. She loathed Len.

Stephen stumbled over Molly sitting on the stairs in the gloom one evening. He was nipping up to make coffee in the top kitchen hoping to avoid everyone when he fell. The cup broke. She mumbled an apology and brought her legs up. She'd been daydreaming. 'I broke the cup, I'm sorry. Are you alright?'

Stephen was fine; he gathered the mug bits. 'Steal another from him,' suggested Molly. Stephen smiled and said, 'Do you fancy some coffee, Molly?'

'Make some, I'll join you.' He clambered back down to the main kitchen and put the kettle on.

They sat opposite each other sipping his tinned powder, the smile of thanks as he handed her a cup stayed, as if she'd forgotten to remove it. He racked his brain to think of something to say when she asked, 'What are you trying to work out?'

With a smile he said, 'What you are doing here?' She put down the cup, 'Just waiting.' She asked about him and he summarised the drama student thing and living there because it was close to the college. She noted he travelled in his mini, so was it that close? She summarised their lives – moving about, place to place, doing this and that. Neville had family investments they lived off. She was tired; she needed to take things easy. She put up with Len Boyd, but she couldn't take to him.

It wasn't a satisfactory response. Molly was being evasive but he couldn't probe further into this weary, disillusioned, enigmatic woman as the kitchen filled with others ready to cook. Neville came to give her a little handheld device which was part of the intercom he and Len had now rigged up in every room. In amidst the hubbub and with everyone occupied except observant Stephen, she suddenly spoke into the machine.

'Nothing to report. Nothing has happened. I get a feeling I'm being watched.' She looked straight at Stephen. 'I'm cutting out now as I can see the watcher. He is quite open. Will report later. Over and out.'

Stephen smiled, a little unsure, but Molly beamed at him. 'So now you know. I am a spy!'

'Are you?' he responded. He knew he was being mocked, but couldn't move beyond it. Susan solved it by indicating she wanted to talk privately, so they went to her room as Shirley was out. Susan had given herself to the organ master and it had been a huge letdown. Stephen nodded sympathetically, not sure how to respond to this one either. Shirley returned so Stephen escaped to his room.

Neville knocked. Was there no peace for Stephen? 'I gather you are curious about us?' So, Molly had filled him in already. 'What do you want to know?'

'How long have you known Len?'

'Thirty years, give or take. In Coventry, I was teaching and we shared digs. He was a junior reporter, did amateur theatre spots and obits. Old Will Sykes was editor and passed his love of Shakespeare to Len, or rather Len nicked his ideas.'

Stephen felt like a reporter himself asking questions about Len. Molly came in yawning. 'Time for bed, Molly? We must go, Stephen, nice talking to you.' As they reached the door, Neville turned and told Stephen, 'We're going to see Molly's family to tell them we're getting married.' Stephen mumbled congrats to cover his astonishment. They were together, yet not. This could be the perfect spy couple – known Len for decades, so he wouldn't suspect them. But Stephen did.

The door-chimes went as they left the front room. Molly answered to Mills and Haines. They asked to come in. Molly told them, 'No, Mr Boyd has given instructions; you may not. He's at Northampton, back next week.'

'Not at the party where Gary Ericson was last seen, were you?'

Molly took charge. 'No, and we know nothing about him beyond what has been mentioned in the house. If you want my opinion, I think Mr Boyd did it but you will not prove it. I refer you to the Al Capone case. They couldn't get him for murder, larceny, racketeering, drugs and assault. They got him on his tax returns.'

On that she shut the door in their faces and went to bed. That was how much she hated Len Boyd.

The next day Len threw their possessions out the window into the front garden and changed the lock. That was how much he hated traitors. The trusties all got new keys.

**-8-**

The Glasses squatted in number 19. They banged on walls, rattled windows and lit a bonfire in the back garden so smoke blew over 17's back patch, aka a garden. Len flew into a rage when he caught sight of Molly in the garden with binoculars looking at his house. Then, after a blood curdling scream one night they were heard of no more. Hedda was convinced Len had strangled the pair and hid them under number 19's floorboards. Only Stephen gave them any further thought.

Susan's weekend in Southend came and went with little more to be said. The Johns, Paula and Stephen were disappointed for her (they wanted details). Susan decided that she wouldn't carry on, suddenly afraid his wife would find out and make a scene. Gary slid back into her mind and triggered a bout of tearful regrets. Shirley was quite supercilious about it until she rushed away to the toilet to be noisily sick.

Toilet retching became regular and Shirley realised she was pregnant, just a day or two after Hedda twigged it. For Hedda every sneeze in the house was the prelude to a funeral. Word spread and it was Susan's turn to be superior.

Shirley confided in Hedda and got the comfort, 'you are silly woman.' It could only be Max's, apparently. When word of that spread, everyone was flabbergasted. Len didn't let on that he'd heard.

Official post piled in the hallway, gathering dust. When the pile got ridiculous, Len took it out to the back and set fire to it, dancing like a madman as it curled and vanished. But Len decided to show Stephen some private papers he'd kept, hidden in a suitcase behind the junk in the cellar.

From twenty, thirty years ago there were crumpled letters from the revenue, councils, debt collection agencies, businesses; some from individuals that Len was convinced proved that he was a wanted man from his youth. They had it in for him. The papers proved little except Len's chaotic lifestyle and administration, but Stephen agreed that Len seemed to attract problems.

Hedda had a friend who came about once a month, Donald, in his 40s. He told everyone who'd listen that his life was slipping away, and it was. Still living with his mother, thinning on top, driving a scrapheap car and unable to decide to marry Barbara or not (he'd only known her seven years) he was a session musician who came for tea from Hedda's cracked cups, a slice of cheesecake and pseudo-sympathy.

Donald always politely shook hands with any residents he encountered and made small talk about the injustice of love, regardless of how many times he'd met them. Susan's weekend was of passing interest; Shirley's misfortune occasioned a belly laugh. They talked trivia, with Hedda delighted in embellished stories from the asylum that was the house. The continuing police interest alarmed Donald and he offered to help her move away.

'I know I'm not your son, but I can help.'

'Na! My son sends money when he can. I do not need much.'

Paul confirmed to Stephen that Hedda did indeed have a son in Germany, but never saw him. What Donald was really getting concerned about was the summer invasion of foreign students that Len insisted on having and made his offer every summer. They paid well and most of his residents were on summer vacations anyway. 'Na! I manage, zank you, Donald.'

He stared at the single photo of a radiant 19 year old girl standing by a piano. It was Hedda, when she was somebody at the start of a promising career before two world wars, a husband shot for desertion and coming to England in the 1950s to make a new life. It was a sadly obscure existence in a house where her horizon was defined by memories, a few young people and the peculiar Len Boyd.

As he walked past her room, Len recognised Donald's voice so knocked and stuck his head round to shake hands with Hedda's visitor and snag a piece of cheesecake which he wolfed down. Donald prattled on, recounting the news Hedda had just told him. Susan and Shirley – Len had had no idea, it appeared. Hedda's mad look to silence Donald was missed.

Len got the full picture. He hid his feelings and offered to take Hedda on a drive to Northampton. She'd pestered to go for months and he'd put her off. Now when he offered it was too late, she was tired already. But Len knew that, which was why he offered.

The awkward scene was rescued by Paul arriving to tell Hedda about a new duet for piano and violin he'd found, to support Donald's idea that Hedda should go away while the foreigners were here (so he could have Linda round all night in Hedda's room) and to wangle some cheesecake. Len slipped away. He must have been in a great mood, or why would he have brought Tony back with him?

-9-

Tony was just 16 or thereabouts. A tall, gangly, fair-haired boy with no chin but plenty of teeth. He always wore a crumbled grey suit with a chewed-string tie, just like Len. He was English but had lived most of his life in Australia. He thought he was full of surprises, but to most in the house the only surprise was that he wasn't called Bruce. Nobody had met an Aussie not called Bruce. In fact none of them had ever met an Aussie.

He was somebody high up in Len's organisation of self-helpers. He'd been through it all and had achieved the highest level, funded by God knows what. But now he was penniless, dependent on Len's goodwill and was to pay nothing 'for a week or two.' He was an orphan, all alone in the world apart from Len and the collective madness that grabbed the believers.

He moved into the Hole for two nights before transferring to the cellar. Len provided him food and he shared a bowl of veggie mash every night made by a tut-tutting Hedda. Aside from that he ate only the odd slice of bread he stole from the metal cupboards. If anyone cooked while he was around, he'd sit and talk to them looking hungry.

It was a period when Stephen was more taken up with his college activities – exams, a show to direct and a day visit by his mother who was horrified at the run-down state of number 17 and the wild, manic appearance of Len.

His main focus was first year Jackie. The custom was that first years did crewing and technicals for older students' shows. They were close during the show and as it ended she accepted his offer of curry and chips at the Bamboo restaurant under the tube line bridge.

Then back to 17. But the lounge was full of Len, Tony, a bunch of weird visitors and Shirley gripped in a giggling fit. He got Jackie upstairs but John S came back in a foul mood about a rebuff and needed to talk. Hedda wanted to tell him that Shirley seemed to be in favour with Len and Paul wanted to discuss the show he'd loyally come to see that made little sense to him. So it was well into the night before everyone settled and Stephen got on with making Jackie feel relaxed. But she wanted to borrow his brush to clean her teeth and then hear more backstories about the people she'd just met.

He combined the tale with gently stroking her. She responded fairly warmly, as she did to everything, but after a time Stephen realised she was asleep. He snuggled beside her and hoped it would be better in the morning. But he couldn't sleep. A fresh attempt to rouse Jackie produced nothing so he got out and went for a drink in the kitchen. He heard a thud upstairs. John B came rattling down the staircase and saw Stephen. 'It's Tony, come and look. The stupid bugger tried to gas himself…'

Tony was partially out of the upper kitchen, quietly choking, frothing from his mouth, his eyes facing upwards. 'What?' John B barked, 'give me a hand to get him in the air.' They struggled with the gibbering juvenile and dropped him on the porch outside, leaving the door open. John went to dial 999 allowing Stephen to look in on Jackie who had woken and was wondering. Others appeared from their rooms. Stephen leaped upstairs and turned off the gas oven. The window was open so it wasn't a serious attempt.

When he returned to the porch, John B was telling the runt to stop snivelling. The boy was crying, large tears rolling down his face. 'There was a bit of fun in the lounge and they all went off to Northampton, even Shirley. Don't know what happened to the baby here. That's right, bring it up,' he snarled as Tony heaved all over the path, his shirt and tie. 'Did you call the ambulance and the police?'

Stephen nodded. 'Will you go with him to the hospital, I've got Jackie here?'

'You must be joking,' giving the boy a kick. 'He'll recover.' Tony looked up at him. 'I'm so lonely, you don't understand.' This looked as if it would make John start punching Tony again but an approaching blue flashing light stopped him.

A surly man in a light-grey uniform barked, 'Gassed himself, you think?'

'I didn't say that,' retorted John, playing the Len game.

'Looks alright to me. We'll take him in.' Tony was unceremoniously placed on a stretcher and taken away, having aroused most of the lace-windowed Crescent.

The next morning Stephen and Jackie overslept and had to get up in a rush. That evening, Tony was back with nothing different except a smell from his fetid shirt. But within minutes of Len and Shirley returning and having the event reported by an excited Hedda, Tony was out, bundled off in Len's car with no goodbyes just as Susan came home in floods of tears having just slept with the organ master for the last time.

Tony left no possessions beyond a few dirty magazines and a transistor radio, which were bagged and forgotten. Susan insisted they all went to a cinema that night, as she was feeling angry about the affair. So, unable to find excuses, Paul, The Johns, Stephen and Susan saw a romantic one at the Odeon where Shirley didn't usher.

They had a good time, all in all, so it was a surprise when they got back that Susan provoked a row with Shirley leading to them fighting like cats and dogs. All her pent up anger came out. Hedda shrieked and the boys tried to separate them. Len returned in the peak of the desperate, rough struggle. He got a scratch for being too close. He slapped Shirley across the face as hard as he could. The fight stopped.

The next morning she left, her bags packed and a taxi taking her away. Another departure. Another unexplained mystery to those who cared.

**-10-**

John S embarked on a 'world' tour with a girl who claimed to be an heiress. Tony reappeared, looking outwardly no different and 'helped' Len get the house ready for the summer invasion of foreign students. Nobody talked to Tony, so nobody knew how he was feeling after his nightmare. Hedda finally agreed to have a few days away arranged by Donald, so Paul moved into her room and got Linda to stay with him. He was in seventh heaven; she was on the pill.

Stephen worked on his book notes besides college stuff. He wanted a good end of term – after one show first night he brought Jill, the college Everybody's. She stayed two nights. Next, he took Lou to the pictures and proceeded to put into practice some of the technique books he and Paul had been reading. She wasn't on the pill – not all were, even in those free love days – so Stephen risked it. It ruined the summer holiday waiting for her to write or ring to say she was knocked up. Carol came back one night, but the house freaked her out so she left early.

Stephen was pleased with his tally. Term ended. The main players went back to their home bases and forty French students from 12 to about 18 with one male teacher swarmed in. There were mattresses everywhere. Hedda returned to her room but had to pay extra to keep it. Len must have found it financially worthwhile. Each morning he managed to produce bacon and eggs for the lot, but according to Hedda, nobody ate any after the first morning.

They spread themselves over the whole house, constantly moving and jabbering. Lights on and off, endlessly. They ate main meals in a church hall, endured daily outings and were supposed to have English lessons every morning. It was beyond the male teacher, so he let them free roam. Some of the other 600 who'd come with them in a fleet of coaches loved the chaos of number 17 so came for leisure time too. Tony's role was unclear. The French didn't warm to him, but he knew card tricks, shared dirty magazines and did a silly amusing impersonation of Len.

Len's yellow toothed smile was fixed. Stilted conversations with the teacher were surreal, according to Hedda. It was into the chaos of garlic-reeking babble one evening that Mills and Haines called. They stood in the hall absorbing the storm, having been let in by an uncomprehending French youth. When Len appeared they asked him about Gary, about the Glasses and about a woman called Shirley Roberts.

He denied being Len Boyd or ever knowing those people. It was a circular conversation until Mills demanded when Len had last submitted a tax return. Len said he had 'no comment' at which the two officers brightened up and said they'd be back with a search warrant. Before they did, though, Tony suddenly left, bound for Australia. Nobody later fathomed how a minor was able to arrange it, raise money and depart without telling Len or Northampton.

But go he did. He was there Wednesday, on Thursday he wasn't.

There was a rash of food poisoning, so the house looked like an improvised war zone hospital. An official called Robinson called to check up on Tony for his passage to Australia and was puzzled that he'd left already and that Len claimed to have seen him only once at a house in Bromley. He left after a cup of coffee with Len with no clear idea of anything.

**-11-**

The new academic year brought Paul back to the house, to Hedda's great relief, swiftly followed by Stephen. They were put in together; John B was not returning and Susan had finished at the Academy and had embarked on a year's teaching course. She'd changed organ masters and would be visiting whenever she had a London lesson. John S's world trip got as far as Amsterdam where the girl had had enough.

The French students had wrecked the place – on top of decades of wear and tear and Len's crazy schemes. Hedda pestered Len to decorate. He reluctantly agreed and said the upstairs double bedroom would become 'luxury'. He started on stripping wallpaper and then lost interest.

At college, Lou returned pregnant. When Stephen got a chance to ask her, she was convinced it was from Roger, a former schoolmate she'd bumped into during the vacation. Stephen was relieved, but then the poor girl was called home as her father died unexpectedly. A college lecturer passed away suddenly and word reached the house that the Glasses had been killed in a car crash near Northampton.

Paul, who had a way with old people, knew another old dear he visited in Norwich. When she too suddenly slipped away, Stephen was at his desk writing with the transistor on loud. When Paul came to tell him, tears in his eyes, Stephen nodded and said, 'yes, ok,' as he usually did when Paul was making music. Then he realised Paul was distraught.

So after a summer of sex, madness and disappearances came an autumn of deaths. On top of that, Stephen's second most recent play was to be performed at college and all the people he'd known who were not blacklisted or actually dead were invited. Susan planned to fit an organ lesson round a visit. Lou returned from the funeral having lost the baby and Stephen comforted her as best he could.

New arrivals, true to form, turned up all hours. Joel, a Canadian in his 30s was researching state power and its excesses and went in with John S and a piano. Len liked the man at first and helped with his thesis from his wide experience of state oppression, saying that he had some papers on it in a drawer somewhere. Jody, a Scottish girl about 20, moved into the attic, a hippie of the 'tune in and drop out' variety. Len'd found her in London at the Covent Garden centre and brought her to the house before she went to Northampton for 'training.' Joel often tiptoed up the attic 'to see if Jody was ok' which fooled nobody.

In a rare moment of neighbourliness, Len had a coffee-in – the lounge was the centre for everyone without excuses to cram in and try some of his blends and sparingly diminish two packets of digestive biscuits. Once they'd discussed Len's plans for a recording studio and a ballet rehearsal room that 'weren't quite yet ready', Joel lit up a gigantic pipe and filled the place with pungent smoke. He said it made him look more like a Brit.

He reported he'd seen a Mind Test advertised at Covent Garden and had been tempted. Len assured him he should go for it. 'It's a pattern for living, a code of morals and ethics that overcomes obstacles to personal fulfilment.' It was awkward, because most had heard it a million times before, Jody was going to do it soon at Northampton and Joel was winding Len up. When he went outside to make more coffee, 'if anyone fancied a top up' people began to wonder if they could politely get away. The break gave Len time to think.

Len gave Joel some leaflets from a cupboard and insisted he tried a French blend he claimed he'd been given in the summer. Joel took a few sips. The door chimes stopped it as Len dashed to open on a nondescript man in a suit as lived in as Len's, Denis. 'This is the man to ask if you want to know about clearing obstacles to living, Joel, this is Denis. He's done every course available and is a successful businessman with a sizeable set of investments behind him, more than repaying what the courses cost.'

Denis looked anything but successful. But after all had left bar Joel, he sat and watched while Len and Denis exchanged banalities. Len reported how busy he was with jobs in the house and how so many of his visitors couldn't be trusted. Denis launched into a point about the novel *Nineteen-Eighty Four* and something called Big Brother. Len knew just enough about it to nod enthusiastically.

'It's less than twenty years away, but by 1984, you see, certainly we'll all be puppets to their games, reprogrammed at will, controlled to oblivion and any dissenters will be recycled, their body parts removed to keep the controllers perpetually young and healthy.' Joel was fascinated; it was right on for his dissertation. They droned on about disappearing people and the police and bureaucracy.

The door chimes went again. Everyone else was otherwise engaged so Len opened. It was Mills. 'Good evening, Mr Boyd, I understand you have a Mr Denis Jarvis visiting you. May we have a word?' Len's response was, 'Mr Boyd, as you know is not here and neither is Mr Denis Jarvis.' Denis sighed and went through to the hallway, 'It's ok, Len, I'll see them.'

He walked straight out the house and stood on the path till Mills and Haines joined him, just out of hearing through the open front door. Joel yawned and said he needed to get some sleep as he stood up, leaving Len to peer through the dirty lace curtains trying to hear what Denis was saying to the law. Len was outraged that Denis would do that. He thought Denis must be an actual police infiltrator.

Joel dashed to the upper kitchen where Hedda was dishing out cheesecake to Paul, Linda and Stephen and reported the last conversation and the police arrival. That Denis should openly be conversing with cops was certainly remarkable. Within a few minutes, Joel went pale, started sweating and complained of a fierce stomach ache. Paul suggested, only half-joking, it must have been the coffee as Joel staggered off to his bed.

**-12-**

After weeks of preparation and problems, Stephen's play was staged. The first night audience was kept outside for 20 minutes while the set was hastily screwed tight. It was weird, of course, speaking of his student days, the drama, relationships and the fringes of lunacy he'd been part of. The hilarious section went especially well.

The gang from 17 came. Hedda looked like something from the 1920s, Len had put on a less dirty shirt, Paul brought Linda who was pleasing for some of the straight students to look at, John S borrowed a cowboy costume for some reason and Susan came from the Midlands and sat beside Stephen as his hands churned the programme to pulp during the show.

All the way back and once in the lounge, they talked it over and over. They recalled unimportant parts, to Stephen's mind as if they'd watched a slightly different show. They all claimed to have loved it, mainly as Stephen had written it. No one understood it, but that applied to over half the audience and the media too.

Joel recovered, but not soon enough to see the play, packed his bags and left, promising to look them up when he was back in the UK. They all knew he'd be forgotten the moment he closed the door, and so it was. Jody followed a week later, after confiding in Hedda that John S had tried to rape her on the stairs. When Paul heard he thought it better not to bring Linda into the house for a time as John S was in a caged animal phase.

John S's behaviour was increasingly odd, even by 17's standards. Stephen discussed it with Paul and they compared notes. His part-time architecture work was lucrative but John S obsessed about being a famous pianist. He was moody, bizarre in comments and facial ticks and was writing a concerto called 'Tribute to Sex.' He then announced he was buying a house just two streets away, a 'proper house'. Hedda said he was, 'Na! He's a madman.'

Mad or not, he pulled the girls, despite his Neanderthal views on women. Night after most nights, in they came. A thin girl who looked about 15 stayed a week; a German au-pair who lived just up The Crescent was amazed when Len brought them breakfast in bed. There was Lisa, a mature woman on the run from an abusive husband. A black-eyed, lovely Jewish girl called Rachel would've floated Stephen's boat too, if she'd been free. He was amazed to learn she was not a model but a shop assistant. Two Susans, some Amandas, an Elizabeth and a Beth, some Annes and even a Violet. Still they came.

Perhaps it was a cover for something. Stephen became increasingly suspicious of who and what the real John S was.

Paul, who Stephen had trusted completely, was mocked as a 'poof' by John S when he told him not to kiss Linda in the corridor at which he was defended by Hedda and Linda both. But what did Stephen know about Paul, really?

It was when John S became ill that Stephen seriously began to think it was Paul who was the real menace. He wouldn't see a doctor, but his translucent face, the sweats and stomach cramps (not unlike Joel's symptoms, they remarked) got worse. He lay in bed, hour after hour, quietly dying.

They visited him as and when. Stephen tried to ask him about what he'd eaten or drunk lately, now sure John S had been poisoned. Paul came in with a cup of raw egg and cold milk mix that his mother swore by when he and his brother were kids.

On one visit, Stephen's sleeve was pulled and John S whispered that he was being poisoned; he wasn't simply ill. Stephen recoiled from his dog breath but had to agree with John S's conclusions. 'Before you came here, there was a man who was poisoned and escaped. After a few days the cops came knocking because he'd been found floating in The Thames, poisoned before drowned.'

'Have you any evidence?' demanded Stephen.

'Are you blind? How long have you lived here? Look at the people! Len poisons whoever he likes. Fancy a cup of coffee, Stephen?'

It was food for Stephen's thought. As he left, John S asked him, 'have you ever wondered why next door has been empty so many years? How many bodies do you think there may be in there? Do you know who owns number 19?' Stephen didn't. 'Len Boyd.'

As he left the invalid, Len looked suspiciously at him and asked him to look at a new ad he'd inserted in the local paper. *'Home from home accommodation. Come and join our family. Self-help in a progressive environment. New luxury room available. View now.'* 'What do you think?'

Stephen checked Len. The man was serious. 'But the luxury room is not even decorated yet, Len.' Len didn't think that was a problem.

Over Christmas all was quiet. Just Len, Hedda and a handful of people from Northampton with nowhere else to go. John S got better enough to move to his new house.

When everyone returned in the New Year, Len told them that he had sad news.' John S fell through the glass roof of the conservatory at his new house. No, he's not dead. But he's broken every bone in his body and he may not walk again.' He seemed genuinely upset. So, for Stephen then, Paul was the poisoner, not Len.

### -13-

A young guy called Reggie Duke, his woman called Gyp and a big beautiful dog moved in. Len normally refused animals and didn't like the look of Reggie, but Len was short of cash, so they moved into the 'luxury' room. The dog roamed the house, jumping up and licking faces, pleasing everyone but Hedda and Len.

Duke was a folky-rocky-pop singer who'd cut an album and got an advance on the release. He rubbed Hedda up the wrong way, so the dog was chased up and down stairs all day while his owner waited for record sales to start and fame to arrive. Most others just ignored him and Gyp who was of an indeterminate nationality with poor English. 'Hey man, where's the freak keep his coffee?' said Reggie, rushing into the kitchen where Stephen was eating a packet curry and reading a novel.

'Back of the beaten up cupboard, behind you,' Stephen responded without looking up. He was indifferent to the fact that Reggie might take a tampered tin. 'Hey man, where you at, we ain't seen much of you?'

Stephen was obliged to look up. 'I've been busy....' and told him his college life in a nutshell. This made Reggie quite hostile as a college for drama students was beyond his comprehension. He was obviously seriously disturbed, but Gyp came in at that moment, looking for him. Stephen made the mistake of looking at her, which made Reggie say, 'Don't even think about her, man, she's mine.' Stephen was happy to let him have her; he didn't need a doped out girl belonging to a mental case.

Len arrived; a bad moment. He saw that Reggie was drinking his coffee and told him it was not free. Reggie took big exception and they argued, culminating in a threat to set the dog on Len and rip his throat out. That was the first round. The second was Len staring at them, standing in shadows, appearing without warning. Hedda urged him to throw their things out and change the locks. He would've but he'd taken a phone call earlier to say that Reggie and Gyp had gone to the Rent Tribunal about the cost of their room.

Reggie took things from the kitchens, used the phone without recording/paying for his calls and didn't clear up dog mess inside the house. There was going to have to be a fight. Reggie had to go; but Len had to win the case. A lock was fitted to the phone which inconvenienced everyone. Reggie simply ripped off the entire dial and tapped the top till the operator answered and connected him. War had been declared.

Len joined the Caterers' Association for legal advice which consisted of classifying 17 The Crescent as a Guest House. In the wait for the hearing, one evening, Stephen was in his room with a delightful blonde from college called Maria and was hoping for great things. Len and Reggie met on the landing. A scuffle started, so Stephen summarised for Maria as the two men thumped, pushed and scratched each other with the dog enjoying the game. Gyp stood ready with a chair to hit someone.

When Stephen opened his door a fraction, Len shrieked to call the police before Reggie killed him, just as his head was being rolled across the greasy wall, his glasses twisted at an unnatural angle. Len splintered Reggie's guitar across the younger man's head causing blood and shrieks, as Stephen darted across the landing to the phone. He tapped for the operator and called 999. The protagonists were exhausted, and sat exchanging verbal insults.

Stephen checked they'd stopped punching and said he was opening the front door for the police. Len and Reggie were instantly angry at police coming, so he skipped down and waited outside. Upstairs he could hear Len wiping the wall and Reggie picking up his wrecked guitar. He looked in on Maria who was lying on his bed reading his notebook. She nodded she was fine.

Ambulance men arrived and cursorily checked both men. Neither warranted taking in. Then the uniforms arrived, two young beat bobbies. They demanded statements and names of witnesses and immediately regretted answering the call to attend since neither man was helpful. They looked down as two other men walked up – Mills and Haines. The uniforms were sent packing and Mills said, 'well, good evening, Mr Boyd and Mr Duke, known and respected far and wide, the pair of you.'

It was the last straw for Len who barked at them to get out, but they claimed as 999 had been called they had to be there. They enjoyed a quick look round, knocked on some doors and goaded Len nicely. 'We've decided to await the outcome of your Rent Tribunal, Mr Boyd. Good evening. Mr Duke.' And they left, the front door still wide behind them. Stephen made Len and Reggie a cup of the filthy coffee, engaged in surreal small talk and slipped away to his room where Maria was getting ready to leave. He persuaded her to stay as it was late; she reluctantly agreed but her body language made it clear nothing else was on offer.

In the morning Reggie, Gyp and the dog were gone. Everyone was convinced Len had smashed their heads with rocks. Stephen was asked to go with Len and Hedda to the Town Hall to make a statement for the rent appeal. Reggie never showed. After a tortuous hike down corridors and sitting in front of a desk, they each gave a few thoughts on the character of Mr Duke. Hedda's was mainly, 'Na! He is a brute.' Len rambled on about freedom to rent out a house to deserving and appreciative guests. Stephen said as little as he could.

Next they had to traipse to the Caterers' solicitor, Mr Sieffs, who demanded the cheque for fifty pounds that Len was told to bring before he'd even bid him good afternoon. He then explained that Caterers' Association advice was basic. Specialised advice needed an upfront, nominal payment and if services were less in the end, he'd get a refund. As if.

Sieffs would brief a barrister for the hearing, so Stephen knew this would cost Len dearly. He asked Len to speak and made notes; he invited Hedda to speak and looked at her as if watching a film. He nodded a bit when Stephen gave him a summary of events. As they were leaving, he took Stephen aside, handed him his card and congratulated him on being the only sane man in the building. Probably.

The Tribunal visited to inspect the 'luxury' room, which was a total shambles. And a week later, all nervous and Len spruced up as best he could, they went to the Town Hall again and sat on one side of a line of tables. There was nobody on the other side. The barrister spoke at length, Sieffs nodded, Len looked confused. The chairman expressed surprise that a simple case required a barrister, but there it was. The finicky Clerk asked the room if Mr Duke had been properly informed of these proceedings. Nobody knew, except Len who had opened his notification and ditched it.

After Len was asked questions, the tribunal declined to hear either Hedda or Stephen and took exactly six minutes of huddle before declaring that Mr Boyd's attitude had been hostile and unhelpful and that after consideration they ruled 17 The Crescent was a paying Guest House, so they had no jurisdiction. Case dismissed.

Len treated everyone to coffee and doughnuts that evening to celebrate. The nightmare cost him over two hundred quid. There were lessons to be learned, but Stephen wasn't sure Len actually learned them.

**-14-**

The summer saw the end of his college years. Strawberries and sunshine, the final welter of exams, productions and 'we must keep in touch' mingled with news of those securing jobs in teaching or the performing arts industry. Stephen had no particular job; his plan was to go back to East Anglia and write, including the story of the house. He was confident the film rights alone would fund his lifestyle.

That was his pipe dream, but he knew that despite superficial freedoms and 'doing your thing', the state had become so much more intrusive in the past few years. So, he crammed all his stuff – clothes, books, notebooks and poems – into his car and away to the east. He had a long August weekend back at the house to see Maria who was also in London at that point, though she had another year to do at the college.

He had a final walk round, allowing time in each area to bring back the memories, checking them against notes. Len found him. 'I am writing that book now, Len.' Len nodded, considering it. 'I am writing about what I have seen, what impressions I had...'

'And what did you see, Stephen?'

'You know what I've seen.' But what Len meant was that there were some things he saw that could be written about and some things he saw that not only could he not write about but he hadn't seen them in any case; they didn't happen. It was the Len view. 'Be careful what you put on paper, Stephen.'

'Yes, I get you, Len. The people who came and went, the unexplained mysteries. I have to set it down, how our freedom is an illusion in many senses is a story worth telling.' The shadows of evening were beginning when Hedda appeared from her old room.

'Na! Paul is in Norwich. He's as crazy as you. He turned down opportunity in an orchestra to go back there.'

'East Anglians rarely leave for long, Hedda.'

There was no more to say, so Stephen went home. He had ten days in Germany with his sister and Maria came to stay a few days. He went to Edinburgh to see her in a college production at the festival. He told himself he was in love with her.

Working a few hours a day in the family art shop, he started writing the book. He stuck with it hour after hour and made good progress. By October he had a draft of 92,000 words and felt a final outing to London would be useful. Besides he hadn't got a photo of the front of the house for his cover.

He met Maria in town on a Friday night to see a crap play. His car was towed away so they tubed to Kings Cross and hitched a ride in a police van to the pound and a fine. Typical of the way the authorities constantly watched and hassled people. His draft had been on the back seat, anybody could have read it.

Len, having done half a redecoration job on the luxury room spoiled by Reggie, gave it to Stephen and Maria. Tired as he was after a full day, Stephen couldn't sleep so he left Maria in bed and found Len in the cellar.

'Len, I've finished the book. I've set matters straight, changed names and nobody in a year or two will connect it with here or with you. My only worry is Paul.'

Len didn't react. 'I know that Paul poisoned John S. I know the truth and I've said it.' There was a long pause before Len said, 'I had a letter from bureaucracy the other day. As you know, I don't usually open them, but this was disguised as a personal letter. They said I had no choice under law, I had to answer their questions. Nothing has changed. The truth will not be allowed to come out.'

'You think I should alter the truth?'

Len didn't reply so Stephen left him. He cleaned his teeth in the cold running water of the bathroom. The house was silent. He looked in on Maria – fast asleep – and went back to the cellar. Len was exactly as he'd left him. 'Can I borrow a typewriter, Len?'

'Upstairs in your first room.'

Stephen climbed up, cleared the table of junk and found paper in a box under the table. He redid the references to Paul being the poisoner, leaving it more open-ended, less obvious. And it was done.

**-15-**

Through the late autumn Stephen edited and retyped his book. The need for longer term work suited to his training and talents and other things to write about kept filling his mind and absorbing time. London seemed the place to be if he was to get anywhere, so he applied for English supply teaching in east London to tide him over and got an instant acceptance.

While he lived in a variety of rented rooms and shared flats of the student variety, meeting some strange oddbods, none was in the Len and his residents' league. Maria was busy at college; it was good to have a regular girlfriend he could see at least once a week.

His typescript began a long journey from him to a publisher, back and then to another publisher. Some took weeks, others returned it at once, clearly unread. He replaced the front cover when it got tatty. When he ran out of publishers he tried literary agents in alphabetical order. He spent a fortune in envelopes and stamps. If any commented on it beyond a standard rejection, it was to say that the characters were unbelievable and the story showed a worrying paranoia on the author's part.

Film industry agents didn't want it, 'at this time.' He got leads on American, Australian and even Swedish publishers. Nobody wanted his book. He gradually realised that he was the victim of a conspiracy. Of course nobody wanted the book – they'd been ordered not to take it. It was too hot; it showed a dark side of society suppressing individualism. He feared for the safety of his precious manuscript, so he carried a copy with him to schools every day in case they broke into his accommodation.

He put a copy with his bank in a sealed envelope for their vault and signed over the seals. The building had the illusory air of security and integrity beyond all the pomposity and seriousness. He posted three copies to his mother on different days with instructions to hide them properly and not together. He sent one to Len who promised not to read it, but as it had been to endless offices Stephen no longer worried. He even sent one to Paul. He kept two further copies himself, one of which mysteriously disappeared within a week and the second he sent to his sister with instructions to deposit in a different bank in her university town.

A letter arrived from Len, sent on from his mother. It was a tatty scrawl but said he should visit 17 as soon as he could. He thought Hedda may have died but she was mainly alive when he arrived next evening. Len was himself.

Linda had written to Hedda to say that Paul was desperately ill in the Norfolk and Norwich Hospital, in a coma. He was not expected to pull through. He'd been poisoned.

They thrashed it around over coffee. 'Why?' 'It makes no sense.' 'Who?' None had any answers.

After a time, Stephen asked, 'did he poison himself?'

Len shrugged. It was clear that if someone had hit Paul, any of them could be next.

Two weeks later Stephen fixed a weekend in East Anglia, Maria with him and they'd visit Paul. He rang 17 for news.

They'd just heard from Linda that Paul never regained consciousness and passed away.

Stephen knew he'd never go to that house again. He had to look out for his safety and those of his loved ones.

-16-

Len put 17 The Crescent up for sale. It took months to shift largely because of Len's improvements which added to the sense of a handyman's nightmare TV set. The small front garden he concreted over to make a pull-off for a car. It cracked and pitted immediately. Broken furniture, bits of timber, bricks, hard bags of plaster and bags of old papers were piled into a decrepit shed at the back. Once it was crammed full, Len tossed in a gallon of petrol and a match. The fire brigade were called by a neighbour and the Council sent a letter saying they intended to prosecute him.

Each time a sale fell through, Len knew the authorities had it in for him. He increased his asking price periodically and took in no new guests. When number 19 was sold – Len seemed not to own it after all - Len knew he'd been singled out for victimisation. That house next door had been empty for years but as house prices started to rocket in the early 1970s, a retired Jewish couple bought it, gutted it and turned it into three decent flats.

Hedda was moved to a sheltered accommodation area in Hertfordshire. People she knew who cared about her rallied round and chipped in. She was obliged to store a tea chest of Len's most precious paperwork he wanted to keep private. She was dead within two months, dead from boredom developing into lethargy.

Susan lost contact after writing to say that she'd never been happier – she'd met a 50 year old, twice divorced singer and they were going to buy a house in the north. Stephen never heard any more from or of anyone who'd shared the 17 experience. So, he moved from supply to a one year teaching post and began to fear that his life was planned out. All that drama training was wasted. All that writing was going nowhere. He wondered about Len occasionally.

Then out of the blue one evening his mother rang to say that Len had visited her! With no warning, Len in a better suit with a reasonable tie and fairly clean shirt and a pale boy called Lawrence in tow had turned up at her house in an ancient camper van, stuffed with files and papers, broken artefacts and junk.

She was dismayed to have to entertain the pair to coffee for two hours, she talking about Stephen as they had nothing else in common. He told her of his dream to establish self-help cells in local communities, all linked to Northampton, monitored by him. When no meal was offered, they said they must go find an East Anglian cottage to buy as the first part of the hub and on to Norwich to see Linda and Paul's parents.

When she had the presence of mind to 'mislay' Stephen's actual current London address he left her with some drawings of an eco-building he'd designed, with heat that rose up a central core and all rooms interconnected. She promised to pass them on. And so they left, his mother reporting that far from 17 The Crescent being history, it was alive and well in Len's van and head.

**-17-**

Over the Easter holidays, Stephen and Maria went home to his mother. It was a chance to catch some fresh air, help her with gardening, enjoy food cooked for them and revisit old haunts. The smell of the sea; the wind that rarely dropped away. Home. Bliss.

Maria didn't feel great – Stephen wondered if she might be pregnant – and left her with his mum while he had a solo walk along the shingle beach. He was working on a sex novel, all his previous work sitting in boxes in his mother's loft. He knew he was being followed, but nobody was in sight beyond some fishermen ahead. It was just a feeling, but it discomforted him

A car stood outside his mother's house. Two men were sitting in her lounge in earnest conversation with her. Maria met him as he entered the house, looking at him deeply in the eyes. 'What's wrong, Maria?'

'I don't know, Stephen, is there anything wrong?' She dropped her voice. 'One of those men is a cop and the other a doctor. They've spread panic in your mum's head and I don't feel too good, either.' Mother emerged from the lounge. 'What's going on, Mum?'

'I don't know, Stephen, what's going on?' She was talking in riddles too. 'I knew that house and that man were trouble, always knew it.'

Stephen led into the room. The larger, uglier man, having taken lessons from the Mills and Haines coursebook announced himself as 'Inspector Booker, Norfolk Constabulary.' The other stood up and offered a small, effeminate hand, 'Doctor Mendez.'

Stephen replied, sarcastically, 'well a cop and a doctor. Am I honoured?'

Mendez did the talking. 'We're concerned about you, Stephen. It's been reported from your school, from some of your friends and from our enquiries about the past, that you are – '

'I am not ill!' Stephen barked.

'No, of course you're not,' replied Mendez in the tone of a man agreeing the moon is made of green cheese on Fridays. 'The police have come into our investigations as our work often overlaps these days. Police and medicine.'

Booker chipped in, quite aggressively, 'we are making enquiries about the unexplained death of Paul Starkey. Did you know him?'

'Yes, I knew him quite well, although we weren't close. We shared a house with others.' Stephen gave them a potted account of his time at 17 and the key people, leaving out much of the weirdness, his suspicions about poisoning and about Len. Booker told him enquiries were ongoing about Gary Ericson, the Glasses, Shirley, John B, John S, Hedda, Tony and … Len Boyd. He further stated that the house was being ripped apart by a team of trained officers at that very moment.

Mendez, when Stephen failed to be surprised or moved by the news, told him that his manuscript and some of his poems were worrying a few mental health experts. In short, they thought he was borderline paranoiac schizophrenic, with a highly developed persecution complex and a fertile imagination. He could be helped.

An hour later the discussion was still going round in circles. Booker looked at his watch. 'Well, Stephen you have made your position clear, but we have our jobs to do. Enquiries about the missing people will be suspended till Dr Mendez clears you for questioning. So, you will go to the hospital near Norwich and then we will talk again. Dr Mendez reckons a week, ten days at the most. You are entering this treatment voluntarily.'

'And if I don't?'

'We have powers under the Mental Health Act.'

'So, I am damned if I do and cursed if I don't. You, the system have got me all ways. This is the death of individual freedom. I will be one of the disappeared. Somebody else will be asked about me, as if I was just a statistic, a brief traveller on the road of life that was mapped out by others.'

Dr Mendez nodded warmly, as if he liked Stephen's poetic turn of phrase.

'Monday morning, then, Stephen. We'll send a car.' They left, politely thanking his mother as if it had been a social call. Once they'd gone it was a long time before his mother, Maria or Stephen could think of anything to say.

**-18-**

On Monday he was driven to a Victorian building outside Norwich and shown into a room that was his alone. Roomy, tall ceiling and lots of light from the barred window. At their first session, Mendez asked him to start at the beginning and tell him about the house. Stephen, by then, was happy to play along. This would be material for a book that would be accepted, that would shock, would blow the lid off this repressive society… He'd make it third person to throw them off the trail.

'Stephen arrived at 17 The Crescent on a September 1967 Saturday, about 11. Coffee time. Anytime was coffee time but Len offered Stephen coffee to welcome him to the house. The circus, the rolling freak show that was number 17 in The Crescent, a quiet, curved road of ordinariness in suburban north London. And it was at that moment that Stephen decided he'd keep notes – Len and his house were a rich source of material for a book one day.

He'd got a small, top floor room to one side …'

# A Reunion of Clowns

When Bob Mann in London picked up word on social media that his old friend and fellow clown, Richard Adams, had passed away in Lowestoft, he knew he had to go to his funeral. But he was too late; it was weeks ago.

So Bob determined to make the journey there, something between a pilgrimage and a penance. He'd left Lowestoft and Richard's lifestyle years ago. But they'd had some fun back in the day and even at the reunions till they stopped in the 1980s. So, Bob made his mind up and his long-suffering wife, Megan, went along with it, offering to join him to help him stand upright and walk, offering herself as an extra stick.

Richard and Bob were boyhood friends; Bob from the poorer Roman Hill Primary School and Richard from the allegedly better St Margaret's Primary. They met at the 14th Lowestoft cubs and then were thrown together when they both passed the 11-plus exam and went to Lowestoft Grammar School in September 1959. They also shared adventures in the Scouts and later the Seniors.

Even as he started to pack a few things, Bob thought back quite fondly through a selection of his memories. If the weather was good, he and Megan would go out to the huge wooded area at Herringfleet with its deep lake and scouting history. Years before the then Lord Somerleyton had given over a vast area for local scouts to camp and as the boys grew older and acquired their own motorbikes and scooters, they used it for extra-curricular activity.

He recalled the clearing on the top of the rise where tents were normally pitched, midges in the air and a small sheltered corner of loose shrubbery and bracken. Richard Adams with a girl; he with another. Richard got where he wanted – all the way – Bob got nowhere. The story of much of their lives, though Bob wasn't completely without success. He smiled, as he looked at himself closely in the bedroom mirror.

'Good morning, folks, the time is just coming up to five past the hour and you're in tune with the Bob Mann show on your favourite station...' Megan looked at him from her dressing table, putting her head to one side, quizzically. 'You haven't played the old DJ game for a while, Bob.' He'd always wanted to be a pirate radio jock; but even with his friend's help, had never managed it. At least, he hadn't committed a crime by doing it, thought Megan.

'No, well, I haven't given that a lot of thought for years. But if we're going to visit, I'm thinking. He won't be there. It'll be a half reunion of clowns.'

'Remind me. Clowns?'

'You remember, I told you. At school. Freddie Dowling, taught us French before we gratefully gave it up. He once threw our homework books at both of us in anger, saying something like - you two should be a double clown act, as you've given me a pain with laughing at your puerile attempts to master French. It stuck. Give a dog a bad name, you know. We played up the clowns and once I'd moved away, he called my very first trip home to see everyone, a reunion of clowns.'

Megan neatly laid their things in the suitcase, masking a sigh. His memories would keep returning, most of which she'd heard a million times before, but at least her Bob didn't have dementia. It wouldn't hurt for him to relive some of the past, even without his partner of old; especially without him.

She'd never taken to Richard Adams, nor his Sunday magazine, trophy wife Marcella, never understanding why the woman stayed with a man who was a serial womaniser and dodgy businessman. Still, each to his or her own and this would be the last trek she'd have to make to Lowestoft with Adams now deceased. Bob's parents and family had long gone. She'd put up with visits three or four times a year ever since she met and married Bob in the late 70s.

It was the one that turned out to be their last that she recalled the most when Richard had tried it on with her in buckets. He'd had half-hearted attempts before with her, but perhaps out of a rare fragment of consideration for Bob, had not pushed it. But that occasion was when they'd gone to some big anniversary event at the old grammar school and Richard Adams was the guest of honour speaker - very full of himself over it. Megan thought he saw her as his reward, part of the recognition the local entrepreneur was finally receiving.

His speech had gone down well, even though he'd started off with, 'It gives me great pleasure, and has done since I was 14...' That raised a few eyebrows. But once he got onto his businesses and how many local people he employed and some of his plans for the future, people of the current and past generations generally warmed to him

He'd done the tour for Bob and Megan in his chauffeur-driven roller, showing off more businesses he'd acquired since the last trip. He'd got people from their past working for him – women particularly who Megan had heard described in what they used to get up to. He even had one running a prostitution network he seemed to be controlling by long arms, across East Anglia. She was delighted when Bob and he drifted apart after that, though always regretted giving Adams any joy at all that time.

She drove them out of London towards the east. He wanted to put on some 60s' music, but respected that Megan'd get plenty of that era over the next few days so they chatted about domestic trivia. Onto Eastern Avenue, Megan wished they'd gone north to pick up the M25, as it was a working and school day, traffic was heavy. A line of teenagers at a bus stop in school uniforms, summer skirts short on the girls, set his mind back.

He remembered chatting up Jenni at break times, lunchtimes and occasionally getting to take her home after school on the back of his Lambretta. The party they went to – there seemed to be one most weekends in his circle of sixth form friends. Richard had lined himself up one for time upstairs and Jenni seemed keen. She was, albeit their political and other views were not compatible. He recalled it was going well, even with Adams and a girl and two others in there, till a load of drunken boys came in to see what was going on.

The school dance, probably the Christmas one, a band of local lads playing a Searchers' hit, two Animals' and one Stones' song they'd mastered. The girl he took preferred to dance and hang out with someone else. The boys who snuck out during the music and watched while one of them sawed the wooden struts on a bench by the sports block. The clowning in the corridor that turned serious when Richard somehow acquired a key that let them and two willing girls into a classroom upstairs.

The headmaster's horror when a girl fell pregnant and how he'd lectured the older boys. That turned out to be a mere prelude to his reaction when three more followed suit. Richard made a fortune out of sourcing and selling condoms for them, but demand exceeded supply. The pill was around, but wasn't easy to get, till Richard did a deal with a doctor who'd got himself into some financial bother that Richard found out about. That too was an opener for Richard's business acumen – he started to arrange willing girls for shy boys.

On one occasion the mad idea cropped up among a group of the boys that they'd each arrange one blind date and pick names from a hat. Richard wanted a rule that there were envelopes from which each girl had to draw one before the date; half contained rubbers, half didn't. But that part of it didn't take off.

Bob had a job to find anyone willing, but finally hit on one, a friend of his sister, who didn't seem to mind what might happen – she was flattered to be going out with an older boy. The scene for all the dates was to be the Rugby Club Christmas dance in Yarmouth.

Bob had zero interest in rugby or any other sport, but wasn't going to miss out. He drew Eliza Catchpole. He didn't know her … oh, no, as soon as he saw her he muttered, 'Oh, wait a minute, I've got a bit of a dodgy tummy …'

Everyone laughed. Ever the clown. Short, dark curly hair where he liked blonde and willowy, but her legs were OK and she was well developed for her age. He wondered where Richard had found her, never doubting for a minute that Richard had in fact found most of the girls. Richard pressed an empty envelope into his hand as they parted, to say hello to their new dates.

So he found himself on the school phone asking mother to borrow the car – he'd recently passed his test.

The meal was good and they chatted together and with others quite freely. The dance was fine, though he took a lot of ribbing about 'cradle snatching' and 'his sudden interest in rugby,' despite others being less interested in sport than getting a girlfriend.

He parked outside her house in the middle of the night, feeling a warm glow from an enjoyable evening and they kissed. He was surprised at Eliza's enthusiasm and heard himself asking to see her again.

Saturday evening on the freezing cold prom to the shelter, finding a space among other necking couples. Sunday afternoon in her house while her parents, now recovered, were out. Monday after school, the debating society, she sat next to him and was impressed when he spoke, squeezing his hand secretly, though it only took one to notice for everyone to know.

It was all going so well. He gave up all others for weeks and they started to plan how they'd work it when he finished school and went to training college with Richard. 'Why are you two going to be teachers?' she'd asked. His usual reply was 'to work with 15 year old girls,' but that wasn't appropriate, so he enthused about a good job with long holidays and his real dream was to be a commercial radio DJ now the golden age of pirate radio ships was over.

Yes, all went so well, although they had some disagreements from time to time. She was very young. Then Richard seduced her at a party to celebrate the end of the boys' A-levels. Although she had looked enthusiastic as Bob watched sulkily from an armchair, so perhaps it wasn't seduction.

It was afternoon when Megan and Bob reached Lowestoft and went straight to Richard's house, their old car crunching the gravel. Fancy, posh, one of the best areas of the town, Gunton Cliff, overlooking the North Sea. Extended, state of the art, expensive. Richard's house spoke of power, wealth and him. Marcella answered the door herself, perhaps the staff had been let go.

'Hello Bob,' she smiled, without any warmth. 'And Megan,' offering her cheeks for continental kissing to them both. She stepped back to allow them in. Megan remembered it all too well, and felt a chill, as if Richard Adams was still there, looking at her, mentally undressing her before actually doing it. Bob looked around the hallway and sighed. 'Lovely to be here, Marcella, and to see you again.

Marcella led them through to the massive lounge, now in the latest of pure white furniture and high tech gadgetry. He stared at a large aerial photo of the former fishing vessel 'Aztec' that Richard had bought to convert to a radio ship and casino in international waters three decades ago. He wished he'd at least tried to do a week or two on it as Richard had offered.

'I was surprised to hear from you, Bob.'

He explained that he and Richard had lost touch, as she knew, and once they moved to their present flat in north London, it had got worse, a different life for them. His parents gone, no reason to come back and he'd only heard about Richard's death long afterwards as they were not great social media followers. Megan sipped coffee and watched, adding nothing. 'I'm sorry we weren't here to support you.'

After a long pause, Marcella nodded; then across to Megan. She'd known about how Richard had played a game not unlike car keys in a bowl one night on their last reunion and ended up with Megan. She knew about all his conquests. Indeed, he freely told her afterwards, partly bragging but also because he needed Marcella as a fixed part of his world, which included bedding women, a hobby he'd never broken free from since his teens.

'Do you know how he died?' Marcella asked. Neither knew. 'He had a heart attack.'

'Lord, a heart attack at his age,' muttered Bob, painfully aware that Richard was only two months older than he. 'Yes, he was engaging in one physical exercise too many. It was in bed at the office – you know he had that private suite behind the painting in his top floor rooms?' Bob had been shown it. 'He was shagging Jeanette, his personal assistant, the one who took the job title to extremes.' Bob remembered her very well, having come close after Richard left them together in the office on a previous visit.

'You know, you live with a man for decades. You share his life, you go along with his hopes and dreams and his energy fires you. However honest he was, and he told me it all, even you, Megan, you do not really know someone. Not in the way that matters.'

Megan gulped and looked at Bob, who appeared not to have taken in what was just said. But of course, Marcella had assumed that Bob had known all along. That was how it was with Richard. Whatever he wanted he got, no point in making a fuss, what is – that's how it always would be.' If he wanted to invite people round to enjoy excessive food, copious drink and a blue movie or two that was what happened. Getting an invitation to such a night was regarded as a badge of honour and highly sought after among certain sections of the business community.

Bob got up to stretch his leg, 'You're right, Marcella, I never really knew him inside. Oh I knew him a good deal through those teenage, college and some business years. But as we grew older, he developed his businesses but stayed a boy in many ways. Every girl, every woman later, was a fresh journey and challenge, though the end was always the same. He loved the chase, the conclusion was his reward. When I stopped wanting to screw every female with two legs and all the rest, I went in a different direction.' Neither woman responded.

Marcella refreshed their drinks. 'Napoleon once said, apparently, that if you want to understand a man you need to understand how his world was when he was 19. Well, that explains Richard, in a way. He was forever into that hippie, free love shit. And like a boy who never acquired the taste for dark chocolate...'

'That was me,' smiled Bob. 'I still like only milk chocolate.'

She went on, 'Did you know the spare room you stayed in was wired to a control area in the cellar? Microphones, camera, the lot. Richard wanted to keep tabs on you.'

'Not very hippie shit, that,' laughed Bob but still rather shocked.

'I've kept the lists he made, the folders and the slides, if you want to look,' Marcella offered. Bob didn't fancy it, not after all this time, to Megan's relief. After the speeches and celebrations back all those years ago, Richard had shown Bob his files. Every encounter was recorded, almost all for them both as they usually happened at the same time. He'd collected slides of many of the girls, including some as they were then, older and some looking the worse for wear. Who they'd married or lived with; children they had; work they did. It was an extraordinary archive.

'Knowledge is power, my old spotted dick,' Richard had laughed, 'you never know when you might need to check something about anyone.' It was the Eliza Catchpole slides that had upset him – in fact, they were the only ones that touched him at all. She'd moved on, been married twice and was working in a club in Norwich that Richard 'had a stake in.' With all his success, why did Richard have to take her? Bob was surprised that it still mattered to him.

Even their teacher training days were there. The parties, like school ones but more doped and people taking more alcohol and the young people with longer hair, clothed from charity shops and market stalls. The young women now sporting names like Poppy, Rainbow, Purple Haze and Love Flower in their accommodation including one occasion where they'd actually shared a girl and another who put out happily despite being six months pregnant.

There were moments in cars, carparks, forests, open fields. A college lecturer old enough to be their mother had been accommodating one night. The teaching practice and the near panic that gripped Bob when they found themselves taking two loudmouth, physically mature fourteen year old girls for some bowling, drinks in a pub garden so they didn't go inside and a session back at the men's student accommodation.

Illegal even then, it was also a foolish risk that just excited Richard, but Bob couldn't take advantage of the situation, able to imagine what teaching them would be like. Maybe that was what began to differentiate them. Bob had always gone along with Richard's drive, energy, madcap ideas, clowning and solutions. But Bob began to discover a conscience, an inner voice that said women are more than possessions.

When Richard decided to abandon the teaching route and Bob declined to join him in leaving, it was perhaps the beginning of the end of their friendship. But there were many reunions, their respective weddings to come that brought them together, usually lost in Memory Lane for at least part of the time. Megan could only wonder how much reliving the past Marcella would do now, if any. Would she move on? Move away? Go back to her native south coast? Richard had been successful financially, so she must be comfortably off.

She took a little notebook from a drawer and looked at Bob for a long time. 'He said one day, some time after you'd lost touch, that if you ever came here, be sure to ask you about… let me see. Ah, yes, about Bernadette.' Bob swallowed and thought back. 'Doesn't ring a bell, that one,' he muttered fooling neither Marcella nor Megan.

Early on in his teaching days he'd encountered Bernadette, a sixth former at his school. He was not teaching that age group, so it was not so obvious that they were hitting it off. One night after the pictures, Bob had her spread-eagled on his lumpy mattress as he realised she was crying. He stopped at once and tried to work out what was wrong. It surely wasn't that bad? 'I'm so unhappy….'

She then launched into an explanation of how lousy her young life was. Dead father, mother in a wheelchair and a brother who had gone AWOL, destined for Her Majesty's pleasure according to Bernadette. He put his arm round her and hoped she'd cry it out and he could resume what they were doing. 'I want you to kill me, Bob.' He wasn't sure he'd heard her rightly. But she repeated it.

'What?' She seriously thought that their kindred spirits had become so close that he'd see her misery and agree to put her out of it. His reaction told her that wasn't going to happen. It was his fastest exit from a relationship ever. When Richard was told, he found it hilarious and promised to look Bernadette up and do it. After he'd had his way with her, naturally.

But Bob wasn't going to confess all that now. Not unless Richard had actually done something? But why would he?

They bid Marcella goodbye and prepared to head back. She said, 'Eliza Catchpole is over at Normanston, if you want to visit before you leave. She's been there a couple of years.' He considered. 'Wasn't that the cemetery?' Marcella nodded, 'Still is, though it's nearly full now.' And she left them to climb in their car and depart.

As Megan drove back to London, Bob thought it was just one more of the unsolved mysteries of Richard Adams. The face of the clown masking a mish-mash of simple and complex emotions, abilities, skills and talents that used people, situations and ideas to his own advantage.

He revisited some of the sites, places and spaces of their sexual antics. Some were familiar because his mind returned there from time to time. Others were freshly interred. And Eliza dead too. And all those wasted opportunities and those truths untold and those lies and fantasies lived out. What was it all for?

But he said none of it, letting the miles fly by.

Megan said nothing either, thinking back to the last time they'd come back from a reunion in Lowestoft after she'd been used, partly quite willingly, by Richard Adams and how long it had taken for her and Don to settle to a new normality that allowed the past to sit in a kind of perspective, and the future a more shared expedition.

That had all been a very long time ago. Richard Adams was gone. Bob really needed Megan now for however long they had left together.

# Open Relationship

## -1-

Jon was desperately keen to try an open relationship. This was the early 1970s, after all, and he hadn't managed it in the more liberal times of the late 1960s. He knew time was running out in the sense that responsibility was coming. At least, that was what everyone told him.

Cathy was not so keen. In fact, she was very far from certain that it was a) what *she* wanted and b) the right thing to do, even to make Jon happy.

He went into a bit of a sulk, which was not unusual. The upcoming conference was the ideal opportunity. Indeed, he felt that their line of work was the perfect setting to do it without any nasty repercussions and acceptance in a shrugged-shoulders, 'let it all hang out man' sort of way.

Their company – Tide's Reach Theatre – was well established and they'd worked long and hard at it for a good six years. It had risen from the ranks of pathetic, basic, very amateur and being extremely embarrassing to a successful and somewhat in-demand ensemble, known for presenting quality, well-researched theatre in everything from schools to colleges to civic theatres to community projects.

History made modern and relevant. Characters people could relate to. Stories that stayed in the mind. Jon was good at coming up with snappy clichés to promote their work.

He was also determined to have the open relationship and no, he wouldn't be jealous. No he didn't want to lose what he and Cathy had. He wanted his cake and to eat it.

Cathy sighed as he manipulated conversation yet again to open relationships. She knew men thought about sex every six seconds, but his thoughts were rather more specific nowadays. He failed to grasp that she wanted more than a quick roll in the hay so Jon could have one elsewhere.

He cited the case of Jimmy and Yvonne who'd been in the company last year – she was married, but on tours she happily slept with Jimmy every night and without any detriment to anybody, as far as they knew. She cited love and commitment,

Another day, another travel across all directions in London or out into Hertfordshire, Buckinghamshire or Essex. Another need to put off discussion about anything but getting there, relying on memory if they'd been to a school before or their curled A-Z maps if it was new.

And another performance. Sometimes two in the same centre. Collect the money and off. They employed a generally flexible team of around eight, but a core group of four who worked any day and every day they could get the work. Everyone got on generally well, given how much time they spent together and the pressures of devising or scripting, rehearsing, making and/or sourcing costumes and props, endless loading and unloading, performing and home late. Sometimes very late.

Cathy and Jon had been among the founders and it grew out of their passion for performance – they'd been at drama college together – but over the years with the need to build a business from the ground up in a competitive and uncertain environment, it became the baby they never had. Business was their marriage.

That was why Jon felt that to experiment, to experience relationships with others outside the circle would benefit their own. Cathy was dubious. She was actually opposed to the idea believing that after one time, nothing could be the same again. They'd been out socially with a few couples and some singles they'd met along the way, but quite deliberately, nothing had developed.

Once in the early days, and only once, Jon had been caught at it with a girl they engaged who was a brilliant singer and saw a year in the theatre group as useful on her CV and a good stepping stone. Step to what, nobody was quite sure.

She was gone within the week and Jon had to swear to Cathy it would never happen again. Things gradually smoothed over and when he started again about an open relationship, it was very much from the angle that it would only happen if they both did it.


-2-

The event was an annual shindig at Easter in some university campus or other, enjoying the facilities while students were away. It was a practical course with a few lectures from the great and worthy in theatre, young people's drama and various performance skills.

It attracted around fifty people, a mix of teachers, students, actors (usually resting) and miscellaneous others who thought it would do something for them. Improve confidence? Give them performance and teaching ideas?

Jon and Cathy had taken over the organisation of it on behalf of the Youth Drama Association. They just absorbed it into their company work – booking venues, accommodation, speakers and practitioners, taking money, troubleshooting.

With just two days before they headed north on the Easter Monday, Jon went into overdrive with his open relationship campaign. He took Cathy out for a meal at the local pub and once they'd finished chatting about the company, bookings, finances and then the conference, she smiled at him, knowing where their chat was going next.

Reading the smile as encouragement, he said, 'Cathy, I know I've been a bit of a bore for ages now, with all the talk about open things, you know.'

'Bit of a bore?' She swallowed the rest of her wine.

'Alright, a big bore. It's just that you know we have become so totally focused on the work and the business, I fear we're separating ourselves bit by bit. Our relationship is dying, in effect, and we can't do anything with the business always our top priority.'

'I know. I know. How long is it since we went out for a meal like this?'

'Couple of years?'

'More, I think.'

'Well, there you are. That's not good. Cathy, I just don't want to lose you. What is behind all my push to try open is that I fear one day you will come across some bloke who'll sweep you off your feet and you'll fall head over heels, walk away in his arms from all we have made and from me...'

It was an award-worthy speech and she mock-clapped it.

'It's not just to have lots of extra sex, then, sex without commitment, responsibility or love?' She raised her eyebrows while he looked at her.

'No, Cathy, it's just that I want us to come closer together, honestly, with a fresh set of experiences that we can bring to each other.'

There was a lull while she scraped her spoon round her dessert plate and considered the absolute absurdity, illogicality and selfishness of his argument. She knew their relationship might be vulnerable to him being swept off his feet equally. Or disease. She wasn't prepared to risk losing him or all they'd built so long and hard. Yet she knew him. If she did go with someone, just the once, he'd be unable to handle the jealousy. It would eat him alive.

Perhaps she'd call his bluff. 'We'll see what happens at this conference, then. Let's see who is there and how we all get on.'

Jon raised the final dreg in his glass.' To the conference.'

With a spring in his step they walked back to their apartment arm in arm. They were the closest and most affectionate that they'd been for months.

And after that, it was heads down on all that had to be done to get things packed, correspondence up to date and head north to set up and be ready.

**-3-**

Jon had a self-appointed role at the event as co-ordinator. He usually didn't participate in any sessions. Cathy joined a practical group, always the one with the fewest delegates and really threw herself into it.

They were in separate bedrooms as all the student accommodation was single spaces. Jon surreptitiously moved his to another corridor away from Cathy's before people started arriving and settling into their spaces.

They did the meet-and-greet in the foyer, welcoming old returnees and newcomers alike. Jon thought there were several possibilities, early to mid twenties, a couple of blondes, one with a very winning smile and one who was very ditzy and clearly needed extra encouragement and support.

Among the men that Jon imagined might interest Cathy, there were one or two contenders. Picturing them with her didn't trouble him at all. No, it all felt good.

There was also Tom, a little overweight and in his thirties nearer the top of the age range. He was a committee member and lecturer who loved these occasions, not to learn anything because there was nothing left for him to learn, but to extend his own open relationship experience as widely as possible, preferably, one a night.

Jon happened to know his wife had left him. Jon was always wary of him because he never missed an opportunity to chat Cathy up, touch her arm or back and indicate that she was missing out on his charms, big time.

By dinner time, everyone had arrived and unpacked in their rooms. Dinner was the first time all gathered together and Jon enjoyed making a speech of welcome, giving the emergency and practical details even though they were clearly spelled out in the brochure and explaining that he would be around through each and every day and evening in case of difficulties.

The school-meal-plus dinner was served and people chatted happily throughout as drama/theatre people do to everybody and anybody. Then it was into the first group sessions. Jon sorted out one man who wanted to change groups and the ditzy woman, Selina, who didn't know what she had signed up to.

He floated round the corridors, having a quick look in each area where the practitioners were introducing themselves and getting started on warm ups. Selina gave him a smile, as if he was an old friend and Jon thought she'd do in the absence of anyone else.

He checked twice on Cathy's room where she seemed happy enough, taking charge of some improvisation. Tom was in the same group, which Jon wasn't comfortable with, being quite charming and making the women smile warmly. There was also Andy, an older man with an air of superior cunning, Jon thought.

After the first sessions almost everyone gathered in the bar and new friendships began, a lot was drunk and a great deal of nonsense was talked. Jon noticed that Tom was after one of the students; Andy was ensuring Cathy's glass was full and Selina waved to him across the crowd.

He pretended he hadn't seen her as he mingled, answering questions about breakfast timings, the last night party he was organising, the availability of pay phones and another who wanted to change group, even at this stage.

When Andy went to the toilet, Jon made a beeline for Cathy and she said without preamble, 'OK, Jon, let's try it...'

It took him a moment to take it in. She had said OK. Blimey! He gulped. He tried to analyse how he felt. Yes, he was jealous already!

Suddenly filled with anxious, frantic activity, he dashed about so people thought he was busy dealing with an emergency, while he was simply trying to find someone, anyone, to blot it out and do what he wanted.

But it was the first night, not the last. Many were tired from their journeys. Nobody was in the mood to be picked up or anything like it. So, he got nowhere. He hared off to Cathy's corridor and was relieved to see Andy saying goodnight, quite casually and seeing her into her room before walking on to his own, some distance off.

Of course, the man could return and saying goodbye was just a ploy. But there were three more nights to go. Jon allowed himself to be reassured. He'd talk to Cathy in the morning and call the experiment off.

As he entered the corridor of his own room, there was Selina struggling with her door key, her hair falling down from the casual pile on the top of her head, her tights with a small hole on the back of the slim left leg.

Jon stopped, took the key from her and opened the door with a flourish. 'Your room, Selina!'

'Thank you, kind sir, what am I like?'

Her face was extremely close to his and suddenly she was breathtakingly attractive and available. 'Would you like a quick nightcap?'

He began to mumble his excuses when she closed the door on them, pulled a bottle of Scotch from her suitcase and went to the bathroom for a tooth glass. 'Only one, oh well, I'll use a cup,' she smiled, pouring into a help yourself coffee cup and behaving clearly not at all ditzy.

'Cheers, Jon. Tell me the story of your life?'

Jon had a swig – it was very agreeable – and sat down on the only chair. He began to talk about Tides Reach Theatre, about how they came to be involved with the Youth Drama Association and about Cathy. After a time he steered away, as Selina's eyes were starting to droop.

'That's enough about me, what about you, Selina?'

'Oh, we've got more nights, haven't we?'

'Yes, but ...' He was going to continue with the fact that he might want to find someone else, that he had to talk to Cathy, that he didn't want to be bound to this girl, at least not straight away.

He looked across at her. She was beginning to sob, gently. He let it go a moment, wondering if she was aiming for an Oscar, but no, it seemed quite genuine. He crossed the room and sat beside her on the bed, putting his arm round her shoulders.

She reached away to set the cup down, then leaned back into him. 'I've come here because I have broken up with my boyfriend, Karl. He is an absolute bastard, a Grade A shit....'

Selina launched into a dramatic tale of unconditional love, sacrifice, betrayal, vengeance that Jon filed away even as he was being told it, thinking it could be useful for a piece of drama.

Not only ditzy when she wanted to be, a natural victim and a fairly good teller of narratives, Selina was clearly unstable. After a few sympathetic noises, Jon made a move to leave, glancing at his watch and knowing tomorrow was another heavy day.

'Have you got any rubbers, Jon?' she asked out of the blue.

He gulped. 'No, no, I haven't... why?'

'If you get some, we can pay them both back, your Cathy and my Karl...'

'But I didn't say I wanted to get back at Cathy,' he spluttered.

'You didn't need to, Jon. Goodnight.'

**-4-**

At breakfast, Jon made his way as the cheerful good morning host into the dining room which was already quite full. A decent fry-up with fruit and pancakes had been laid on and everyone was tucking in. Cathy waved to him as Andy sat opposite her, his tray loaded. Jon made for a table with a very attractive blonde who had made herself up fully, even at that time of the day.

Tom cut across his path, moving at a pace, 'Morning, Jon,' and sat opposite the blonde. Jon stood, momentarily annoyed, looking for a table when he saw Selina making for him. She was unavoidable.

Several others joined them at the table, giving them neither privacy nor space, for which he was grateful. As people got up to find their groups and continue the practical sessions, she bent to his ear and whispered, 'Don't forget. Find a chemist shop.'

The conference took on a routine, rhythm and drive all of its own. Temporary friendships were formed and the sessions were reported variously by individuals he asked. When they all came together for the set lectures, there was a buzz that spoke of success. Jon was pleased.

In the dining room and in the bar after the evening session, everyone became louder and more over the top. He noticed that Andy and Cathy were virtually joined at the hip. He observed that Tom had made a friend of the blonde. Selina didn't leave him alone.

Not until bar time began to give way to bedtime did she grab his arm and say, 'I am looking forward to this, Jon'.

Two things he didn't do that day was talk to Cathy at all nor go to a chemist. In her room he took a second glass of her scotch and feigned falling asleep before he had to explain anything to her.

The rest of the week rolled past with Jon getting more desperate to find an alternative woman to Selina. He did wonder about going to find a chemist, just in case, but never actually did it. He kept thinking that something better would turn up.

His attempts to talk to a woman long enough to make a hook up even a possibility were both comical and pathetic. Even those few women who were on the look out themselves had seen how Selina had claimed him and knew that somehow he belonged to Cathy anyway.

He bought an outrageously costly bottle of scotch from the bar to replace Selina's on the third day and went to her room that night determined to push it further. She was pleased to find him more approachable and even momentarily affectionate, but less happy that he hadn't bought condoms.

They fell asleep, sharing the bed but nothing more. The next morning it was like nothing had gone wrong. She cornered him at every meal. She was quite committed to her group who were preparing a shared performance for the final evening and was anxious that he approved their ideas.

After all groups had shared and inevitable speeches and thanks, Jon's party was all set for the off. They had booked a large room with a temporary bar. Everyone had contributed to it and Jon had gone to town to pick up extra booze, snacks and condoms.

'Have you done it with Selina?' Cathy asked him from behind as he came out of the gents. 'He wheeled round and saw they were alone. 'No, have you?'

'No, I haven't. But I'd like to.'

'With Andy?' The man had made himself popular with almost everyone during the week.

'Yes, with Andy.'

'Right then, that's fine,' shrugged Jon, feeling glad he'd bought condoms for Selina but decidedly agitated about Cathy and Andy. She looked at him hard and long. Two people went to the toilets; she said nothing.

'Jon, I can see you are not comfortable with this. So, I'll hold him off till midnight. If you haven't knocked on his door and disturbed us by then, you have your open relationship.'

Without waiting for his reply she returned to the party. Jon stood a few moments taking that in. What he'd wanted so long was a mere couple of hours off. Yet, yet...

About 11pm, with a final look round the party and noting absolutely no woman who wasn't avidly talking to someone or in a group, he nodded at Selina and they left. They said nothing on the walk, ignoring a pair who emerged from a room on the way.

Selina wondered about his silence. Jon wondered about Cathy. He knew she'd go through with it. He had just under an hour to do it with Selina and then get to hers and stop her from doing it with Andy.

Jon turned down Scotch and went straight for a clinch with a willing Selina. He moved them both to the bed and started to relieve her of her clothes. When it came to the condom moment, he reached over to his trousers, but she pulled him back, 'Just do it, Jon, do it now...'

So he did. Putting Cathy's face onto Selina and imagining Andy on her, it was very quick. It was unsatisfying for them both and at once a surge of loathing for Selina swept through him.

She didn't seem to mind that it was dire, cuddling down ready for the night. Jon forced himself to look at his watch and make a move to leave, time was ticking. As he moved off the bed, his foot caught in the crumpled coverlet and he crashed headlong to the floor.

Assuming it was some game he'd suddenly started, Selina got the giggles, and full of energy after their sex, jumped on top of him and started tickling and shrieking, oblivious of the people in rooms on either side.

As Jon's desperation to leave mounted, his fury rose and the more she wrapped herself around him. He held his arm out for the watch – a few minutes short of midnight.

With a savage push, he was free of her and wrestled into his clothes. She, hurt, lashed out at him with fists and nails and spitting venom. 'You've had what you want and now you want to run off? You must be bloody joking.'

He bolted down the corridor, leaving her naked in her doorway still berating him loudly. Out of the building and across a patch of garden as a short cut to Cathy's room. He hurled himself through the main door and down the corridor and as his watch showed midnight he pounded on her door with both fists.

'Cathy, Cathy, don't do it, it's me, stop now, Cathy. Cathy!'

There was no sound within. She must have done it! Oh no. He heard a door along the corridor open and somebody peered out. But it wasn't her.

Her comment came back to him as he leaned against the wall, thinking, his heart racing, 'knock on his door'... Oh, no, they were in his room. He dashed off, nearly knocking someone else over two doors up who'd just emerged in a dressing gown to see who was making so much noise.

Thinking unclearly as he ran, he made a wrong turn towards Andy's room, before realising he was in the wrong block altogether. Outside again, and as he dashed over the soil his foot caught on a plant, he stumbled and fell with a thump, twisting his ankle in the process.

Nobody heard his yells, as much in anger as pain. One or two saw him dragging himself into the next building. Nobody in Andy's corridor saw him fetch up outside and look at his watch. Ten past twelve. Too late. She'd given him what he had long wanted.

Conference over, lifelong friends made and some to be forgotten. Jon avoided everyone after he'd got his foot bandaged up in the university first aid room.

Selina avoided him completely, so that was something. Tom said a fond farewell to his third woman of the event, so it had been a great week for him. Andy and Cathy parted in the car park and promised to write to each other.

Cathy drove her and Jon to London in an atmosphere that was frosty, to say the least. They gave a lift to a young woman who went along with Cathy's view that Jon was swinging the lead over his foot injury.

Once back in their base, an apartment with a small workshop out back for costumes and props, they had a blazing row. Cathy was disappointed in herself and in him. He was furious at her for doing it and not giving him just a few more minutes.

He lied and said he didn't have anyone. Cathy laughed out loud at that statement and again when Selina took to ringing several times in an evening, every evening.

**-5-**

On the first day of the new summer term, Jane arrived at the theatre group operation. She'd seen it and liked it at her audition and was ready to start work. Of course, she'd have to be trained to fill the gap left by their long term team player who'd had a better offer.

Jane felt reasonably confident. She needed this. At almost 30, she knew time was not on her side and that it would be a great opportunity. She should surely work her way up for promotion and she might find a man she could keep. She needed to be in charge of things.

She had little experience of practical performance but had completed primary teacher training. Cathy found some of her little traits annoying – slightly old fashioned language, a deep laugh and some strange eating habits picked up from a previous boyfriend.

Her reluctance to do exactly what she was asked to do irritated both Cathy and Jon, but he was more forgiving of her generally. She was only 5ft 2ins tall, with curly red hair and exceptionally pale, somewhat freckled skin. Once they started trying on costumes, Jon noted her legs were a little too thick for his tastes; but there was something about her.

The company were still talking about what they knew and guessed of what had happened between Cathy and Jon at Easter. The pair could barely be civil to each other.

The ideas for the new show were just not relating enough to the junior school age group, so they had to improvise a lot. While they were traditionally good at that, it did demand a level of co-operation and give and take that the pair at the top was unable to give.

There was one incident when the normally calm Cathy let her feelings show about the way Jane was a) talking to Jon and b) tackling a scene, so much so that Jane seriously considered either a) walking out or b) killing her. In itself it was very little and a director of improvisation has to deal with a million moments like it in any piece of work. It was just that Cathy implied that Jane's understanding of a woman who'd been let down was too superficial.

Soon Jane would talk freely only to Jon. In fact, she would not talk to Cathy at all unless she had to. The others were a little concerned at this, but hoped things would settle down.

It was just that in the van between gigs, in the apartment cum office and even in one failed social event, tensions were high. Jon and Cathy kept rowing, mainly about That Night, and were soon unable to keep it to their private times.

None of the others attempted to broker the peace, so Jane did. She asked them to sit down and talk rationally because she as a newcomer was 'finding it difficult to work in this atmosphere.'

Jon thought it was a good idea and said Jane was a brave person; Cathy accepted it but soon twigged that Jane had an ulterior motive. She was after Jon and would ditch Cathy at the first opportunity!

The peace attempt achieved nothing beyond giving Jane more information about how and what happened. Following that, Cathy decided to go out for a meal with Andy, partly to annoy Jon and partly because she was getting to know him better on the phone.

Jon was so pissed off that when Selina made another of her annoying calls, he suggested she come up to London on that same evening. If Selina was surprised at his turn of mood, she said nothing and agreed she'd stay with her sister who lived at the other end of the tube line. She was happy to accept Jon's offer.

She arrived in her full ditzy dress costume with a lot of fluttering and giggles to go with it. She caused a stir when they entered the local pub, where they sat by chance at the table he and Cathy had last eaten at. Selina took the opportunity to pour out her troubles afresh and particularly how she had put her trust in Jon…

Jon began, as she ran on, to resent the price of the meal and the thoughts of Andy and Cathy out somewhere better, so without feeling any real desire for the woman, he decided after a couple of glasses of ale to get his money's worth back to the apartment.

It was clear that Cathy and Andy were already upstairs in the apartment, so he led Selina into the workshop. Excited to look around the heart of the theatre company and thinking that Jon was now hers, she was willing and warm. However, with Jon's mind full of Cathy, it was a perfunctory act on his part.

Jon became aware that someone was watching from the corner. He froze. Selina looked across to see Jane staring at them. Selina, speechless, leapt up, dressed rapidly and stormed off damning him as a pervert into voyeurism and every Satanic practice known.

Embarrassed, John pulled himself together and asked Jane what the hell she was doing there. Jane herself was quite unconcerned and explained to him that she'd been sleeping in the workshop till her new accommodation was sorted. Jon promised to let Cathy know and there'd be no problem.

He had to wait in the van till lights went out and he could creep in and sleep on the settee, thoroughly pissed off. As he lay, awaiting sleep, he wondered if he could push it further with Jane – but was he that attracted to her? It would, though, really get Cathy's goat.

The work of their term ground on and by half term, only the mutual loathing that Jane had for Cathy remained in the air, as Jon and Cathy came to some peace arrangements, triggered by the emergence of the secret that Andy, despite all he'd said, was married and his wife had found out about Cathy.

-6-

The main summer term tour was to primary schools in rural Shropshire, 15 of them in a week, with a decent set of expenses and fees paid by the schools and the local education authority. It was a regular tour and normally Cathy and Jon looked forward to it.

They stayed in a pub with guest rooms for accommodation which arose originally because one of the group's parents kept the pub. That fell through when the mother went down with shingles and the venue was closed.

Rather than cancel the tour and knowing they could afford neither normal hotel nor B & B rates, they persuaded Tom to accommodate them as he lived in the county. Well, Cathy metaphorically flashed her eyes and tits on the phone and Tom was hooked. He'd never stopped fancying her.

Tom remained the most successful womaniser they knew, if even half of what he claimed was true. His wife had long left him and their large out of town bungalow with four bedrooms off a central corridor.

Although it saved the tour, Jon was irritated in anticipation of Tom trying it on with Cathy as he most assuredly would. Jon was entertaining hopes he and Cathy could ride out the present difficulties and settle to an open relationship. She dismissed Jon's fears with a shudder.

Tensions rose during and after a morning drive, an afternoon performance, take way food in the van and arrival at Tom's just as he reached home from his lecturing job, Jon and Cathy rowed in his front garden while the rest of the team unloaded the cases.

The evening was marred by the atmosphere, which would have been theatrically priceless if it could've been bottled. Watching TV, having a bottle or two and trying to relax, Jane smiled a lot and flirted with Tom, which quite bothered Jon, to his surprise.

Come bedtime in the main guest room, Jon wouldn't let it go and they rowed in stage whispers.

'You know you fancy Tom? So go and fuck him. I don't care.'

'I don't fancy him but at least he cares about me, so if you keep on, I will go and fuck him.'

'Go. There's the door.'

She stormed out, down the corridor to Tom's room, the sound of his door being flung open and slamming shut. Then silence.

After a bit of futile listening, Jon tiptoed down the corridor to the bathroom, avoiding Tom's partly open door – the slam had let it swing back a little way. They seemed to be just talking softly. It was as he emerged, washed, that he couldn't help himself stopping to glimpse through the gap. Tom was really pushing it with Cathy now, stripped and lying on top of her.

As Jon turned, clenching his jaw tight shut, Jane whispered from her dark doorway, just a few steps along the corridor.

'Jon, you can get back at the bitch, if you want to.'

Jon looked at her, trying to take in what she said and calm down a bit. 'You can get back at Cathy that bitch, if you really want to.'

'How?' Jon mumbled, still not sure where this was going.

'You can have me. Here and now. No strings. But she won't like it.'

She stepped back into her room, inevitably drawing him towards the doorway like a puppetmaster. 'I'm here, Jon, no strings, I promise...'

Jon stepped inside her box room, closing her door behind him, put down his bog bag and towel as a new feeling replaced his frustration and anger and hurt about Cathy.

As Jane's lips met his, her pale skin seemed fine. Her red hair was set off perfectly in the bedside lamplight. Her annoying little ways melted like snow in the rising sun. As her legs opened to him, they no longer seemed fat.

He took her, as offered. No strings. It was just the release he needed. He crashed out at once.

As he woke, stretching from being rather cramped on the single bed and trying to extract his arm to look at his wristwatch – they had a show to do in a school first thing – Jane smiled at him, reminding him what they'd done.

She reached down her hand and made sure he wasn't in any hurry to leave. As she knelt beside him, she said between mouthfuls that if he wanted, she could move her things in with him tonight and the bitch could move straight in with Tom.

He had little head space to ponder that, before she sat astride him, inserted him and encouraged him to comprehend that it was a very sensible idea, that this was the promise of more to come.

In the situation they were all in, it would have been impossible to keep a relationship with Jane secret. So they carried on openly after the tour. Cathy loathed it and hated them both. But said nothing, ever and whatever the provocation.

Jon and Jane stayed together in the spare room or the lounge. They sometimes stayed in the workshop and occasionally at her flat which she shared with three other girls.

One afternoon, Cathy walked in on them after rehearsals. They weren't going to be together that night, as Jane had to visit her sick mother. So Jon pushed for a quickie on the settee in the rehearsal room.

Cathy's question for Jon froze on her lips as she came in to see his backside between her thighs. Jane saw her come in; Jon didn't and carried on. As Cathy stood stock still for a moment taking in the scene on the bed with Jane's tights and knickers on the floor, she reached down and held him and kissed him so he came at once.

Only then could Cathy force herself to move away, disgusted and disappointed equally. Jane was pleased as punch; Jon thought it was through his efforts.

Jon's general well-being eased much tension within the ensemble. Only Cathy remained put out, but in the interests of the business she waited and watched, suffering in silence.

She opened up to Rachel, one of their casual performers who came and went, and shared her remaining hopes and dreams for the business, wondering if the relationship with Jon could be saved in any meaningful form.

Rachel suggested it could, given their long history, provided Jon didn't escalate things with Jane. Cathy replied that she had no intentions of giving up her business half to Jane and Jon was stupid at times, but even he in a moment of madness wouldn't throw it all away.

A few weeks later, Jon had his moment of madness.

He was in bed with Jane, Cathy upstairs above them. They were using a condom because it was mid month and she hadn't yet gone on the pill. Jon wasn't enjoying it so much. She slipped him out but kept her hand holding it on him.

'What's the matter, Jon?' she whispered into his face.

He whispered back. 'It's just this thing. I hate them. Can't we risk it and take it off?

'Do you want to risk it?'

'Do you?'

After a beat, she asked him, 'If I get pregnant will you marry me? I don't want to be a single mum?'

Without hesitation, his voice husky with instant lust, he said, 'I will.'

She snapped it off and put him back inside. It was all over in seconds.

And Jon's open relationship was closed, firmly and permanently.

# The Dreams of Nigel Barnes

'Remind me to worry about half the roof tiles blowing off and decapitating you...' Nigel said.

It wasn't a joke. He was a born worrier. Throughout his childhood, accepted by all his family and even himself as 'nervy', he would fret anxiously about bad things that might happen or good things that he was bound to miss out on.

It wasn't so much that he was envious of what others had. It was more that he feared blessings would be strangled at birth by curses.

And the dreams. His parents told him he dreamed most nights as a child, often waking in a sweat and able to recall vividly a war he'd fought, a mountain rescue that'd gone disastrously wrong, a crime that had engulfed him and his loved ones or an indescribably dark place he arrived at every single time.

One of his earliest and most frequently recurring dreams was that he was kneeling down looking at something that was really important when he was hit from above by someone standing over him. He was hit on the back of the head and fell forward, bleeding to death.

His parents didn't exactly blame themselves. Rob Barnes had befriended a young woman who'd been the victim of a violent boyfriend, a girl who was instinctively drawn to the bad boys. Lorraine was glad to make friends with Rob, he was different. He listened to her, he cared and he worried about her.

At first, that was what won her to him. Nobody had cared a damn about her before; Rob was obsessively concerned about her well-being. She agreed to become Mrs Barnes when she was two months pregnant and all the family – the ordinary Barnes and Lorraine's dysfunctional mix – were delighted.

From this starting point, the Barnes children were given an as excruciatingly ordinary life as possible. Nigel was the youngest of three. Christopher, three years ahead of him was a remarkable sportsmen with lashings of promise; Janet his senior by a year was a talented artist, dancer, singer and great all round creative clearly destined for marvellous things.

Nigel was a thinker. And a worrier. First his infant school teachers, then those in the junior school, learned to be careful about what ideas, images, stories
and dark deeds were taught which feed Nigel's mind. At secondary school, nobody had time to notice much about him beyond that he was 'very quiet; needs to make more of a contribution.'

Other students were called 'dreamers' because they'd be easily distracted or just be preoccupied with thoughts, memories and imaginations. Nigel was a *real* dreamer. His fear and doubts were in control of his mind, yet he could still hear new things, obey orders, do school work.

It was as if he were functioning on two levels simultaneously, but felt instinctively that to analyse it overmuch wouldn't help. Does a person's intractable problems as perceived by others actually make them who they are?

In the awkward teenage season while his peers explored relationships, some more successfully than others, Nigel was rarely part of anything. He'd listen to the accounts of others about their exploits, many of the more ambitious in the boys' heads rather than actually occurring.

But nonetheless, Nigel often wished he could find a girl, talk to her easily, go out with her and show everyone he had a girlfriend. He often looked at his parents, knowing dad was the mould he came from, yet they seemed to have made a go of it.

The fact was that Lorraine had found various ways of coping with Rob's obsessive fears and worries, as often as not by ignoring or brushing over them. To the outside world, they rubbed along, though she'd never talk about her own feelings, any regrets she may have had or plans she still entertained.

When she took up with a man who was trapped in what he told her was a loveless marriage, she kept their weekly meetings a complete secret. Her outings to the whist drive at the local village hall were a perfect reason to be out. Nobody ever realised she know next to nothing about card games.

She made the decision to stay married, have her occasional fun – they both had an equal amount to lose if discovered – and being a bit naughty played to her by now fond memories of her disastrous younger years.

Nigel opened up to his sister Janet who'd always liked to hear his dreams and had used them in a festival dance piece she'd won and a painting her boyfriend's father was given because he liked being reminded of 'the death that is to come.'

His family were hopeful when a terrible incident led to referral to a medico of some description, though nobody was ever sure what exactly she was qualified in. Nigel, a regular in the Scouts was in camp one weekend, as normal when in the early hours of one morning in the patrol's dormitory tent he had his hands pulled from the throat of a boy he was trying to strangle because he'd dreamed Christopher was being threatened by two men in dark cloaks and no faces.

It naturally led to many enquiries. Mr and Mrs Barnes thought it prudent to remove Nigel from the Scouts and had to agree to medical examinations as the price for the other little boy's parent letting the matter drop.

Dr Flerssohn, in an accent that wavered between Scandinavian and low Scottish, delivered a lecture that Mrs Barnes felt she'd uttered many times before. To her, Nigel was just another patient.

'Mr and Mrs Barnes, please understand that there is no one-size-fits-all for dreams. There is no way of curing them, stopping them or being certain of their interpretations. But we can draw some conclusions and try to help Nigel control and rationalise his dreams and his fears.'

Mrs Barnes nodded madly; she was distraught. Mr Barnes was more philosophical, having been subject to crippling fears of heights and road accidents all his life. The doctor went on, 'Every minute detail, every aspect of a dream may be important, and usually they're forgotten when waking. Nigel seems to cling on to shreds of them.'

The three adults looked at Nigel, slumped in his chair, staring at his hands in general and his finger nails in particular. 'Every symbol may mean a memory, a fear, a feeling or something from the deep unconscious. A person who suppresses memories may find they surface in dreams and then later in everyday behaviours.'

She asked about animals, insects, birds, vehicles, places, faces, objects, films and books that he'd mentioned or they were aware of as evidence from his fearful dreams. In the spirit of the times, she spoke to his parents; Nigel himself was not important enough as a young teenager to have any views of any significance.

'So, his dreams are trying to tell him something, are they, Dr Flerssohn?' his mother asked as they finished with a programme of sessions booked in.

'Yes, they tell us everything, if only we can make sense of them.'

After that time, with exams approaching, Nigel managed reasonably well. His dreams were recorded on a bedside pad that the doctor had demanded, and he found it helpful to look at her notes on what symbols mean in dreams. One recurring one was of an octopus which sometimes came in a variant of being pulled underwater by tangled weeds.

After a year, Nigel was signed off from Dr Flersson's 'care' and left to deal with adolescence as best he and his parents could. Most of his contemporaries were thinking of sixth form and then university; some were hoping for an apprenticeship with a promise of a proper career and a pension eventually.

Christopher, now a weekend sportsman with his secure job clerking in the bank and Janet, married with twins at nursery school and her ambitions of a career in the arts 'on hold', both suggested their little brother might be suited to a factory. Nigel thought he'd like to be a journalist.

The local rag took him on as a junior with no promises, but at 15, then the school leaving age, Nigel began to learn what to look for when sitting in the magistrates' court while the dregs of society were dealt with for a range of crimes and offences that made him dizzy at first.

There were occasional important weddings and inquests to cover, the odd review to knock out from something worthy at the little civic theatre and accidents to report on. He was a regular hanger around at the hospital, waiting for news of and comments about victims of mishap.

He was given Obituaries and Letters to the Editor to knock into shape when the old dear who'd done it for centuries suddenly pegged it on the bus going home one day. Hers was his first eulogy.

His second was for his mother, who took ill with a cancer of the womb that was just not mentioned in polite company in those days and died within weeks of being diagnosed. The obituary was spiked on the grounds that she wasn't well-known enough.

What impressed him most was the obits-in-progress the paper had in stock. Every time a local dignitary said or did something, it was added to their file to make the writing of their tribute when the time came easier and quicker.

He attended more council meetings than was good for anyone, but made sure he noted any anecdotes or titbits for later use. The editor warmed to him, and when the smoking got to the old man's lungs, Nigel was entrusted with a few leader articles.

So, gradually he rose up the ranks from jack of all trades in a grubby, old fashioned newspaper office to the dizzy heights of Chief Reporter with a weekly column under his own name. He once dreamed of standing on top of a pile of other newspaper people, stacked as if in a Mayan pyramid.

By the time he became editor, the paper had been absorbed into a major regional print and media conglomeration and technology had transformed the building, the mind sets and the entire industry of local news. He had a series of dreams about cogs and wheels grinding, a sort of Russian Revolution nightmare with a sprinkling of surrealism.

Now they had websites, social media, podcasts and videos to process as the weekly paper itself became the least important and profitable part of the business. Now news was big business 24/7. News fed on itself and became both its own need for more news and the answer to the journalist's desperate need for something to report on.

Along the way, Nigel befriended a young woman who'd been the victim of a violent boyfriend, a girl who was instinctively drawn to the bad boys. Lucy was glad to make friends with Nigel, he was different. He listened to her, he cared and he worried about her.

At first, that was what won her to him. Nobody had cared a damn about her before; Nigel was obsessively concerned about her well-being. She agreed to become Mrs Barnes when she was two months pregnant and all the family – the ordinary Barnes and Lucy's dysfunctional mix – were delighted.

As time passed and they bought a small terraced house with a little garden, a space to park on the street out the front and a bedroom for them and one apiece for their two children, Lucy kept to herself her concerns about Nigel's fears and his occasional strange dreams.

He often dreamed of losing her to someone from her past who came back for her, or someone she met but Nigel didn't know him. However, their children triggered more dreams and fear-drenched thoughts than anything else. He talked about his fears with his old dad he went to see once a fortnight in the sheltered accommodation he'd fought against entering.

According to the old man it was a tragedy waiting to happen, falls and slips were standard, old people were expendable and 'certain people' left windows open, force-fed elderly stomachs and made them exercise to the point of death.

And for Nigel, there wasn't a safe vehicle on a road, a secure school building, a free leisure space, their own house and garden that wasn't peopled with villains, murderers, perverts and the damned all hell bent on torturing, abusing, killing, abducting or lobotomising his children, Simon and Joanne.

One summer, as they were splashing in and out of a little plastic pool in the garden, shrieking, totally carefree, Nigel and Lucy sat on the grass patch enjoying them. Suddenly the head of the miserable old man who lived behind them, other side of the alley that ran along the back of the houses, appeared and rested its gnarled chin on the fence top.

The ugly, bitter neighbour caught the Barnes by surprise. He snarled angrily, 'how dare your children make all that noise...' Nigel reached for a gun that happened to be in his hand, took aim and put a bullet in the very centre of the man's forehead. He simply repeated his question, 'how dare your children make all that noise...' before Nigel woke, sweating.

He and Lucy found a way of living with how he was, sometimes making a joke of the fears – a door blowing shut, falling from a cliff top or finding a leg on his body that became suddenly paralysed when applying the brakes in a runaway car. Other times, she wondered if he hadn't become impossible to live with.

It was about this time that Lucy took up with a man who was trapped in what he told her was a loveless marriage, managing to keep their weekly meetings a complete secret. Her outings to the pilates and keep fit sessions at the gym were a perfect reason to be out. Nobody ever realised she had no real interest in keeping fit.

She made the decision to stay married, have her occasional fun – they both had an equal amount to lose if discovered – and being a bit naughty played to her by now fond memories of her disastrous younger years.

Nigel read reports in the news, which was after all what he did for their living, and would transpose them onto his family. The school bus crash happened to his family; the deranged hammer killer entered his own kitchen and slaughtered them all while he was at work.

As they grew up, the kids managed him, not letting it spoil anything more than the occasional outing. The trip to the theme park where they were sure to fall headlong from the roller coaster or slip between the wheels of the train was one thing.

The refusal to let them go on a school camping trip in late autumn for fear of a landslide was an embarrassment. In his rational moments and daylight, Nigel knew what he dreaded was nonsense, statistically wouldn't happen and was causing needless anxiety in others.

As his children reached the university and leaving home stage, and his father passed into that great inner turmoil in the sky, Nigel's dreams began to fall into two distinct categories. The first was a dream of a house that he was in that was only partially familiar where there were rooms he'd never known about, not visited and which needed major work.

Lucy put this down to the stress of his father's death and the fact that he knew subconsciously that even at this stage in his life there were things he could yet accomplish with his abilities. It wasn't too late to utilise his assets to the full. Both Simon and Joanne supported their mother and urged Dad to get out more, do more, to embrace his approaching retirement as a new beginning.

All positive stuff. But the second category of dream was of a carpet in their lockup, a rolled up shagpile they had owned when they first set up home together. It was rolled up beneath cases, boxes, gardening junk and the detritus of decades living in the same house.

They'd taken on the lockup about a mile from their house when Nigel had read of some experiment where people physically packed away their fears and objects that worried them, out of sight and mind until the day came when they could face them and throw them away. They'd paid a monthly fee for several years.

Occasionally, in a sudden and rare spurt of enthusiasm, Nigel would start sorting in the lockup, confident some of the old stuff could now be ditched. He was always drawn inescapably to that carpet roll, clambering through the junk to reach it.

Each dream took him further. He looked at it, he touched it, he lay it down and he unrolled it. Finally, its secret was revealed. Inside was a body, perfectly preserved yet shapeless and unrecognisable simultaneously.

The nightmare was so vivid that he could no longer tell if it happened or was another dream excursion.

And no matter how often Nigel dreamed it, the unrolled carpet releasing the body always brought forth a primal scream of terror from Nigel's inner being. Every time. He couldn't stop it, despite knowing at the same time what he was to find. He still had to unroll that carpet.

Nigel began to think that its message was that he had actually put somebody in a carpet decades ago and hidden it in the lockup; that he was guilty of a murder he'd been allowed to suppress.

But now, in Lady Macbeth fashion, the truth was emerging. Nigel had to face it. Lucy was at the point where she really didn't know if she could face the rest of her life with Nigel. The prospect of running off at their time of live with her man friend was not appealing after a few moments' thought.

And the lump on her breast was a worry she knew she'd have to ask the doctor about. When she had the time.

She told Nigel that they'd go into the lockup together. They could see if there was a roll of carpet there and unroll it. They could face it together, whatever it was.

She'd never offered such a practical way of facing head-on any of his irrational fears. He agreed after some thought but took a baseball bat from the hall clothes cupboard left over from Simon's sporting youth, to deal with the body in case it came to life.

Lucy urged him to go ahead of her through the lift-up metal door, mainly so he didn't see the small lump hammer she carried under her arm, under her cardigan. It was for Nigel.

If there was a body, that was one thing and when they called the police she'd tell them he had prophesied it because he must have put it there. But if there wasn't one, then, Nigel would be it.

It took ages to get through, there being more junk than Nigel recalled. It was a tough crawl through boxes, cases, old clothes, Christmas stuff, kids' memories and long since defunct technology.

'My God, there it is!' gasped Nigel, indicating a roll of green carpet just visible under the mountain on top of it. 'I dreamed it was red.'

Lucy nodded. She knew the carpet was there, as she'd put it in place before suggesting they went in. She knew it was green – it was all she could find.

It was a detail that didn't trouble him. With the goose bumps on his arms right up and the back of his neck chilled, he scrambled the carpet free of its coverings. He slowly reached for the roll and laid it down, kneeling beside it, his heart pounding and his breath short.

Lucy got herself into a firm standing position, above him so she could strike down on the back of his head and he would fall onto the carpet making it easier for her to roll him up in it.

After a deep breath and a glance at her, he began the unrolling. Nigel recalled in a blinding flash that oldest bad dream dread, of being felled from behind. He had to save himself from Lucy. Now he knew she was going to betray him.

He grasped the bat tightly and swung round to hit her with it struggling to kneel up, to prevent that fear coming true.

# Groups of Five

When Ali Carmichael broke into the bungalow, she had no idea who the old man was. It was just a convenient one to get into and out without too much chance of being seen by neighbours.

High hedges, a little side path and an open window in the kitchen. Ali was small-built, light on her feet so she easily crept through it and surprised the old fool as he sat watching the news on TV, the loud volume masking any noise she inadvertently made.

People often mistook her for a teenager. That was what first attracted Will, her boyfriend, to her, he always claimed. She soon realised that besides that he liked the fact she could get into places easily in her all-black Lycra and hood, looking like a cyclist if anyone noticed.

Her face looked younger than her thirty odd years too, so if she was ever seen in the context of a burglary, Will reasoned people would describe a young person to the cops.

He couldn't do jobs himself, of course, not with those tattoos so uniquely embedded across his cheeks. But he needed the money she made, badly. And daily. A habit like his didn't come cheap.

She stepped round the old man, barely giving him a glance. He'd gone down with minimum clouting from the wooden club, probably because the shock of being smashed from behind had set his old heart in a whirl anyway.

Once she'd stowed the club safely in her backpack, it was a matter of seconds to search the lounge where he lay, the kitchen, the bathroom and his bedroom. There was a little conservatory and a small garden shed that was not only unlocked, but left open.

She took the two hundred odd quid he'd put in envelopes around the place. She grabbed his wallet with merely a quick check that there were a couple of cards and a small wad of notes. His passport was out of date but could still fetch something. He had an old PC but she found no other electronic devices.

But there must be more. She knew from experience that these old people generally horded knick-knacks, family treasures, old coins and medals, books and sometimes documents of interest and value.

In the hall was the trapdoor to the loft. She stood on a chair from the diner, unclicked the heavy door, lowered it and caught the aluminium ladder that extended easily to the floor.

Her surgically gloved hand found the light switch as she climbed up. No loft window, so no tell-tale light on in daylight. The contents of his loft were orderly, logically stored, but the layer of dust told her nobody had been up there for a long time.

Partly out of a fragment of respect for his system and partly because she didn't want to miss anything – Will was strong on that, strongly violent – she went through his boxes and files carefully.

The usual box of old coins, a handful of historic medals would make a few quid but no more. There were some old women's clothes boxed, so either it was a late wife or the old man liked dressing up. Had to be the former, Ali smiled.

Conscious that she shouldn't spend too long up there, she quickly checked the strong plastic boxes piled up on the far corner. Family History. Children's Childhood. Before We Met. That comprised photos and letters of the time before he and his wife were together.

'Ahh, bless', said Ali aloud as she put the lid back. Then she saw the box labelled Lord Fenton High School. The memories came flooding back. So, he was a teacher, then?

It was soon clear that this house belonged to Mr Flanders, the drama teacher. That was him on the floor downstairs. My God, he'd surely recognise her if he caught sight of her face.

She remembered the first day she met him, in Year 10, about a fortnight into the autumn term after she'd been kicked out of all the possible option lessons in turn - cookery, environmental studies, crafts, IT for leisure, personal economics and dance.

Only drama remained as her last, untried chance. She entered the smelly drama studio twenty minutes into the hour period with her usual walk that spoke of attitude, and went straight up to Mr Flanders, sitting while the class were in small groups improvising something noisily. He smiled; he actually smiled warmly at her.

Of course he knew who she was, her reputation went before her. He'd been warned drama was next on Miss Carmichael's shopping list but he shouldn't give her more than a single chance. She wasn't long for Lord Fenton High.

Flanders had been a drama teacher early on in his teaching career and then gone off for a chequered phase in politics before returning to take over at Lord Fenton where his own children had been. His results supported his claim that drama was so often the only subject some students could achieve in.

It was the only GCSE subject nobody can pass on his or her own, students could be themselves and it was a creative, imaginative time of respite from the grind of other lessons. He was an enthusiastic advocate of its benefits.

'I'm Ali Carmichael,' she said defiantly, as if expecting him to go off on one and provoke her to temper so he didn't even have to start her on a trial.

'Hello, Ali, I'm Mr Flanders and you're welcome. This is a practical subject though there is some coursework later on. If you are prepared to give it a go, I promise you will enjoy being creative, make-believe, working with others, exploring some challenging issues and you should get a good GCSE at the end of Year 11.'

She nodded, not expecting that. She looked round the room.

'Ali, they are working on an idea in which one of the group of friends is a traitor and has done something, stolen something or lied to and about another. They are going to share what they have in about ten minutes and we will discuss it as a class. Would you like to sit and watch and then join in the next piece after this?'

'No, sir, I'll join in now.'

'Is there a group you could work with?'

'Them,' she said nodding at a group of girls and one boy a drama teacher normally wouldn't want together, but he smiled at her as she went over, spoke briefly to the group and got stuck in.

It was the start of a commitment to the subject that Ali made and though some days she would kick off, usually because of somebody or something outside the lesson, she was a keen student in drama, suffering fools poorly and leading to the point of occasional bossiness wherever possible.

One day, Flanders began by saying that a new directive had gone round and all lessons now had to take account of English and Maths. To a universal cry of what rubbish this was, he explained that English was easy – all of them spoke it all the time so communication through English was fundamental and clearly demonstrable.

Maths, however, he had scratched his head over. He said, 'Get into groups of five. Don't just go with friends. There are 25 in the room, so it's exactly five per group.' After some shuffling round, to his surprise they did it, without argument.

'James, how many in your group?'

James was puzzled, it was obvious. Flanders urged an answer. 'Five, sir.'

'Good, that's five per group. Tracey, if we take two off your group and they go to that group, how many in your group and how many in that one?'

Tracey looked round, unsure, but came up with, 'three in this group and six in that one…'

Everyone laughed and she put it right. 'OK, that's our maths for today, counting and if anyone asks, that's what we did. Now, let's do some drama…'

It was part of the growing trust the students had with Flanders and he with them, a shared touch of rebellion and that everything was different in drama. Even 'groups of five' became an in-joke and although he made them swap around, five was the magic number of effective improvisation.

His almost unique selling point in the school was that he listened to and was genuinely interested in young people. Students with low ability, he seemed to find ways they could do well in the group work. The high fliers blossomed. The already troubled and disaffected, he got through to in almost every case.

He could see potential in some unlikely characters and for that, several generations of adults alive and working and raising families today were very grateful. In every group of five, maybe three were doing well, one was on the border and one was lost. Ali understood that.

Not that he was soft touch. He enforced rules like politeness, punctuality, respect for others and a strong work ethic as hard as other staff. But there was a sense with him that students wanted to co-operate, to please him and succeed for and with him.

Ali Carmichael warmed to that and put herself out when he asked her to stretch herself, almost every time. She was soon assigned to help a couple of less able students in the class and she grew in confidence in performance that was neither arrogant nor indulgent.

She was unaware that other teachers expressed surprise to Flanders that she was still in his class and doing well, by all accounts.

His lesson plans were preserved in folders which she flipped through. The sessions on body image she'd enjoyed particularly as she was small and somewhat behind other girls developing and it had helped her.

Those on punishment she had contributed to enormously, and even found the historical and cultural aspects of punishment absorbing. It just didn't rub off in other areas of the school.

In the Y11 file she came across the work on *Romeo and Juliet* that Flanders had made palatable with parallel work on *West Side Story* and some good 'what if...' scenarios – what if Romeo had fallen for Juliet's sister; what if Romeo was gay, that sort of thing.

The practical exam preparations were not a good time for her. She discovered Flanders' '101 Starting Ideas for devising drama' which had been useful and recalled the process her group had gone through to start their exam piece.

But a month off from the exam, she was suspended for a week for an incident with the bitch who taught her PE, so she missed a lot in every subject. It was only drama that bothered her.

When she returned, her group of five wanted her out because she'd missed a lot of group decisions and tried to change things when she returned. It took all Flanders' diplomacy skills to negotiate a settlement that allowed Ali to change two angles that affected her but left all other decisions intact.

She unearthed notes on students' predicted grades, copies of reports, class lists, ideas for future work and a few photos he'd taken during group work to satisfy the demands of Ofsted's inspection system and to offer students for their drama coursework.

Suddenly feeling that she'd seen enough of Mr Flander's teaching stuff, she left the box marked Wedding and Early

Marriage. She'd had a trip down memory lane, got some bits so Will would be OK for an hour or two and it was time to leave. Anybody could come to the door from family to medical to neighbours.

With the ladder stowed back, she checked in her bag and made sure that everything was secure. A message on her silent phone told her Will had found another likely place two streets off and she knew she'd have to do at least that one and another before they moved to a different part of town. The police always piled in resources if there was spate of robberies.

In the days of her schooling she'd learn to put up with no crap, to fight her corner and with Mr Flanders she'd learned that co-operation, creativity and self-belief could pay dividends.

But Will needed his fix. He'd make her pull a trick tonight if she didn't come up with enough and she'd rather break and enter than that.

Ali Carmichael returned to the lounge. Flanders hadn't moved. 'Sorry Mr Flanders,' she muttered, looking at him. You tried and I nearly made it. But I'm not your fault. Thank you. And thanks for the groups of five.'

Still Flanders didn't stir.

She looked closer and realised that he'd never move again. He'd gone to the great drama studio in the sky.

'Sorry, Mr Flanders' she said again.

And she left the bungalow to fulfil her next task, if not her real potential in life.

# My Friend, The Don

I first met Giovanni - Joe – Palazzi when I stopped at a junction to let his driver emerge from a small country lane onto the more main road I was on. There was a queue ahead, so it was no sacrifice.

Well, I say 'met', when what I should say is that I first saw the man. He was in the back seat of a long, black limo. I don't know about cars, but this was a nice, top of the range impressive motor. His chauffeur waved thanks and I noticed that one of his passengers was staring at me as if I was an alien and clearly asking the driver something.

I later learned that Joe had asked his hired driver in astonishment why I'd stopped to let him out when I didn't need to. He'd been given a reply something like, that's what's done in England, occasionally, even these days.

Joe Palazzi was in his early sixties, a tanned Italian American, always well-dressed and carrying a bit of extra weight but doing so with the ease and natural power that a man used to getting his own way does.

This impression was reinforced by the three well-built bodyguards who accompanied him everywhere. Grim-faced, smart suits, cropped hair, ties and dark glasses though it wasn't very bright in late October, these guys spoke of gangster movies and clichés.

My second sighting of him was again through the car. I saw it three vehicles ahead of me as I drove to St Bartholomew's

Church, the other side of Norwich. I had a free morning and knew I ought to use it to do a bit of homework for my family history class.

Mike, who ran the class brilliantly, had been on at me in the nicest, politest way for several weeks to get out into the field, look up a few actual grave headstones and arrange an inspection of parish records in person. I had reached an impasse in my searches.

I was reluctant to spend out on any of the paid ancestry sites, being careful with our money. My wife called it parsimonious but as I kept reminding her, none of us knows how long our retirement savings have to last. And we wanted to leave the kids something beyond memories and a family tree.

My other problem was that from me there were my two parents, four grandparents, eight great grandparents, sixteen great, great grandparents and so on forever. Free sites, particularly the Mormons, had got me back to the late 1700s/early 1800s with basics like births, marriages and deaths.

Others in the class were happily shelling out for copies of certificates, census returns, military records and last wills and testaments of their ancestors. If they didn't get the right surname, locality or approximate dates, they bought in vain.

So, pushing back the need to fork out by taking a photo of a couple of family graves I was pretty sure were in St Bartholomew's churchyard, Mike would encourage me by letting me borrow his site subscription and make progress back in time.

The car turned down the lane towards the village. I followed it, wondering if they weren't all going to the same place I was!

As I pulled into the little gravel, tree lined carpark, keeping as far from the black limo as I could, out came the three heavies and fanned out, looking to and fro before the main man himself stepped out.

Blimey, it was either a film shoot or they really were some sort of mafia hoodlums. One of them had a folder and a map while the others kept a hand in their long coat pockets, as if holding a gun each.

At that point I didn't know they were Americans, so I thought it distinctly possible they were armed and up to no good. To have driven off now would have aroused their suspicions.

For some reason a moment from a film I once saw came to mind. An old woman was dying, mother to a hoodlum. He swore that some other villain would be in the ground before his mother and was laughed at for it. At her torrentially rained on funeral, we saw a hand and an arm in the loose soil at the bottom of the grave as his mothers' coffin was lowered so we knew that that baddie was indeed in it before her.

The bodyguards watched me, hawk-like as I emerged from my car, picked up my notebook and made to set off among the graves.

The man in charge recognised me from that car courtesy moment. He smiled, made a slight hand movement to put the guards at ease and came towards me. 'Good morning,' I managed.

'And good morning to you, sir.' American! They wouldn't have brought their guns into the UK unless the man was a bigshot politico. He held out a large hand. I took it, warm and crushing.

'The name is Giovanni Palazzi, known as Joe.'

'Henry Fisher, known as Henry,' I responded, kicking myself for the flippancy of my response.

But he was smiling. 'Henry, I never forget a face. In my line of work, I can't afford to. I remember that you let my car out of a little side road and that was an act of kindness.'

'My pleasure, Joe.' We were still smiling, despite one of the guards maintaining a close eye on me. I was beginning to feel that Joe Palazzi was actually an interesting guy, the sort of man I could talk to, which is more than could be said for most of the people I meet these days.

'What's your business, Henry?' Thinking back on it, he meant what was I doing in the carpark of a tiny rural church on this weekday morning. But I replied, 'Oh I've had an interesting set of careers. Most recently I was teaching in a high school, I have been involved in politics and I have run a small business.'

Joe tried a different tack. 'You from these parts, Henry?'

'Not that close, but part of my family came from here. I'm doing some family history research, it's a bit of a hobby I've recently taken up. I am certain that at least two of my ancestors are buried here and I just want to take a photo of their graves and see the parish register inside, if the man turns up as he said he would.' I pointed vaguely at the church, at the graveyard.

'My story too, in lots of ways. I have English ancestors on my mothers' side – God rest her soul – and as I get on and the years ahead are fewer than those behind I want to understand my roots better.'

'Yes, we're roughly of an age, Joe. I have grandchildren and soon great grandchildren. I find seeing yourself as part of a line stretching forwards and backwards is quite something...'

Joe beckoned to his sidekick holding the folder and map and showed me the material. I shared my notebook, but I didn't have a map. The churchwarden I'd spoken to on the phone told me to look in the west, nearly south west corner for my family graves, close to a large sycamore tree.'

I told Joe about parish records, the census in the UK every ten years and how dates could not be relied on. People didn't always know exactly how old they were. Some might get married in the twenty-first year, for example, but in it they turned twenty two. Baptisms might not be done straight after birth. People may not always have been married, though they claimed it. And if a man remarried after widowhood, it was fiendishly complex.'

He maintained interest, but I could see that he was more focused on me as a person than what I was saying. 'Henry, that's interesting. I pay people to do the leg work for me, but I like your enthusiasm. Good luck on your search.'

With another handshake, we parted ways. His map took him and his party to the east and I trudged off through heavy undergrowth, well beyond the area where two old sheep grazed to keep it tidy, hoping I'd know a sycamore when I saw it.

It took me over an hour to locate one grave with my grandmother's family name on it. The photo was taken – details could just be made out – but as it was getting on, I abandoned my search for the brother. Perhaps he was in there too and nobody had chiselled it on the stone.

Still hopeful of a single photo persuading Mike to let me in on his paid for research access, I tried the main and vestry doors of the church. Locked. So much for the churchwarden's offer to help.

In the car park, my old Ford Escort stood alone, the limo gone. I would happily have talked with Joe Palazzi some more sharing fragments of my life but equally, learning something of his. One of many things I'd learned teaching teenagers was that nobody is too old to learn something new every day.

There was a note on my windscreen. Churchwarden? No, it was Joe inviting me to have a drink with him at the Maids Head Hotel in Norwich and the cell phone number of his assistant.

Unwilling to use credit from my old trusty pay-as-you-go mobile I drove home before calling him back on my landline that was on an evening calls deal. The henchman had few conversation skills and no interest in me except to agree a meeting time the next day as he'd been ordered.

It was a fair walk from the civic carpark so I had to walk briskly, hoping it wouldn't be an overlong meeting, with parking by the hour so very costly in Norwich. Joe was relaxed yet still with a presence that had waiters hovering, ready. The heavies sat at a distance, two on one table and one nearer the door. Joe ordered coffee.

That later became lunch and it was dark before I got back to the car and had to dig deep to pay the parking. But Joe was charming, fascinating, determined and clever. I took to him as a man, though I have always found it easier to talk at length with women.

Indeed, I developed the response to the question people ask, 'how are you, Henry?' the clever line, 'Do you want the male answer or the female one?'

To the answer, 'the male one' I'd say, 'I'm fine, thanks.' To the female one I'd say. 'We haven't got time!' It usually raised a smile and meant I didn't have to add more. Most people in the end are happy to talk about themselves.

Joe had me talking, singing like a canary in East End criminal world parlance.

He soon had my life story and the background, the stories behind many of the bones of what I'd done so far in life. He got feelings out of me, reactions and understood many of my foibles and eccentricities.

But he didn't confine it to that. In return I listened amazed, intrigued, shocked at times but always absorbed in the story of a man raised in a criminal fraternity and a school of hard knocks. He nutshelled his rise through the ranks, being blessed with an understanding of people that saw behind their masks.

Without being obvious, he'd discover extra facts and pieces of a puzzle. To a joke about turning 70 next year, he asked when it was, what I intended to do to mark it and what was the exact date as he wanted to send a card. Oh and where should he send it?

To information about my wife Sally and our kids, he asked to see a photo and got their names and some facts. Oh, he shared pictures from his wallet, facts about his kids and grandkids, too. But he soon turned things back to me, always smiling, always friendly.

People trusted him, he understood and I could believe it fully. He was ruthless or compassionate when needed. He could read people, perceiving their hopes, dreams and fears. He was successful.

The term 'Don' was more for the movies he said, but he didn't contradict people if they called him Don Palazzi out of respect.

Yes, he'd done many things that were illegal, immoral and thoroughly unpleasant. But in a strange way, I understood. Joe was honest in a human sense, and although I couldn't work out why I was being entrusted with information I could surely pass on to the law or sell to the media, I was at the same time flattered that I was chosen to hear it.

As we said goodbye and he suggested another meeting, he said, 'Thank you, Henry. What I have discovered in the UK so far is that there is a simplicity and honesty about most people and I am tired of being constantly on the lookout for my enemies. I want all my businesses to be legitimate, I want everything to be straightforward and legal. Transparent, as they say nowadays.'

'That's good, Joe. And anything I can do to help, let me know.'

'Henry, you will be spending some time with me while I'm here, so I want to send you a little gift to say thank you to Sally…' As I started to protest it wasn't needed, that in friendship I'd be happy, indeed honoured, to spend time with him, he smiled and said, 'Never offend a don by turning down a gift, Henry, you've seen the movies!'

It was a joke, but deadly serious.

Two days later Sally told me we had a payment of five hundred pounds in our bank account from PELAZZI and what the hell was that all about?

I added to what I'd already reported of our meeting and concluded that I had clearly given enough information for a man like Joe to find out a lot about me, including my bank account. She was alarmed and not at all grateful for the money, but I had to admit that I was delighted that Christmas was now partially covered.

For our next meeting Joe suggested the beach at south Lowestoft, as a relative had come from thereabouts in the old beach village, the heart of the fishing community. We met by the Claremont Pier and I explained that in fact the beach village was the north end of town, and I'd be happy to take him there but he should prepare to be disappointed at what they'd done to the area since the heritage was demolished in the 1960s.

We enjoyed a walk on the south prom, despite a fair breeze straight off the sea. I had my winter coat on; Joe was just in his suit jacket. His guards walked to our side and rear, clearly on edge, despite there only being a few dog walkers, a jogger and some old dears sat on benches.

After a drink in the Hatfield seaside hotel, we drove in our respective cars to Whapload Road where we parked and walked the length of it right up to the caravan park and Sparrows Nest Gardens as I explained things - the pubs, the cramped unhygienic hovels and the relentlessly harsh lifestyles fisherfolk led in a tight community known as 'The Grit'. Joe liked that.

Before he was driven off to St Margaret's Church with its extensive graveyard for a look at some records he knew had been arranged for him, Joe and I talked more about what he could do to make his business safe and his children and grandchildren secure in an age that was enjoying digging up the past and punishing the living and the dead.

I was out of my depth, really, but many skills acquired by someone in his or her late sixties are applicable and I enjoyed sharing ideas with him. I was sufficiently versed in American culture from books and films to make some sense to him.

As we got onto the general topic of money, I thanked him profusely for his gift to my bank and congratulated him on somebody's research that had made that possible. He smiled and said it was elementary. With the few details he had, birthday, address, mother's name and car registration his minion had opened a credit check site in my name and got details of my bank so after a bit more cyber digging he had access to my account.

I blurted out that he could have emptied the account instead of putting money in! He smiled again, 'Henry, we are friends.' It was awkward, but I raised the matter of Sally's unease about his gift while desperately not wanting to offend him.

He said he understood. Would I open a private account she didn't know about? I couldn't do that. 'Is she afraid I am money laundering through your account?' Yes, she was and so was I. There was also the matter of explaining to the tax man an unexpected sum of money.

'I am not money laundering. I don't need to. How about if I put you on my payroll as my adviser on British matters? I'm thinking of opening some import-export facilities in London, maybe. You could be invaluable.'

I was over the moon. Yes, I'd have to pay high tax, but this was an extra revenue stream I'd only dreamed of and I did enjoy talking with Joe, surely it was a win-win.

As I predicted, Sally was suspicious but softened a little after hearing everything would be above board. The salary payments started at once and to call them generous was an understatement. What it encouraged me to do was to be available for Joe on the phone and to his people by emails, on demand. When he flew to the UK, he was my full time job and I loved it.

I respected his judgements and decisions. Even if my advice was not required, I felt I knew him well enough to offer it, especially if his plans could cause him problems in Britain. I was able to swallow his past as that of a man now in repentance.

At Christmas all my family received quality gifts appropriate to their tastes and interests – again, carefully researched. Yes, I was somewhat troubled by conscience. I mean, what was the origin of all his wealth and generosity? Had people died so he could splash his cash and buy a friend?

That line of thought went nowhere. I'd worked hard on the right side of the law all my life. I didn't need to know the origins of his money. If I worked for a bank did I need to bleed my heart over how many mortgages were defaulted?

For about a year, this is how it continued. I'd talked about downsizing to a more convenient house, as my old knees were feeling the pressure of stairs. Our problem had always been that a bungalow costs top dollar and there was huge stamp duty of buying another house anyway.

I hoped I could afford it soon, but then Joe offered to buy my house! I said, after profuse expressions of gratitude that he didn't need it and he would be wasting his money. He brushed that aside and went ahead with buying it, paying legal and tax costs, bought me a new bungalow out of town and all the costs associated with that.

This was the single biggest act of generosity I could imagine, short of laying down your life for someone else. I begged him to come to dinner in our new house, something he'd politely declined all this time. I asked if he'd meet my family at the same time and laid on a lavish do.

The guards arrived early and checked the place out. Joe made a nicely judged entrance, charmed Sally and was kind and generous in conversation with all my family, even joking about our mutual obsessions with family history research.

The grandchildren either were being babysat at home or were allowed to watch videos in our spare room. The two teenagers were with us for dinner, both nervous till Joe put them at ease.

With the warm glow of success, approbation and an immense liking for my friend, the Don Joe Palazzi and his world, we were about to sit down at a somewhat squashed dinner table when the doorbell rang.

Police swarmed in and I was arrested on a variety of fraud, money laundering and false accounting charges.

Joe's legal adviser turned up before I was taken away, handcuffed, but short of checking his passport and those of his guards, they had no interest in our guests. It was me they wanted.

'Thank you, Mr Fisher. That's quite a story, very imaginative. Especially as we have found no Don Palazzi anywhere in the world. You'll have plenty of time to write that as a film script while you're inside. Make some money when you finally get out, if you ever do,' said the officer with a smile once they'd recorded my statement.

# Who Will Speak At My Funeral?

As they grew older, it became more of an issue. With some people living so much longer than expected and outliving their nearest and dearest, it became more urgent.

Just who would speak at their funeral(s)? Who would be the last man or woman standing on the shelf of life? Who would utter the choice words, recall the best moments and reduce the audience to both tears and laughter?

They'd all done their stints of speaking at the funerals of others, but who would care once it was down to the sole survivor?

Like a great Tontine – a lottery popular centuries ago when people paid in and the last living one claimed the prize, often decades later – this lottery of life with many people reaching truly ripe old ages, meant that most busy younger people had no clue, no patience and no interest in your time.

The men in the informal club gave up their weekly meetings for lunch as they became fortnightly, then occasionally a drink or coffee and then nothing at all. It was too much trouble. They'd been moved into different sheltered housing or actual care homes. And one by one they dropped off, some without knowing their elbows from Tuesday.

Those who could recall enough stopped sending Christmas cards and it was if they'd never been a little group of like-minded men from an era now long gone. Most had families, at least alive if not always nearby. For a few, they had no family and as friends passed on, there was little of that social lifeblood remaining.

One who had a family but'd lost them along the way was Godfrey Withinshaw. In his very late 90s with all his brain faculties but not his physical ones, Godfrey still lived alone in a supported living arrangement of bungalows looking onto a pleasant set of formalised gardens, manicured to within an inch of their life.

From his moderate works pension and his basic state one, he paid for the help he needed. He had no social or pleasure outgoings and bought no clothes or personal items. He had a ragged, white beard to save on shaving and his straggly hair was long as he couldn't pay for it to be cut.

His podiatry, eye, hearing and diabetes were sorted by the NHS. He had no teeth of his own so needed no dental treatment. He barely walked anywhere, hating the frame they'd given him, so he never wore out his shoes.

He'd reckoned when his son lost his battle with cancer in his 70s and his daughter had died in a car crash in her late 60s, that what he had would last him.

The problem was that he had long outlived his plan. By twenty years. There wasn't much left. Nobody to leave it to, anyway. But what he dreaded the thought of was being given a pauper's funeral because there wasn't enough cash left. Not that he'd know then, of course, but it troubled him now

He was of a generation that regarded a failure to afford a funeral as a burning disgrace, a shameful indignity. At the back of his mind there were a few shares that he hadn't looked at for years, but he couldn't think where they were or even how to sell them. He hoped they'd pay for his funeral.

One day, feeling quite low, the TV blaring pointlessly from the corner, he said to the young woman who was giving him a chair wash, 'Oh Lord, who will speak at my funeral?'

She, a bright young thing, around twenty five as far as Godfrey could guess, smiled and nodded her head. 'Funeral, yes, is good.'

He sighed. She was foreign. She didn't understand. She certainly wouldn't speak at his funeral.

***************************

Many people regarded her work as depressing and not something to be talked about. Most accepted that it had to be done, but didn't want to think of it. How could anyone get into such a state that Marina's department had to step in?

Marina worked with two others in the council section responsible for welfare funerals, still often referred to as 'paupers' funerals'. Under public health legislation, local authorities have a duty to dispose of the dead if nobody else takes responsibility.

In practice for decades this has been because no surviving relative can be traced. After transport in a van, a simple, very brief service is conducted before a burial in a communal grave or a cremation, often early in the morning before the places get busy.

The only people present will be the officiate and someone from Marina's department. It's as dignified as it can be and allows people in the rest of society to carry on their busy lives unaware that another forgotten citizen has left them.

Very rarely, if a body was found after a long time, the media would pick up on it and friends and relatives would come forward. Even more rarely, an old

person might be known as a war hero or responsible for something worthwhile for humanity. The media, particularly social media, would go to town on it and hundreds would turn up to pay their respects for someone they never knew but was worth celebrating.

Even more rarely, the public would chip in to fund the funeral. Or support the abandoned dog or cats once cherished by the lost person.

She and her colleagues were assigned other work in the legal affairs and electoral registration departments when not tracing relatives and arranging Public Health funerals. Marina sometimes talked in general terms to any of her friends who would listen and really only her old granddad properly talked about it with her. He had a growing interest in funerals and how they should be run.

She said that in recent times, they'd found an increase in cases of relatives being found or living in plain view, but *refusing* to take responsibility. That was an entirely new twist on social consciousness. And it saved them money, the average funeral now running close to £5000.

Marina knew the stigma once associated with such funerals was long gone, along with illegitimate babies and being unemployed. Dickens would turn in his grave. But the fact was that local authorities were being required to pick up the bills for these funerals as people exercised a choice – let others pay for their family funeral.

There was a case recently where she had laid on a simple affair with a burial in a part of the civic cemetery where unmarked graves were aplenty, only to find car loads of 'mourners' who turned up with wreaths and tasteless grave trinkets 'to send her off properly.'

They were direct family. They got the taxpayer to fund the funeral. One of them even had the gall to make a long speech at the graveside because 'somebody should speak at a funeral' and what a gem his old great grandma had been and how they'd all miss her terribly.

*********************************

Godfrey passed away in the middle of the night. He was discovered in the morning and moved to the old barn in the complex used for these occasions. Normally, after a check in their files, they'd ring the nearest and dearest and offer to have the departed moved to a funeral home.

At the relatives' expense, naturally.

They found no known relative. Old Godfrey hadn't had a visitor for years –
somehow he'd just slipped through the net. They advised the council who arranged for him to go to the cheapest undertaker, at public expense while they collected the paperwork and started searching.

There were Withinshaws in a few parts of the country, mainly the north west. Enquiries drew a blank. Godfrey definitely had no family alive. There was a suggestion that his son had had a child but Marina couldn't find a birth record that matched, and neither a marriage certificate nor death report.

Going through his box of possessions that'd been delivered to her desk, she found an old passport, but the Passport Office could shed no further light. He was military, but the records were sparse and gave nothing beyond his enlistment date, ranks, service in the Far East and discharge.

He'd kept his medals in little boxes. A shopping list that he'd hung onto for some reason. A picture of his wedding, he with his children and one military reunion he'd attended in the early 1960s. There were some gloves and a flat cap that had seen better days and a small selection of out-dated and well worn clothes.

There were some old 45rpm records of 1950s rock 'n' roll, but no record player. The wife's wedding and engagement rings were there. Various packages and containers of pills and his medical notes were as expected.

There were no private letters beyond those from his bank when he'd paid off his mortgage three decades ago. He didn't seem to have a solicitor. She asked his bank for help but that came back with no information about next of kin. She had to conclude there was nobody.

The only unusual item in the box that was not found in many effects of these people was a scruffy notebook with his scrawny handwriting of the era when he learned to read and write, headed *Who Will Speak At My Funeral?*

She sat to flip through his notebook. It was thoughts, achievements, tragedies, anecdotes and jokes from the lives in his little group of old codgers and buffers ready for him to speak at their funerals.

Each page contained a full name, date of birth and death of the departed. When Godfrey hadn't delivered the oration, he'd put in the name of the man who did. Eventually, it was down to Godfrey to deliver them all and on the last page he'd written, 'who will speak at my funeral?'

There he'd set down the stark details. His birth, schooling, work records, marriage, the children, their deaths and his wife. It was short on anecdotes and details that brought the facts to life.

It gave Marina some further research to connect the departed friends with Godfrey, but beyond the commonality of all having worked at the shipbuilding company that'd gone bust in the 1970s, there was no further evidence, no more light on whether he had any surviving relatives.

After a final appeal on social media with the information she had, she closed the file on Godfrey Withinshaw and authorised the welfare funeral. She was touched by his selfless seeing on their ways of so many old folk and how he would bring them to life not as old buffers, but as real, living personalities still in their younger glory days.

And his heartfelt cry – *who would speak at my funeral*? He wasn't complaining; his generation rarely did. He just wondered who would say a few words. He must have known that as the last man, nobody would speak.

Marina notified her friendly contact in the local rag and put it out on social media that old Godfrey Withinshaw was being cremated, Godfrey the man who'd been one of the most remarkable unsung heroes on our area. People should show respect.

The chapel at the crematorium was packed. It was a thirty minute slot and after a medley of rock from his record collection, Marina stood to speak. The crematorium official raised an eyebrow, never having seen a council staffer speak at a pauper's funeral before.

Marina spoke, reading from her notes and Godfrey's book. 'Godfrey Withinshaw was born....' And so she went on for twenty minutes, telling the tales, anecdotes, achievements and jokes he had recorded and/or spoken about others, all as if they applied to Godfrey himself.

By the end of it, most people were amazed that he'd done so much, made so many people in life happy, stood so tall in the community, yet died unknown.

She concluded, 'Godfrey wrote in his notes, who will speak at my funeral? Well, we all have spoken by being here. Thank you.'

www.ingramcontent.com/pod-product-compliance
Lightning Source LLC
Chambersburg PA
CBHW051241260626
47162CB00002B/545